唱吧！
英文歌謠
聽歌謠說故事

Gloria Lu 編著

Let's Sing and Learn
English Songs

二版

Contents

1 Are You Sleeping?

Are you sleeping,
Are you sleeping,
Brother John,
Brother John?
Morning bells are ringing.
Morning bells are ringing.
Ding, ding, dong!
Ding, ding, dong!

你在睡覺？
你在睡覺？
約翰弟弟，
約翰弟弟，
晨鐘響了，
晨鐘響了，
叮，叮，噹！
叮，叮，噹！

這首膾炙人口的童謠，原曲是法文版。但在英語系國家，還是有許多人用法文傳唱。在法文版，英國國教晨禱的鐘聲使用羅馬的旋律，到了英文版，鐘聲就改成美式鐘聲了。

注意一下法文版，歌詞中可是要 Jack 起床敲鐘，所以，鐘聲根本還沒響呢！

Frè - re   Jac-ques,   Frè - re   Jac-ques,   dor - mez vous?   Dor - mez vous?

Son-nez les ma-ti - nes!   Son-nez les ma-ti - nes!   Din, dan, don.   Din, dan, don.

 法文版

Frère Jacques,
Frère Jacques,
Dormez-vous?
Dormez-vous?
Sonnez les matines!
Sonnez les matines!
Din, dan, don.
Din, dan, don

英文版

Brother Jacob, brother Jacob
Are you sleeping?
Are you sleeping?
Ring the morning bells!
Ring the morning bells!
Ding, dang, dong.
Ding, dang, dong.

2 Ten Little Indians

(2)

One little, two little, three little Indians,
Four little, five little, six little Indians,
Seven little, eight little, nine little Indians,
Ten little Indians boys.

One little, two little, three little Indians,
Four little, five little, six little Indians,
Seven little, eight little, nine little Indians,
Ten little Indians girls.

一個，二個，三個小印第安人，
四個，五個，六個小印第安人，
七個，八個，九個小印第安人，
十個小印第安男孩們。

一個，二個，三個小印第安人，
四個，五個，六個小印第安人，
七個，八個，九個小印第安人，
十個小印第安女孩們。

Indian [ˈɪndɪən] (n.) 印第安人
- *Look at those Indians.*
  瞧瞧那些印第安人。

這是一首教導孩子數數兒的歌謠。早期的曲名是〈Ten Little Injuns〉（印第安人），由流行歌曲作者 Septimus Winner 在 1860 年間，為一個歌舞表演所精心打造的，原文較長，意指十個印第安男孩一一遭到事故，最後一個不留。

在莎士比亞的戲劇《凱撒大帝》（*The Tragedy of Julius Caesar*）中，十個印第安男孩變成了十個羅馬士兵，這些命運坎坷的士兵們，一一遭到不測，最後一位因為凱撒過世，悲傷過度而亡。後來，一些戲劇和推理小說都借用了這個故事，可見影響之深遠。

3 Happy Birthday to You

Happy birthday to you.
Happy birthday to you.
Happy birthday, dear friend.
Happy birthday to you.

祝你生日快樂，
祝你生日快樂，
祝親愛的朋友生日快樂，
祝你生日快樂。

Wishing you happy
Birthday

Happy Birthday
to you~

在美國，有三首歌是美國人最常唱到的歌，分別是：美國國歌〈The Star-Spangled Banner〉、棒球歌曲〈帶我去看棒球賽〉（Take Me Out to the Ball Game），以及這一首祝你生日快樂歌〈Happy Birthday to You〉。

1893 年，兩位美國肯德基州路易維爾市（Louisville）的教師姐妹花 Mildred J. Hill 和 Patty Smith Hill 編寫了這首歌，最早的用途是教室問候曲，收錄於《幼稚園故事歌曲》（*Song Stories for the Kindergarten*）中，原本的曲名為〈Good Morning to All〉。

1935 年，這首〈生日快樂歌〉終於受到版權的保護，1988 年，樺樹集團股份有限公司（Birch Tree Group, Ltd.）以約二億五千萬的價錢，轉讓給華納兄弟傳播公司（Warner Communications）。如今每年約創造一千兩百萬的版稅收入，到 2030 年版權才會期滿。〈生日快樂歌〉已榮登《金氏世界紀錄大全》最膾炙人口的歌曲寶座。

4 Hot Potato

One potato, two potatoes,
Three potatoes, four,
Five potatoes, six potatoes,
Seven potatoes, more.

One potato, two potatoes,
Three potatoes, four,
Five potatoes, six potatoes,
Seven potatoes, more.

一顆馬鈴薯，兩顆馬鈴薯，
三顆馬鈴薯，四顆，
五顆馬鈴薯，六顆馬鈴薯，
七顆馬鈴薯，還有更多。

一顆馬鈴薯，兩顆馬鈴薯，
三顆馬鈴薯，四顆，
五顆馬鈴薯，六顆馬鈴薯，
七顆馬鈴薯，還有更多。

「燙手山芋」是很常見的兒童遊戲，遊戲方式是把燙手山芋扔給他人。1565 年，馬鈴薯傳入歐洲，十六世紀中葉，西班牙開始耕種。1846 年，「燙手山芋」開始被引申為「避之唯恐不及而想立刻丟棄的事物」。1885 年，加拿大開始收錄這首歌，原版本是「One potato, two potato, three potato . . .」，為便於唸誦，potato 的複數未使用 potatoes。在本書，因英語學習之需要，改為複數形 potatoes。

potato [pəˋteto] (n.) 馬鈴薯
- *Potatoes are yummy.* 馬鈴薯好好吃耶。

5 Hot Cross Bun

Hot cross buns!
Hot cross buns!
One a penny, two a penny.
Hot cross buns!

If you have no daughters,
Give them to your sons!
One a penny, two a penny.
Hot cross buns!

熱騰騰的小餐包！
熱騰騰的小餐包！
一個一分錢，兩個一分錢。
熱騰騰的小餐包！

如果你沒有女兒，
就給你的兒子吧！
一個一分錢，兩個一分錢。
熱騰騰的小餐包！

古希臘人在春分時，會以 bous 麵包獻祭給月亮和眾女神，象徵迎接重生、生生不息的大自然力量。西元 350 年之後，開始用奶油或糖霜在麵包上做成十字架形狀，象徵耶穌乃「永生的活糧」。人們認為，將熱十字麵包（cross bun）掛在家中，可以驅魔避邪，甚至治療疾病。

在克倫威爾（Oliver Cromwell, 1599–1658）治理期間，復活節前的六週封齋期（Lent, Lenten Season）才能烘烤販賣十字麵包，英國復辟後，禁令開放。今天，小販的叫賣聲「Hot cross buns!」，聲聲喚回孩提時光的回憶。

bun [bʌn] (n.) 小餐包
- *We all love buns a lot.* 我們都愛吃小餐包。

6 The Muffin Man

Oh, do you know the muffin man,
The muffin man, the muffin man?
Oh, do you know the muffin man
Who lives on Drury Lane?

Oh, yes I know the muffin man,
The muffin man, the muffin man.
Oh, yes I know the muffin man
Who lives on Drury Lane.

喔，你認不認識那位賣鬆餅的人？
那位賣鬆餅的人，那位賣鬆餅的人！
喔，你認不認識那位賣鬆餅的人？
那位住在杜利巷賣鬆餅的人？

喔，是啊，我認識那位賣鬆餅的人，
那位賣鬆餅的人，那位賣鬆餅的人！
喔，是啊，我認識那位賣鬆餅的人，
那位住在杜利巷賣鬆餅的人。

lane [len] (n.) 巷
- *There's a baker who lives on Drury Lane.*
  有一位烘焙師住在杜立巷中。

muffin [ˋmʌfɪn] (n.) 馬芬鬆餅
- *The muffins you baked are delicious!*
  你烤的鬆餅真好吃！

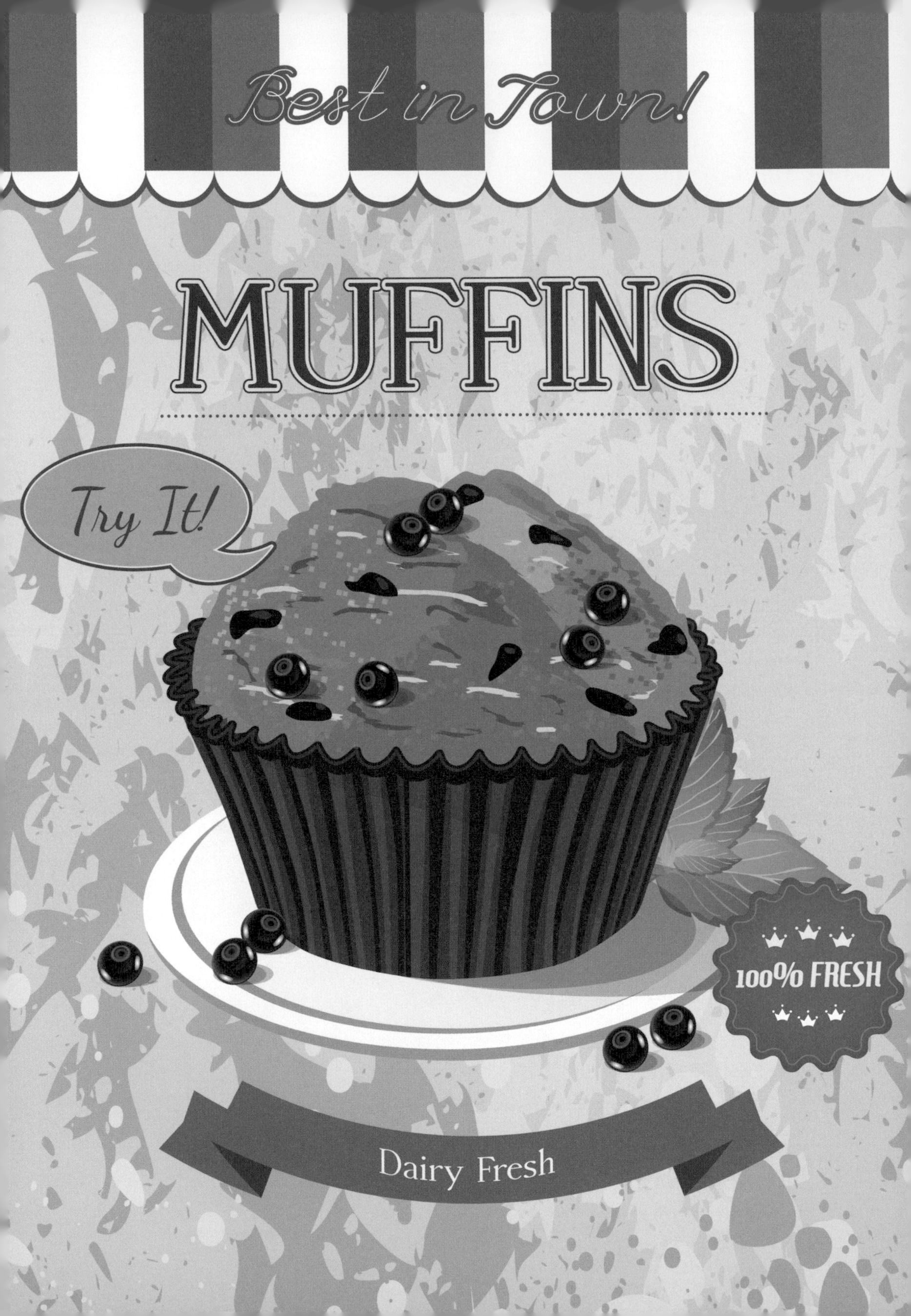
Best in Town!
MUFFINS
Try It!
100% FRESH
Dairy Fresh

Blueberry Muffins

1 1/3 cups all-purpose flour.
1/3 cup all-purpose flour.

Flour

2 teaspoons baking powder.
1 cup fresh blueberries.

1/2 teaspoon salt.
1/3 cup butter, cubed.

1 egg.

3/4 cup white sugar.
1/2 cup white sugar.
1/3 cup vegetable oil.

1 teaspoons ground cinnamon.
1/3 cup milk.

Directions

Ireheat oven to 400 degrees F (200 degrees C).
Grease muffin cups or line with muffin liners.
Combine 1 1/3 cups flour,
3/4 cup sugar, salt and baking powder.
Place vegetable oil into a 1 cup measuring cup;
add the egg and enough milk to fill the cup.
Mix this with flour mixture. Fold in blueberries.
Fill muffin cups right to the top,
and sprinkle with crumb topping mixture.
To Make Crumb Topping:
Mix together 1/2 cup sugar, 1/3 cup flour,
1/3 cup butter, and 1 teaspoons cinnamon.
Mix with fork, and sprinkle over muffins
before baking.
Bake for 20 to 25 minutes in the preheated oven.

西元十世紀左右，在英國大不列顛島西南部的威爾斯，人們開始在高溫的石頭上，烘烤添加酵母的 Bara Maen 蛋糕充飢。時至十九世紀，人們改在淺鍋上煎餅。特別是維多利亞時代，家家戶戶鬆餅香四溢，小販沿街叫賣這些新鮮現烤的鬆餅，挨家挨戶遞送香噴噴的喜悅，別具懷舊氣息。而英國的杜立巷（Drury Lane），正是鬆餅人的聚集地。一代代的孩子們，傳唱著兒時鬆餅人叫賣的記憶，久久不散……。

7 Star Light

Star light, star bright,
First star I see tonight.
Wish I may, wish I might,
Have the wish I wish tonight.

Star light, star bright,
First star I see tonight.
Wish I may, wish I might,
Have the wish I wish tonight.

星光點點，星光閃耀。
今晚我看見的第一眼星光。
希望我可以，希望我能夠，
實現我今晚許下的願望。

星光點點，星光閃耀。
今晚我看見的第一眼星光。
希望我可以，希望我能夠，
實現我今晚許下的願望。

十九世紀末，美國開始流行這首歌曲。人們認為，
當夜幕低垂，望著窗外寶藍絨似的天空，對著第
一顆映入眼簾的星星許願，願望就能實現。在各
種文化中，星星象徵著希望與指引光芒。古埃及
人認為，星星是往生者快樂的靈魂；蘇格蘭人視
星星為上帝的亙久的愛，陪伴著你驅走孤寂；在
現代科學裡，星星是宇宙運行的一份子。對人類
而言，星星是純真的願望。晚安，我的願望！

8 Little Green Frog

"Gung, gung," went the little green frog one day.
"Gung, gung," went the little green frog.
"Gung, gung," went the little green frog one day.
And his eyes went "aah, aah, gung."

「呱，呱，」小青蛙向前跳。
「呱，呱，」小青蛙向前跳。
「呱，呱，」小青蛙向前跳。
他的眼睛「嘎，嘎，呱」。

這首童謠出自法國童話作品《Cabinet des Fées》。童話研究者德魯·蘭格（Andrew Lang, 1844–1912）將它收錄進《蘭格世界童話全集》裡。故事中，王子 Saphir 奉父親 Peridor 之命，前往尋找一隻華麗斑斕的鳥，途中巧遇一隻小綠青蛙。小綠青蛙前後三次指引王子秘密進入皇宮，但前兩次王子都因沒聽小綠青蛙的警告，弄醒了整個皇宮的人而行動失敗。第三次，他終於找到了這隻鳥，也巧遇仰慕已久的鏡中女孩，原來女孩便是小綠青蛙，兩人最後結為連理，傳為佳話。

frog [fɑg] (n.) 青蛙

- *The frog has a pair of funny eyes.*
  那隻青蛙的一對眼睛很有趣。

9 Row, Row, Row Your Boat

Row, row, row your boat
Gently down the stream.
Merrily, merrily, merrily, merrily,
Life is but a dream.

划，划，划著你的船兒，
輕輕地順水划，
開心地，開心地，
開心地，開心地，
人生不過一場夢。

這首韻文蘊含著深刻的人生哲理，細細品味，便能體會弦外之音。划著承載著我們靈魂的身軀，每個人拚命地力爭上游，想要出人頭地。但是，有多少人真能功成名就、流芳萬世呢？

在人生走下坡的時候，不要戀棧塵世的浮華，其實，溫柔地對待自己和週遭的人，不經意間就能發現世間的美好。用喜悅的心，敞臂迎接人生的每個階段，哪怕是下坡呢？人生如夢，用生命編織夢想，讓夢想精彩生命吧！

merrily [ˋmɛrɪlɪ] (adv.) 快樂地
The boy laughs merrily. 那個男孩笑得很開心。

10 Bluebird, Bluebird

(10)

Bluebird, bluebird, through my window.
Bluebird, bluebird, through my window.
Bluebird, bluebird, through my window.
Oh, Johnny, I'm tired.

Bluebird, bluebird, through my window.
Bluebird, bluebird, through my window.
Bluebird, bluebird, through my window.
Oh, Johnny, I'm so tired.

藍鳥，藍鳥，飛過我窗前。
藍鳥，藍鳥，飛過我窗前。
藍鳥，藍鳥，飛過我窗前。
哦，強尼，我累了。

藍鳥，藍鳥，飛過我窗前。
藍鳥，藍鳥，飛過我窗前。
藍鳥，藍鳥，飛過我窗前。
哦，強尼，我好累。

bluebird [ˈblu͵bɝd] (n.) 藍鳥
• *Look over there! It's a bluebird.*
  看那邊！有隻藍鳥。

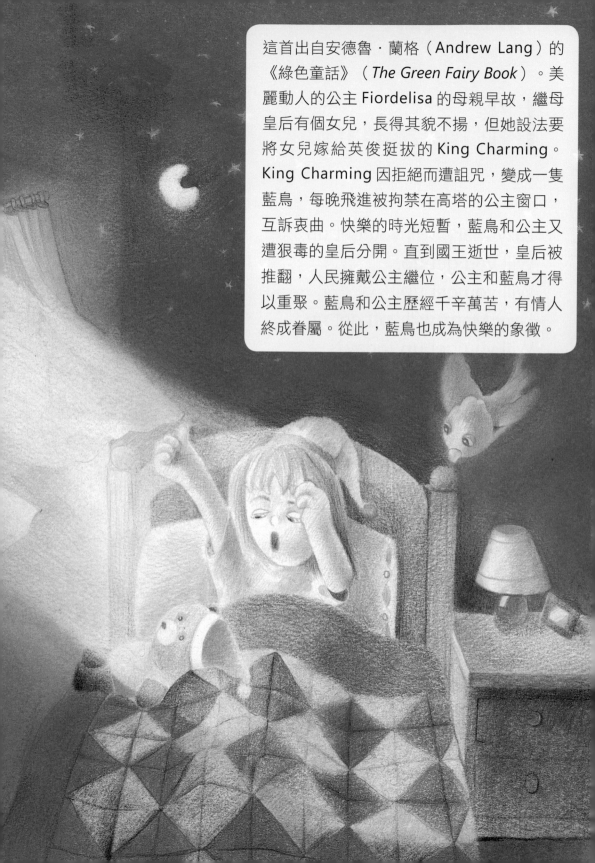

這首出自安德魯・蘭格（Andrew Lang）的《綠色童話》（*The Green Fairy Book*）。美麗動人的公主 Fiordelisa 的母親早故，繼母皇后有個女兒，長得其貌不揚，但她設法要將女兒嫁給英俊挺拔的 King Charming。King Charming 因拒絕而遭詛咒，變成一隻藍鳥，每晚飛進被拘禁在高塔的公主窗口，互訴衷曲。快樂的時光短暫，藍鳥和公主又遭狠毒的皇后分開。直到國王逝世，皇后被推翻，人民擁戴公主繼位，公主和藍鳥才得以重聚。藍鳥和公主歷經千辛萬苦，有情人終成眷屬。從此，藍鳥也成為快樂的象徵。

11 Lazy Mary

Lazy Mary, will you get up,
Will you get up,
Will you get up,
Lazy Mary, will you get up,
Will you get up today?

No, no, Mother, I won't get up,
I won't get up,
I won't get up,
No, no, Mother, I won't get up,
I won't get up today!

懶惰瑪麗，你要不要起床了？
你要不要起床了？
你要不要起床了？
懶惰瑪麗，你要不要起床了？
你今天要不要起床了？

不要，不要，媽媽，我不要起床，
我不要起床，
我不要起床，
不要，不要，媽媽，我不要起床，
我今天不要起床。

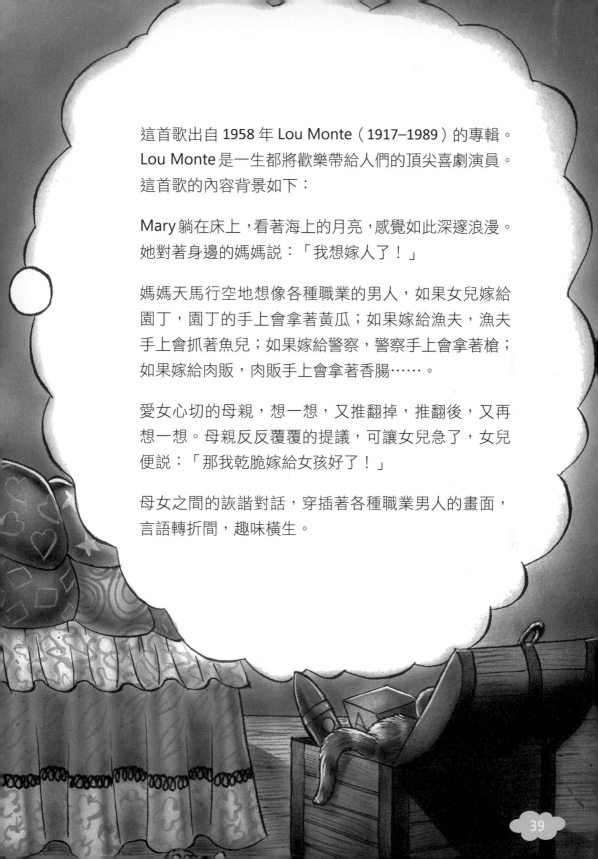

這首歌出自 1958 年 Lou Monte（1917–1989）的專輯。
Lou Monte 是一生都將歡樂帶給人們的頂尖喜劇演員。
這首歌的內容背景如下：

Mary 躺在床上，看著海上的月亮，感覺如此深邃浪漫。
她對著身邊的媽媽說：「我想嫁人了！」

媽媽天馬行空地想像各種職業的男人，如果女兒嫁給
園丁，園丁的手上會拿著黃瓜；如果嫁給漁夫，漁夫
手上會抓著魚兒；如果嫁給警察，警察手上會拿著槍；
如果嫁給肉販，肉販手上會拿著香腸……。

愛女心切的母親，想一想，又推翻掉，推翻後，又再
想一想。母親反反覆覆的提議，可讓女兒急了，女兒
便說：「那我乾脆嫁給女孩好了！」

母女之間的詼諧對話，穿插著各種職業男人的畫面，
言語轉折間，趣味橫生。

12 The Train Is A-Coming

The train is a-coming, oh, yes!
The train is a-coming, oh, yes!
The train is a-coming, the train is a-coming,
The train is a-coming, oh, yes!

Better get your ticket, oh, yes!
Better get your ticket, oh, yes!
Better get your ticket, better get your ticket,
Better get your ticket, oh, yes!

哦，對啊，火車就要來了！
哦，對啊，火車就要來了！
火車就要來了！火車就要來了！
哦，對啊，火車就要來了！

哦，對啊，趕緊拿出你的車票！
哦，對啊，趕緊拿出你的車票！
趕緊拿出你的車票！趕緊拿出你的車票！
哦，對啊，趕緊拿出你的車票！

美國西部拓荒年代，除了風塵僕僕駕著馬車到西部開拓之外，火車的飛快速度和緊湊的班次，也讓火車成為西部拓荒的重要交通工具。到了 1869 年，結合「中部太平洋線」（Central Pacific）和「美國太平洋線」（Union Pacific）的第一條跨大陸的鐵道完工，立下了東西交通的里程碑。

凱西．瓊斯（Casey Jones, 1863–1900）是一位盡責的火車駕駛員。有一次，因為時程延遲了，他駕駛著砲彈快車（Cannonball Express）飛快地行駛在鐵道上，突然，前面班次的火車出現在眼前，整車的乘客性命，就掌握在他的手中。他沒有跳車逃命，而是堅守崗位，在駕駛座上使盡全力地減緩火車速度。最後，凱西．瓊斯雖然在這件火車事故中不幸喪生，但是他的英勇的事蹟，仍流傳在西部地區晦暗搖晃的車廂裡。

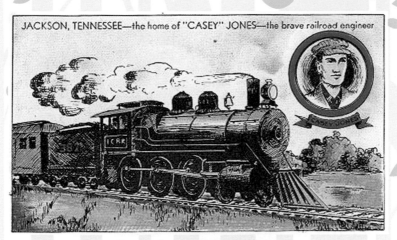

Casey Jones (1863–1900)

13 Go In and Out the Window

Go in and out the window,
Go in and out the window,
Go in and out the window,
As we have done before.

Stand up and face your partner,
Stand up and face your partner,
Stand up and face your partner,
As we have done before.

走過窗戶進又出，
走過窗戶進又出，
走過窗戶進又出，
像我們做過的。

站起來和夥伴面對面，
站起來和夥伴面對面，
站起來和夥伴面對面，
像我們做過的。

這首歌謠長久以來即是幼兒律動和吟唱的韻文，遊戲方式如下：

1️⃣ 所有小朋友手牽手圍成圓圈，假裝是窗戶。

2️⃣ 其中兩位小朋友站到中間，雙手高高互握，在窗戶（圍成圓圈的小朋友）之間穿梭著，像鳥兒飛越窗戶般靈巧。

3️⃣ 數次之後，兩位小朋友雙手分開，個別尋找新的玩伴，繼續玩鳥兒穿越窗戶的遊戲。

4️⃣ 當作鳥兒的小朋友越來越多，窗戶越來越小。
最後，窗戶消失了，所有的小朋友都加入了飛翔的行列！

stand up 站起來
* *Everybody, stand up!* 大家站起來！

partner [ˋpɑrtnɚ] (n.) 夥伴
* *We are partners!* 我們是夥伴。

14 Little Peter Rabbit

Little Peter Rabbit had a fly up his ear,
Little Peter Rabbit had a fly up his ear,
Little Peter Rabbit had a fly up his ear,
And he flicked it 'til it flew a-way.

有隻蒼蠅停在彼得小兔的耳朵上，
有隻蒼蠅停在彼得小兔的耳朵上，
有隻蒼蠅停在彼得小兔的耳朵上，
他輕輕拍牠直到牠飛走。

1902 年，《The Tale of Peter Rabbit》出版，彼得兔於焉
誕生。這本書的作者是波特女士（Beatrix Potter, 1866–
1943）。她出生於倫敦，小時候的玩伴是青蛙、蠑螈、
蝙蝠等。她的第一隻兔子叫作 Benjamin，第二隻才叫
Peter，波特為牠們畫素描，書中描述的主題，是她們家
庭假日出遊到 Scotland 和 Lake District 的故事。波特溫
馨的筆觸和佈景，將英式莊園的特色表露無遺。百年來，
彼得兔的故事已經被翻譯成各種語言，彼得兔身穿藍外
套和木屐的形象，令世界各地的讀者印象深刻。

rabbit [ˋræbɪt] (n.) 兔子
- *The rabbit is cute.* 那隻兔子真可愛。

fly [flaɪ] (n.) 蒼蠅
- *There's a fly upon it.* 有隻蒼蠅在上面。

flick [flɪk] (v.) 輕彈

15 I Caught a Fish

One, two, three, four, five,
Once I caught a fish alive.
Six, seven, eight, nine, ten,
Then I let him go again.

Why did you let him go?
Because he bit my finger so.
Which finger did he bite?
This little finger on the right

一，二，三，四，五，
我抓到一條活魚。
六，七，八，九，十，
我把他放回去。

你為什麼放他走？
因為他咬我手指頭，
咬你哪隻手指頭？
右手這隻小指頭。

alive [əˋlaɪv] (a.) 活著的
- *All of them are alive.*
  他們都還活著。

finger [ˋfɪŋgɚ] (n.) 手指
- *I use my finger to touch the fish.*
  我用手指去碰魚。

西雅圖有一個遠近馳名的派克魚攤（Pike Place Fish Market），他們寓快樂於賣魚的工作哲學，散播給源源不絕的觀光客，圍觀的客人無不被驚險的丟魚表演和出其不意的逗弄，樂得開懷大笑，呈現出奇異的工作方式與創意的生活態度。

這首歌寫於 1888 年，是一首教導孩子們學習數字的韻文，一邊吟唱之際，還要一邊用手指筆劃數字，才能加深孩子們的印象。

唱遊方式為：

1 當唱到「One, two, three, four, five」時，
以手指頭筆劃數字。

2 當唱到「Once I caught a fish alive」時，
以手臂假裝捧魚，魚活蹦亂跳的模樣。

3 當唱到「Six, seven, eight, nine, ten」時，
以手指頭筆劃數字。

4 當唱到「Then I let him go again」時，
合併雙手前後泅泳，象徵魚獲得自由，
離開羅網。

16 Good Night

Good night, baby,
Good night, baby,
Good night, baby,
It's time to go to bed.
Merrily we roll along, roll along,
  roll along
Merrily we roll along as off to
  bed we go.

晚安，寶貝，
晚安，寶貝，
晚安，寶貝，
睡覺時間到囉。
我們開心地晃啊晃啊晃，
我們開心地晃著入眠。

嬰兒迷濛的雙眼和均勻的呼吸聲，讓夜更加深沉了。
輕輕擁抱著，給他一個香香的親親，他的夢裡或許
會多了好幾顆閃亮的星星。有一句話是這麼說的：
「Goodnight, sleep tight.」這個意思是「晚安，睡得緊」？睡得
香甜，怎麼會用 tight 呢？原來，這是因為在中世紀時，床墊是用
繩索交錯編成的，用久了，繩索就會鬆脫。像在莎士比亞時，床
墊就是綑綁固定住的。「Goodnight, sleep tight.」這句話，最早
就是由中世紀的英國開始流傳。把繩索拉緊，「可以睡得緊」，
而且蟲蟲也才鑽不進去床墊裡面，好讓你有一個甜美的夢哦！

roll [rol] (v.) 搖擺；滾動
- *Peter and Mary are still rolling a snowball outside.*
  彼特與瑪莉還在外面滾雪球。

17 Days of the Week

Sunday, Monday, Tuesday,
Wednesday comes after them.
Thursday, Friday, Saturday.
There are seven days in a week.
Sunday, Monday, Tuesday,
Wednesday, Thursday, Friday, Saturday.

星期天，星期一，星期二，
接著是星期三。
星期四，星期五，星期六。
一個星期有七天。
星期天，星期一，星期二，
星期三，星期四，星期五，星期六。

古埃及人辨識了七個天體：土星、木星、火星、太陽、金星、水星和月亮。他們將神聖而重要的時間，用這些天體來命名，產生了星期的名稱：

第一天 → Saturn	第二天 → Sun
第三天 → Moon	第四天 → Mars
第五天 → Mercury	第六天 → Jupiter
第七天 → Venus	

當時，第一天是 Saturn's day（Saturday）。後來，猶太教徒將星期六（Saturday）改成一星期的最後一天。另有一說，星期的命名源自古希臘羅馬神話，後來逐漸被北歐神話同化，以吻合北歐神話的傳說。

18 Trot to Boston

Trot and trot to Boston town
  to get a stick of candy.
One for you,
And one for me,
And one for Dicky Dandy.

跑，跑到波士頓城，
去拿枝糖，
一枝給你，
一枝給我，
一枝給迪克·丹帝。

波士頓是美國新英格蘭的學術及文化中心，是美東最早開發的城市，著名的麻省理工學院和哈佛大學都在這裡。

這首韻文有很多版本，和嬰幼兒遊戲時，可以隨機改編歌詞。將嬰幼兒放在膝上，與大人面對面，邊唱歌邊律動。時而隨節拍抖動雙腿，配上馬嘶聲，假裝是騎馬去波士頓；時而突然張開膝蓋，輔以跌撞聲，好像差點落馬；時而放緩腳步，拉長拍子，彷彿即將歸來。透過這個遊戲除了增加親子親密關係外，也可以增進孩子們的聽覺靈敏度和集中其注意力。

trot [trɑt] (v.) 小跑步
- *The horse trots around the town.*
  馬兒在城中跑著。

19 I Like Coffee

Bluebells, cockle shells, Evey, ivy, over.	藍鈴鐺，鳥蛤殼， Evey，常春藤，翻轉。
I like coffee; I like tea. I like the boys and the boys like me. Yes—no–maybe so. Yes—no–maybe so.	我愛咖啡，也愛茶。 我愛男生，男生也愛我。 是，不是，或許吧。 是，不是，或許吧。
I like coffee; I like tea. I like the girls and the girls like me. Yes—no–maybe so. Yes—no–maybe so.	我愛咖啡，也愛茶。 我愛女生，女生也愛我。 是，不是，或許吧。 是，不是，或許吧。

咖啡和茶是歷史悠久、最受歡迎的飲品，那麼咖啡和茶的是怎麼來的呢？先來看看咖啡吧！西元前八百年，在東非的衣索比亞，有一位牧人發現他的羊在 Kaffa 地區吃了一種矮樹叢的紅莓之後，變得機敏而愛嬉鬧，於是他摘下這些紅莓來烹煮，喝下了世界上的第一杯咖啡。阿拉伯人長久以來也流傳著那又黑又苦的神祕飲料，具有振奮人心的神秘力量。

那麼，茶的起源呢？五千年前的一個夏日，中國的神農皇帝和官員們微服出巡偏遠地區。途中歇息時，奴婢們燒開了水，準備奉水。這時，灌木叢中飄來一片枯葉，正巧掉落在燒滾的開水中。奴婢急得趕緊要撈起枯葉，未料枯葉浸漬了出棕色的汁液。神農氏大感好奇，嚐了一下，沒想到味道甘美沁脾。

這是一首團體跳繩遊戲時，孩子們琅琅上口的打油詩。一邊跳繩、一邊唱和，逐漸加快旋律和頻率，遊戲的緊張氣氛隨之升高，噗通通的心跳和氣喘吁吁的氣息聲，此起彼落。

shell [ʃɛl] (n.) 貝殼
• *Shells are beautiful.* 貝殼很美麗。

20 Color Song

Green and yellow, orange and red,
Black and white, brown and pink,
Blue and purple, pretty colors,
They are colorful.

綠色和黃色，橘色和紅色。
黑色和白色，棕色和粉紅色。
藍色和紫色，漂亮的顏色。
多采多姿的顏色。

音樂悦耳、色彩悦目，兩者完美結合於色彩歌中。孩子們可以邊哼、邊拼字，唱熟了，拼字也熟了；也可以邊吟、邊認顏色，隨著家長或老師的指示，迅速替換歌詞。在西方文化中，顏色有以下涵義：

紅色 ★ 象徵火和血，代表活力、戰爭、危險、果斷、熱情、欲望。

橘色 ★ 常和歡樂、陽光結合，代表熱忱、創造力、吸引力、成功。

黃色　　是陽光的另一種顏色，顯示歡笑、快樂、思維能力、幹勁。

綠色 ★ 象徵自然，代表成長、和諧、生氣勃勃、繁殖力。

藍色 ★ 是天空和海的顏色，常和深度、沉穩聯想在一起。

紫色 ★ 融合了藍色的沉穩和紅色的活力，代表高貴、力量、奢華。

白色 ☆ 代表光、美德、純真、純淨、童貞等，是盡善盡美的顏色。

黑色 ★ 代表力量、優雅、禮節、死亡、邪惡、神秘等。

21 The Alphabet Song

A, B, C, D, E, F, G,
H, I, J, K, L, M, N, O, P,
Q, R, S, and T, U, V,
W, X, and Y, and Z.
Now I know my ABCs,
Next time won't you sing
    with me?

A、B、C、D、E、F、G、
H、I、J、K、L、M、N、O、P、
Q、R、S 和 T、U、V,
W、X 和 Y 和 Z。
現在我學了 ABC,
下次你要不要跟我一起唱?

埃及的象形文字從描摹動物或東西的外觀而來,最後演變成為符號。腓尼基人將埃及字母加以改進,創造腓尼基 22 個字母。希臘人又對腓尼基字母加以改進,創造希臘字母;古羅馬人繼之加以改進,發明拉丁字母,而英文字母就是屬於拉丁字母。

ABC 字母歌可以說是孩子們學英語的第一首歌。在〈一閃一閃小星星〉膾炙人口的曲調中,輕鬆學會字母的順序和讀法。這首歌的旋律源自法國民謠〈Ah! Vous Dirais-je, Maman〉,現在已流傳在世界各地的幼稚園、家中、課堂或操場上。

next [nɛkst] (a.) 下一個的
- *I can't wait for the next singing class!*
  我等不及下一堂歌唱課啦！

22 Pea Porridge Hot

Pea porridge hot!
Pea porridge cold!
Pea porridge in the pot
Nine days old!

Some like it hot,
Some like it cold,
And some like it in the pot
Nine days old!

豌豆粥燙！
豌豆粥冷！
豌豆粥鍋裡放了
九天久！

有人愛吃熱，
有人愛吃冷，
有人愛吃鍋裡的
九天久！

Pea porridge 是用文火燉煮，食材有豆子、穀粒、蔬菜，有時也會加點肉或培根。這是鄉下農家的主食，常常這一餐吃剩，下一餐繼續添食材燉煮，如此煮了又煮，一鍋粥可以反覆煮好幾天。

十六世紀，農民的生活比較苦，沒有大魚大肉，吃剩的食物也不能浪費丟棄。現代人用來取暖的壁爐，在當時是用來煮食的，通常會把全家唯一的鍋子放在火爐上烹煮，成為全家的三餐。食畢，這個廚房也是客廳，有些家庭甚至只有一個房間。這首韻文描述了中世紀農村人們的艱困生活，讓人遙想那些艱苦的日子。

pea [pi] (n.) 豌豆
  Mom says peas are good for me. 媽媽說豌豆對我身體好。

 porridge [ˋpɔrɪdʒ] (n.) 粥
  So, I usually eat a lot of pea porridge. 我常吃很多豌豆粥。

pot [pɑt] (n.) 鍋子
  And, I help clean the pot myself. 而且我都自己洗鍋子。

23 Michael, Row Your Boat

Michael, row your boat ashore, Hallelujah!
Michael, row your boat ashore, Hallelujah!

Mary, row your boat ashore, Hallelujah!
Mary, row your boat ashore, Hallelujah!

Tony, row your boat ashore, Hallelujah!
Tony, row your boat ashore, Hallelujah!

Susan, row your boat ashore, Hallelujah!
Susan, row your boat ashore, Hallelujah!

麥克，快划船上岸，哈雷路亞！
麥克，快划船上岸，哈雷路亞！

瑪莉，快划船上岸，哈雷路亞！
瑪莉，快划船上岸，哈雷路亞！

湯尼，快划船上岸，哈雷路亞！
湯尼，快划船上岸，哈雷路亞！

蘇珊，快划船上岸，哈雷路亞！
蘇珊，快划船上岸，哈雷路亞！

row [ro] (v.) 划船
- *It's fun to row a boat.*
  划船真好玩。

ashore [əˋʃor] (adv.) 向岸上
- *Let's row ashore together.*
  咱們一起划上岸吧！

十九世紀，一艘艘船歷經波濤洶湧和惡劣天候的肆虐，陸續進港，上面載著從非洲運來、倖存下來的黑奴抵達美國。喬治亞海群島遺世獨立地面對著浩瀚的大西洋，成了許多黑奴世世代代耕耘的地方。

來自非洲各地的黑奴們奮力地搖著槳，唱著自編的靈歌，但有誰會去留意這些鄉野小調的價值呢？意外地，這首歌脫穎而出，傳唱不已。這是一首黑奴抒發己懷的歌，Michael 是一位天使長的名字，在悲苦的生活中，宗教信仰和同儕間的取暖，是心靈莫大的慰藉。

24 Farm Song

🎧 24

Cows are mooing, moo, moo, moo.
Pigs are oinking, oink, oink, oink.
Dogs are barking, bow, wow, wow.
Oh, the farm is so much fun!

Cats are meowing, meow, meow, meow.
Ducks are quacking, quack, quack, quack.
Mice are squeaking, squeak, squeak, squeak.
Oh, the farm is so much fun!

牛兒哞哞叫。
豬兒齁齁叫。
狗兒汪汪叫。
哦，農場裡樂趣多！

貓兒喵喵叫，
鴨子呱呱叫，
老鼠吱吱叫，
哦，農場裡樂趣多！

cow [kaʊ] (n.) 母牛
* *The cows are so big on this farm.* 這農場的母牛很大隻。

duck [dʌk] (n.) 鴨子
* *And the ducks are so cute.* 鴨子也很可愛。

牛仔酷帥地在酒吧前決鬥的鏡頭，儼然是美國西部片的代表。這些在農場工作的牛仔，起源於中世紀的西班牙。十六世紀時，西班牙的牛仔們帶著他們的野馬（mustangs），遠渡重洋到新西班牙（後來的墨西哥），牛仔文化因而傳到新大陸。

在農場嘈雜的聲音中，你聽到了什麼？是哞哞的牛妹妹？是齁齁的豬弟弟？是汪汪的狗狗？還是喵喵的貓咪？鄉間的農場動物，成了孩子們最友善的朋友。動物們的聲音，在稚嫩的耳裡都是清晰可辨的。在向孩子們設計、講述故事時，可以出示農場動物的圖片、播放動物音效，或是讓孩子模仿動物叫聲，樂趣無窮。進而可以和孩子討論動物的特徵和習性，或來一趟農場的田野教學，訓練孩子們的聽力和專注力。在旋律中，你嗅到青草的氣味了嗎？

25 Head, Shoulders, Knees and toes

(25)

Head, shoulders, knees and toes,
Knees and toes,
Knees and toes.
Head, shoulders, knees and toes,
Eyes, ears, mouth and nose.

頭兒、肩膀、膝蓋、腳趾，
膝蓋、腳趾，
膝蓋、腳趾。
頭兒、肩膀、膝蓋、腳趾，
眼、耳、嘴和鼻。

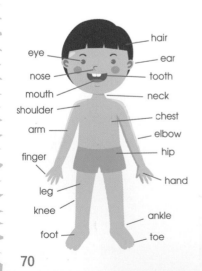

eye
nose
mouth
shoulder
arm
finger
leg
knee
foot

hair
ear
tooth
neck
chest
elbow
hip
hand
ankle
toe

這首歌用來教導孩子們認識身體的各部位。認識自己的身體，也是接受自己、愛護自己的第一步。這首歌也是絕佳的暖身運動，雙手跟隨著歌詞，行雲流水地碰觸身體的各部位，口裡哼著旋律，依序認識自己的身體。

你可以由慢而快，漸增速度，讓孩子們熟稔身體的英語說法，也可以輪流空缺該部位名稱，繼續動作，增加學習的趣味。你會發現，原來寓教於樂的學習如此輕鬆快意，試試看！

70

knee [ni] (n.) 膝蓋

• *He was on his knees proposing to Mary.*
他跪著向瑪麗求婚。

26 This Little Pig

(26)

This little pig went to the market,
This little pig stayed home,
This little pig had roast beef,
This little pig had none,
And this little pig cried, "Wee! Wee! Wee!"
All the way home.

這隻小豬上市場去。
這隻小豬待在家裡。
這隻小豬吃烤牛肉。
這隻小豬都沒吃。
這隻小豬哭叫著：「哇！哇！哇！」
一路哭回家。

beef [bif] (n.) 牛肉
- *We'll have beef for dinner.* 我們今晚吃牛肉。

在英國文化裡，人們給予 pig 不佳的形象，像是：

pig →	對警官的輕蔑用語；性別、種族歧視者
a pig →	貪婪、粗俗、骯髒或沒禮貌的人
pig out →	大吃大喝
in a pig's eye →	不太可能；幾乎不
buy a pig in a poke →	瞎買東西

這首歌用來教導孩子認識自己的手腳。伸出小手小腳，一起邊數數兒、邊唱歌，你對手腳的好奇，將在小豬豬活靈活現的「Wee! Wee!」叫聲中被滿足。

先從手開始，給每隻手指一個名字：

- 拇指這隻小豬上菜市場了
- 食指這隻小豬待在家裡
- 中指這隻小豬吃烤牛肉
- 無名指這隻小豬都沒吃
- 小指這隻小豬什麼都沒有，氣得一路從街頭吼回家——「Wee! Wee! Wee!」

此時適時在嬰兒全身騷癢，逗得他咯咯笑，像極了氣急敗壞的小豬身影。歌詞可以替換成別的動物哦！

27 I Saw Three Ships

I saw three ships come sailing by,
Sailing by, sailing by.
I saw three ships come sailing by,
On Christmas Day in the morning.

我看見三艘船兒駛近來，
駛近來，駛近來。
我看見三艘船兒駛近來，
在聖誕節早上。

I saw three ships come sailing by,
Sailing by, sailing by.
I saw three ships come sailing by,
On New Year's Day in the morning.

我看見三艘船兒駛近來，
駛近來，駛近來。
我看見三艘船兒駛近來，
在新年早上。

這首是英國維多利亞時代的聖歌，扣人心弦的經典程度，足以和〈綠袖子〉（Green Sleeves）這首英國古老的民謠媲美。耶穌啟程前往天國後，基督徒遭受羅馬人的迫害。聖約瑟和三位智者從君士坦丁堡前來，聖杯之謎縹渺在氤氳中。聖誕節當天現身的那三條船，有人說是三位智者，後來象徵聖家庭。「三」象徵三位一體（Trinity）。也有人認為這首歌的來源是十四世紀德國的「頌歌船」，是耶穌搭船而來的神秘傳說。

sail [sel] (v.) 航行

● *They all sail toward the shore.*
他們朝岸邊航行過去。

28 I'm a Little Teapot

I'm a little teapot,
Short and stout!
Here is my handle.
Here is my spout.

我是只小茶壺，
矮又肥！
這是我的把手，
這是我的嘴兒。

When I get all steamed up,
Hear me shout.
Tip me over
And pour me out!

當我燒開，
聽我高呼，
傾斜著我，
倒出水來。

這是一首描述茶壺沸騰和倒水的韻文。蘊積了滿腹的怨懟，你終於達到沸點，聲嘶力竭地吶喊著：一手叉腰，裝作壺把，另一手側伸，做為壺口。小茶壺邊唱、邊比劃著，時而蹲，時而起，時而側身倒水，時而仰天長嘯。水開了！來吧，茶杯們，湊過來分享我的喜與憂！以下是英國的版本：

I'm a little teapot, short and stout.
Here's my handle, here's my spout.
When the kettle's boiling, hear me shout.
Tip me up and pour me out.

teapot [ˋtiˏpɑt] (n.) 茶壺
- *The teapot is so cute.* 這支茶壺好可愛。

stout [staʊt] (a.) 矮胖的
- *He is a stout man.* 他是個矮個兒胖子

handle [ˋhændl̩] (n.) 把手
- *The handle part is funny.* 把手部分很有趣。

spout [spaʊt] (n.) 壺嘴
- *It has a special spout.* 壺嘴也很特別。

29 My Bonnie

My Bonnie lies over the ocean.
My Bonnie lies over the sea.
My Bonnie lies over the ocean.
Oh! Bring back my Bonnie to me.

Bring back, bring back.
Oh! Bring back my Bonnie to me, to me.
Bring back, bring back.
Oh! Bring back my Bonnie to me.

我的邦妮躺在汪洋上，
我的邦妮躺在大海上，
我的邦妮躺在汪洋上，
哦，請帶回我的邦妮。

帶回來，帶回來。
哦！請帶回我的邦妮。
帶回來，帶回來。
哦！請帶回我的邦妮。

英國斯圖亞特王室最後一個熱衷追求皇位的王子查理（Charles Edward Stuart, 1720–1788），別名 Bonnie Prince Charlie，意思是「漂亮王子查理」，bonnie 是法語，他小時候是在法國長大的。

為重返斯圖亞特王室的光榮，王子查理於 1745–46 年領導蘇格蘭人入侵蘇格蘭和英國，歷史上稱為 Jacobites（詹姆斯黨人）叛變。復辟失敗後，王子查理成為支持蘇格蘭獨立的人們心中的痛。這是一首蘇格蘭傳統民俗歌謠，常用於童子軍營火晚會壓軸。

ocean [ˈoʃən] (n.) 海洋

30 The Itsy Bitsy Spider

❶	The itsy-bitsy spider	可愛小蜘蛛，
❷	Climbed up the waterspout.	爬上了水管。
❸	Down came the rain	雨水流下來，
❹	And washed the spider out.	沖走小蜘蛛。
❺	Out came the sun	太陽出來了，
❻	And dried up all the rain.	雨水都曬乾
❼	And the itsy-bitsy spider	可愛小蜘蛛，
❽	Climbed up the spout again!	又爬上水管。

這首韻文來自丹麥，內容描寫一隻蜘蛛的冒險過程。小蜘蛛不知
天高地厚，總是爬上爬下，暴雨一來，牠會面臨什麼樣的命運呢？
唱這首韻文時，常會搭配歌詞作律動，左邊是句子的編號：

❶❷ 兩手食指和姆指相合交替動作，象徵爬的動作。

❸ 雙手合掌向下，抖動手指，象徵下雨的樣子。

❹ 雙手往外甩。

❺❻ 雙手往上，畫出半圓，太陽出來，手指往上抖動，雨蒸發了。

❼❽ 兩手食指和姆指相合交替動作，象徵爬的動作。

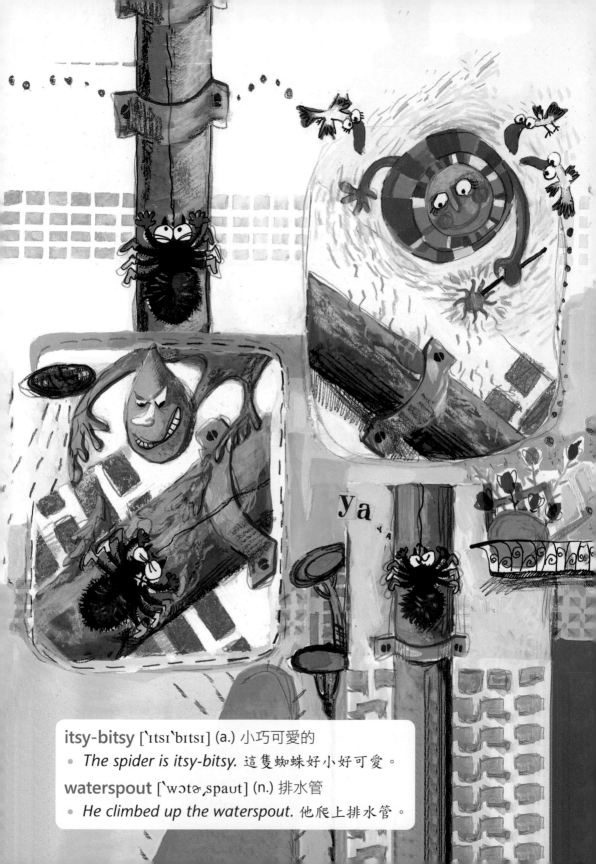

itsy-bitsy [ˈɪtsɪ ˈbɪtsɪ] (a.) 小巧可愛的
- *The spider is itsy-bitsy.* 這隻蜘蛛好小好可愛。

waterspout [ˈwɔtɚˌspaʊt] (n.) 排水管
- *He climbed up the waterspout.* 他爬上排水管。

31 Teddy Bear

Teddy Bear, Teddy Bear, turn around.
Teddy Bear, Teddy Bear, touch the ground.
Teddy Bear, Teddy Bear, show your shoe.
Teddy Bear, Teddy Bear, that will do.

Teddy Bear, Teddy Bear, go upstairs.
Teddy Bear, Teddy Bear, say your prayers.
Teddy Bear, Teddy Bear, switch off the light.
Teddy Bear, Teddy Bear, say good-night.

泰迪小熊，泰迪小熊，轉個圈，
泰迪小熊，泰迪小熊，摸摸地，
泰迪小熊，泰迪小熊，秀鞋子，
泰迪小熊，泰迪小熊，會這麼做。

泰迪小熊，泰迪小熊，上樓去，
泰迪小熊，泰迪小熊，做禱告，
泰迪小熊，泰迪小熊，燈關上，
泰迪小熊，泰迪小熊，道晚安。

ground [graʊnd] (n.) 地面
- *Look at the ground.* 看地上！

prayer [prɛr] (n.) 禱告
- *She says her prayers every night.* 她每晚都會禱告。

switch off 關掉
- *Please help me to switch off the light.* 麻煩幫我關燈。

有一年，美國老羅斯福總統（Theodore Roosevelt, 1858–1919）到密西西比打獵，結果一整天都毫無所獲。朋友們為了討總統開心，便五花大綁了一隻黑熊，準備讓總統大開殺戒。那隻無辜又楚楚可憐的小黑熊，激起了羅斯福總統的同情心，他下令釋放這隻熊，並且發誓再也不獵殺黑熊了。

之後，仁民愛物的羅斯福總統的故事，在大街小巷裡流傳。1902 年，德國玩具製造商生產了第一隻泰迪熊，順水推舟地以羅斯福總統的小名「泰迪」命名。一百多年來，泰迪熊已經是家喻戶曉的絨毛玩具，陪伴每顆稚嫩的心。

32 I See the Moon

(32)

I see the moon,
And the moon sees me.
God bless the moon,
And God bless me.

我看著月亮，
月亮看著我。
上帝保佑月亮，
上帝保佑著我。

傳統上，美國人將月分細分如下：

一月 → 狼月（Wolf Moon）
二月 → 風暴月（Storm Moon）
三月 → 道德月（Chaste Moon）
四月 → 種子月（Seed Moon）
五月 → 野兔月（Hare Moon）
六月 → 一對月（Dyad Moon）
七月 → 蜂蜜酒月（Mead Moon）
八月 → 麥芽汁月（Wort Moon）
九月 → 大麥月（Barley Moon）
十月 → 血統月（Blood Moon）
十一月 → 雪月（Snow Moon）
十二月 → 橡樹月（Oak Moon）

同一個月份裡如果有兩次滿月，第二次的滿月稱為藍月（Blue Moon）。每一次滿月都有不同的意義和神奇效果，所以會配合滿月時刻來進行宗教儀式。每逢滿月，就是占卜的絕佳時機，因為滿月會加強占卜的力量。

這首歌曲由活躍於一九二〇年代的美國作曲家、劇作家威爾森（Meredith Willson, 1902–1984）所作。

bless [blɛs] (v.) 保佑
- *May God bless you.*
  願上帝保佑你。

33 Where Is a Thumb?

Where is a thumb?
Where is a thumb?
Here I am.
Here I am.

How are you this morning?
Very well. I thank you.
Run away.
Run away.

Where is an index finger?
Where is an index finger?
Here I am.
Here I am.

How are you this morning?
Very well. I thank you.
Run away.
Run away.

Where is a middle finger?
Where is a middle finger?
Here I am.
Here I am.

How are you this morning?
Very well. I thank you.
Run away.
Run away.

Where is a ring finger?
Where is a ring finger?
Here I am.
Here I am.

How are you this morning?
Very well. I thank you.
Run away.
Run away.

Where is a little finger?
Where is a little finger?
Here I am.
Here I am.

How are you this morning?
Very well. I thank you.
Run away.
Run away.

大拇指在哪兒？
大拇指在哪兒？
在這裡。
在這裡。

今天早上好嗎？
很好，謝謝。
跑走了。
跑走了。

食指在哪兒？
食指在哪兒？
在這裡。
在這裡。

今天早上好嗎？
很好，謝謝。
跑走了。
跑走了。

中指在哪兒？
中指在哪兒？
在這裡。
在這裡。

今天早上好嗎？
很好，謝謝。
跑走了。
跑走了。

無名指在哪兒？
無名指在哪兒？
在這裡。
在這裡。

今天早上好嗎？
很好，謝謝。
跑走了。
跑走了。

小指在哪兒？
小指在哪兒？
在這裡。
在這裡。

今天早上好嗎？
很好，謝謝。
跑走了。
跑走了。

在英文裡面，有許多以 thumb 組成的片語與成語，例如：

rule of thumb → 以 thumb（拇指）當作 rule （規則），意思指「基本 原則、經驗法則」。

have a green thumb → 某人具有綠色的拇指，指 對栽種植物很有天分。

這首韻文也是屬於 finger play（手指謠）。大人們以兩 隻手指分飾兩角，表演相互對話招呼，並和小朋友一起 練習，最後朝相反方向跑開。在遊戲中可學習各個手指 的名稱，增添學習的趣味。

thumb [θʌm] (n.) 拇指
• Don't put your thumb in your mouth.
不要把拇指放嘴裡。

run away 逃離
• She wants to run away from her family.
她想逃離家庭。

本書將五隻手指的名稱改為現代用法，並加上冠詞，而在傳統的歌謠版本中，五隻手指的名稱則是：

thumbkin
pointer
tall man
ring man
pinkie

34 What Are You Wearing?

Sally's wearing a red dress, red
   dress, red dress.
Sally's wearing a red dress
All day long.

Michael's wearing a striped shirt,
   striped shirt, striped shirt.
Michael's wearing a striped shirt
All day long.

莎莉穿著紅洋裝，
紅洋裝，紅洋裝，
莎莉穿著紅洋裝，
一整天。

麥可穿著條紋襯衫，
條紋襯衫，條紋襯衫，
麥可穿著條紋襯衫，
一整天。

這是一首教導孩子們衣服與顏色的
韻文，可以從孩子當時的穿著開
始，挑起他們的學習動機，然後再
替換其他的顏色與衣服種類，唸到
某個顏色時，穿那個顏色的小朋友
就站起來說「萬歲！」可以採用
《鬆餅人》的曲子來唱誦：

If you're wearing red today,
Red today, red today,
If you're wearing red today,
Stand up and say "Hoo-ray!"

dress [drɛs] (n.) 洋裝
- *My mom bought me a new dress.*
  媽咪幫我買了一件新洋裝。

striped [spraɪpt] (a.) 條紋的
- *He wears a striped shirt today.*
  他今天穿著一件條紋襯衫。

35 Jimmy Crack Corn

Jimmy crack corn, and I don't care.
Jimmy crack corn, and I don't care.
Jimmy crack corn, and I don't care.
My master's gone away.

吉米磨碎玉米，我不在乎。
吉米磨碎玉米，我不在乎。
吉米磨碎玉米，我不在乎。
我的主人已經離開了。

這是一首十八世紀美國南方黑奴抒發心聲的諷刺詩歌，
表面上看來是奴隸在哀悼主人的過世，弦外之音卻是因
掙脫束縛、獲得自由而雀躍。較早的版本中有以下幾句：

When I was young I us'd to wait
On Massa and hand him de plate;
Pass down the bottle when he git dry,
And bresh away de blue tail fly.

黑奴除了田裡的工作、驅趕馬蠅，還要伺候主人的生活
起居。當有一天，主人從發狂的馬背上摔下來摔死時，
奴隸無動於衷，那也是可以理解的。有些馬蠅的腹部是
藍黑色的，但另有一說是影射穿著藍色制服、推翻蓄奴
制的聯邦軍隊。黑奴的心聲，在歌聲中緩緩流出。

crack [kræk] (v.) 使破裂
- *I'm cracking corn.* 我正在搗玉米。

corn [kɔrn] (n.) 玉米
- *Corn tastes sweet and yummy.*
  玉米嚐起來甜甜的很好吃。

master [ˋmæstɚ] (n.) 主人
- *The master is gone.* 主人不見了。

36 Sally Goes Around the Sun

Sally goes around the sun;
Sally goes around the moon;
Sally goes around the chimney top
Every afternoon. Boom!

莎莉繞著太陽轉，
莎莉繞著月亮轉，
莎莉繞著煙囪頂端轉，
每天下午，碰！

太陽和月亮輪替更迭，統治著白天與黑夜。在古希臘神話中，有月亮女神黛安娜（Diana），一彎新月，就像是黛安娜的神弓；在北歐神話中，瑪尼（Mani）駕駛著月車，是月亮的化身。在希臘神話中，阿波羅（Apollo）是太陽的保護神；在北歐神話中，蘇爾（Sol）是駕駛日車的女神。時至今日，解讀太陽、月亮等的占星術，仍盛行不衰。

go around 環繞;四處走動
- *Let's go around and around.* 我們來轉圈圈吧。

chimney [ˋtʃɪmnɪ] (n.) 煙囪
- *Smoke comes out from our chimney.*
  我們煙囪冒出煙來。

37 Oh Where, Oh Where Has My Little Dog Gone?

Oh where, oh where has my little dog gone?
Oh where, oh where can he be?
With his ears cut short and his tail cut long,
Oh where, oh where can he be?

喔，到哪兒？我的小狗到哪兒了？
喔，到哪兒？他能到那兒呢？
他的耳朵短短，尾巴長長，
喔，到哪兒？他能到那兒呢？

tail [tel] (n.) 尾巴
- *The dog's tail is so long.*
  狗狗的尾巴很長。

截短耳朵或尾巴，稱為 docking 或 bobbing。人們為什麼要截短狗狗的耳朵或尾巴呢？據說，這始於古羅馬帝國，當時人們認為，尾巴是狂犬病的來源，所以把狗狗的尾巴截短，以預防狂犬病。

在美國和英國，因應狗狗的種類和用途之不同，主人會將狗狗的耳朵或尾巴截短。例如，在田野裡工作的獵犬或牧羊犬，截短尾巴的目的是避免沾染芒刺或狐尾草，另外長尾巴如果沾附排泄物也不衛生。把德國短毛獵犬和拳師狗等看門狗的耳朵、尾巴截短，牠們看起來更會兇猛。相反地，小狗狗垂垂的耳朵，看起來比豎起的耳朵更惹人憐愛。

這首歌的作者是 Septimus Winner（1827–1902），他是十九世紀的流行歌曲作者，於 1970 年榮獲歌曲創作名人堂（Songwriters' Hall of Fame）的最高榮譽。這首歌在表達主人對愛犬的走失感到很傷心，帶有濃濃的德國口音。在唱這首歌時，可以將 dog 換成其他動物或物品，讓孩子們練習。

38 Pat-a-Cake

Pat-a-cake, pat-a-cake, the baker man.
Bake me a cake just as fast as you can.
Roll it and pat it and mark it with a B,
And put it in the oven for the baby and me!

打蛋糕，打蛋糕，麵包師傅。
快來幫我烤蛋糕。
滾一滾，拍一拍，在上頭寫個 B，
為寶寶，也為我，送進烤箱去。

pat [pæt] (v.) 輕拍
- *Raindrops are patting against the roof.*
  雨滴輕擊著屋頂。

oven [ˋʌvən] (n.) 烤箱
- *Put the cakes in the oven.*
  將蛋糕放入烤箱中。

考古學家在瑞士的新石器時代村落中，發現由濕穀粒做成、在滾燙的石頭上烹調而成的「蛋糕」。「蛋糕」的字眼最早出現在希臘文中，稱為 plakous。起司蛋糕的雛形，最早也出現於希臘。羅馬時代的蛋糕，稱為 placenta 或 Libum，看起來像油酥上疊著起司蛋糕，用於宗教用途。羅馬人最早烘焙含有葡萄乾、核桃和各式水果的水果蛋糕。

烘培技術最早始於古埃及人，1900 年代後期，蛋糕的烘培有了劃時代的進步，人們使用各式各樣的麵粉、酵母和烘培廚具，可以更輕易地製作複雜的蛋糕。在現代，蛋糕普遍出現在婚禮和生日等場合上，並且會在蛋糕上綴上名字和祝福語，用來表達慶祝之意。

這是一首拍手歌，小朋友們可以設計一系列從簡單到複雜的拍手遊戲，可以兩兩互拍，訓練手部反應的靈敏度。

第一句中的 baker man，一般流傳版本中沒有 the，本書為符合文法，加了定冠詞 the。

39 Bingo

There was a farmer had a dog,
And Bingo was his name-o.
B-I-N-G-O,
B-I-N-G-O,
B-I-N-G-O,
And Bingo was his name-o.

有個農夫有隻狗，
他的名字叫賓果。
B-I-N-G-O，
B-I-N-G-O，
B-I-N-G-O，
他的名字叫賓果。

這是英語系國家孩子們的賓果遊戲歌。這首歌通常唱六遍，從第二遍到第六遍，可以用其他的字替換 Bingo 拼出，也可以用拍手替換，考驗孩子們的專心度和臨場反應。

賓果遊戲可以回溯到十六世紀，1530 年，義大利出現每星期一次的國家樂透系統（Lo Giuoco del Lotto d'Italia），時至今日，這個樂透系統的收入仍是國家的一項財源。不過後來法國人將樂透發揚光大，設計成今日賓果遊戲的雛型：卡片上三水平列、九垂直欄的格子中，三水平列都畫上時，就是勝利者。在德國，樂透用於乘法運算的教具，甚至許多遊戲也都以樂透的原理來設計。

那麼，Lotto 這個字，是如何變成為 Bingo 的呢？那得先來認識 Beano 這個字，1929 年，落魄的玩具商人 Edwin S. Lowe 在前往美國佛羅里達州的傑克遜維途中，參加了一個鄉村的嘉年華會。他發現，會中有個 Beano 遊戲區被人潮擠得水泄不通，Beano 遊戲的玩法是樂透的延伸，當遊戲者號碼被唸出時，就在號碼上放一顆豆子，遊戲者可以連成橫的、直的或是斜的線。

這個遊戲啟發了 Edwin S. Lowe，他回到公寓裡，找了一群好友試玩 Beano。當勝利者唸出 Beano 時，他因為興奮過度，舌頭一時打結，唸成了 Bingo。他改良了 Beano 遊戲，不僅成為 Bingo 的創始者，也為自己的事業再創顛峰。

Bingo 不僅指賓果遊戲，後來也用來形容「事情圓滿完成」、「靈光一現的想法」，或是指「猜對了」。

40 All Night, All Day

All night, all day,
Angels are watching over me, my Lord.
All night, all day,
Angels are watching over me.

整夜，整天，
天使守護著我，我的主啊。
整夜，整天，
天使守護著我。

天使（angel）源自希臘語的 angelos，
意思是「精靈的使者」。在基督教中，
天使是一種「靈」，只有神要讓人看
見時，人才可以看到。

天使往往被描繪成溫柔的女性形象，傳說每個人都
有自己的守護天使，無時無刻守在人的身邊。反之，
撒旦（Satan）則是「墮落的天使」，神將他和違
背神旨意的惡魔們（demon）一起趕出天國。

watch over 守護

- *Angels watch over me day and night.*
  天使日夜不休地守護我。

41 I Found a Peanut Just Now

Found a peanut,
Found a peanut,
I found a peanut just now.
Just now I found a peanut,
Found a peanut just now.

找到一顆花生，
找到一顆花生，
我找到一顆花生不久前。
不久前我找到一顆花生，
我找到一顆花生不久前。

Cracked it open,
Cracked it open,
I cracked it open just now.
Just now I cracked it open,
Cracked it open just now.

敲開它，
敲開它，
我敲開它不久前。
不久前我敲開它，
我敲開它不久前。

peanut [ˋpi͵nʌt] (n.) 花生
- *Peanuts are delicious.* 花生很好吃。

crack [kræk] (v.) 使破裂

這首韻文多以〈喔，我親愛的克連婷〉
(Oh, My Darling Clementine!) 的曲子吟唱。
在唱誦時，可以用以下歌詞
代替「Found a peanut」：

Got a stomach ache

Called the doctor

Penicillin

Didn't work

Operation

Died anyway

Went to heaven

114

Wouldn't take me
Went the other way
Didn't want me
Then I woke up
It was a dream
Found a peanut

這首的大意是：
主角撿到一顆腐爛的花生，
他撥開吃下，結果胃痛。
他趕緊去找醫生，
吃了盤尼西林、也動了手術，
卻還是治療無效，
最後只得撒手人寰……
而就在這一刻，
他幡然醒來，才發現
原來只是一場夢！

夢醒，他看到身邊
真的有一顆花生！

42 Long Legged Sailor

Have you ever, ever, ever,
In your long legged life,
Seen a long legged sailor
And his long legged wife?

No, I've never, never, never,
In my long legged life,
Seen a long legged sailor
And his long legged wife.

你可曾經，曾經，曾經
在你長腿生命中，
見過那長腿水手，
和他的長腿太太？

不，我從未，從未，從未
在我的長腿生命中，
見過那位長腿水手，
和他的長腿太太。

sailor [ˋselɚ] (n.) 水手
- *I want to become a sailor in the future.*
  我以後想當水手。

這首歌謠可以當作兩人一組的拍手遊戲，藉以訓練
孩子們的手腳靈活度。建議活動方式如下：

Have	→	拍自己的大腿
you	→	拍自己的雙手
ever	→	拍伙伴的右手
ever	→	拍自己的雙手
ever	→	拍伙伴的左手
in your	→	拍自己的雙手
long	→	張開自己的雙臂
legged	→	拍自己的雙手
life	→	拍伙伴的右手
seen a	→	拍自己的雙手
long	→	張開自己的雙臂
legged	→	拍自己的雙手
sailor	→	拍伙伴的左手
with a	→	拍自己的雙手
long	→	張開自己的雙臂
legged	→	拍自己的雙手
wife	→	和伙伴一起拍雙手

還有一些和水手、航海相關的俚語：

not a good sailor	→	旅途中暈機暈船者
trim one's sails	→	隨機應變，見風轉舵
take in sail	→	抑制欲望
sail large	→	順風航行
strike sail	→	（風大時）急下帆； 為行禮，表示投降

43 We Wish You a Merry Christmas

We wish you a Merry Christmas,
We wish you a Merry Christmas,
We wish you a Merry Christmas,
And a Happy New Year.

Good tidings we bring,
To you and your kin.
We wish you a Merry Christmas,
And a Happy New Year.

我們祝你有個快樂的聖誕，
我們祝你有個快樂的聖誕，
我們祝你有個快樂的聖誕，
還有新年快樂！

我們帶來好消息，
為你和你的家人。
我們祝你有個快樂的聖誕，
還有新年快樂！

tidings [ˋtaɪdɪŋz] (n.) 消息
- *Did you hear of the good tidings?* 你聽見好消息沒？

kin [kɪn] (n.) 親戚
- *All of our kin will come to our party.* 親戚會參加我們的宴會。

這首耶誕頌歌起源於十六世紀的英國。古代英國節慶時,富裕商賈經常雇請樂團巡迴演出,小販則一邊唱歌、一邊兜售物品。有一個名為 Waits 的市立合唱團得到許可,以歌聲迎接來訪的顯貴,或在達官貴人的婚禮上助興。這首歌就是 Waits 的頌歌。

聖誕節前後,Waits 合唱團更加忙得不可開交,在冰天雪地的冬夜,用歌聲唱出耶穌誕生的故事,增添節日的歡樂。Waits 會收到硬幣、無花果布丁、調味的麥芽啤酒或烤豬當作回報。

多年來,在有些版本中,這首歌歌詞中會提到無花果布丁(figgy pudding)。無花果布丁的食材是無花果、奶油、糖、蛋、牛奶、蘭姆酒、蘋果、檸檬和橘子肉、核果、杏仁和薑。這首琅琅上口的耶誕頌歌,讓家庭團聚的溫馨時光備顯幸福。

figgy pudding

44 The Bear Went Over the Mountain

The bear went over the mountain,
The bear went over the mountain,
The bear went over the mountain,
To see what he could see.

And all that he could see,
And all that he could see,
Was the other side of the mountain.
The other side of the mountain,
The other side of the mountain,
Was all that he could see.

大熊爬過大山，
大熊爬過大山，
大熊爬過大山，
去看看他能看到什麼。

所有他能看到的，
所有他能看到的，
是山的另一頭。
山的另一頭，
山的另一頭，
就是所有他能看到的。

這首歌以耳熟能詳、用來恭賀顯赫的功績或榮退的〈For He's a Jolly Good Fellow〉曲調吟唱。原曲為法國歌〈Malbrough s'en va-t-en guerre〉，意思是「Malbrough 作戰去」，可溯源至十字軍東征時代，貝多芬也將曲調放入〈戰鬥交響曲〉（Battle Symphony）中。

45 Polly Put the Kettle On

(45)

Polly, put the kettle on.	波莉，放上水壺。
Polly, put the kettle on.	波莉，放上水壺。
Polly, put the kettle on.	波莉，放上水壺。
We'll all have tea.	我們來喝茶。
Susie, take it off again.	蘇琪，拿下水壺。
Susie, take it off again.	蘇琪，拿下水壺。
Susie, take it off again.	蘇琪，拿下水壺。
They've all gone away.	他們都走了。
Blow on the fire and make the toast.	吹吹火，烤吐司。
Put the muffins on to roast.	放上鬆糕烤一烤。
Blow on the fire and make the toast.	吹吹火，烤吐司。
We'll all have tea.	我們來喝茶。

kettle [ˋkɛtl̩] (n.) 水壺
- *Please put the kettle on the stove.* 請將水壺放在爐上。

roast [rost] (v.) 烤
- *I roasted a chicken for dinner.* 我今天的晚餐烤了隻雞。

這首歌詞是由一位擁有三個女兒和兩個兒子的父親所寫。女孩、男孩會為了要玩什麼遊戲而爭吵,男孩們喜歡玩士兵,女孩們愛玩扮家家酒。當女孩們想排擠兄弟,不想讓他們一起玩時,她們就會假裝要開茶會。名叫 Polly 的女孩把玩具水壺放在爐子上,等兄弟們悻悻然離開時,名叫 Susie 的女孩就把水壺取下來。她們的父親便把這樣的計謀寫成文字,配上〈Did You Ever See a Lassie〉或是〈The More We Get Together〉的曲調,於 1797 年出版。

46 Did You Ever See a Lassie?

Did you ever see a lassie,	你可曾看到一位少女，
A lassie,	一位少女，
A lassie?	一位少女，
Did you ever see a lassie	你可曾看到一位少女，
Go this way and that?	四處走來走去？
Go this way and that way	四處走來走去，
And that way and this way.	四處走來走去，
Did you ever see a lassie	你有沒有看到一位少女，
Go this way and that?	四處走來走去？
Did you ever see a laddie,	你可曾看到一位少年，
A laddie,	一位少年，
A laddie?	一位少年？
Did you ever see a laddie	你可曾看到一位少年，
Go this way and that?	四處走來走去？
Go this way and that way	四處走來走去，
And that way and this way.	四處走來走去，
Did you ever see a laddie	你有沒有看到一位少年，
Go this way and that?	四處走來走去？

lassie [ˈlæsɪ] (n.) 少女
- *The lassie is pretty.* 那位少女很漂亮。

laddie [ˈlædɪ] (n.) 少男
- *This laddie is glad.* 這位少年滿高興的。

Easter Greatings

這首耳熟能詳的歌，是復活節歌曲
〈Did You Ever See a bunny?〉的變形。

這首歌的歌詞被替換成多種版本，例如 bunny、lizard 等。
在和小朋友做這個活動時，可以採用以下的方式進行：

A 誰是 Lassie ？

小朋友們圍成圓圈，中間站一位小朋友，扮演 Lassie。大家唱到「this way and that way」時，Lassie 要比動作，外圍的小朋友就模仿 Lassie 的動作。歌曲結束，Lassie 要盡快找到下一位 Lassie，到中間接續前一位 Lassie 的工作，但是動作不可以重複哦！

B 換版本

將 Lassie 替換成其的字，例如汽車、火車等，也可以加上
聲音，讓活動更有趣。

Happy Easter

47 London Bridge

London Bridge is falling down.
Falling down, falling down.
London Bridge is falling down.
My fair lady.

倫敦鐵橋垮下來，
垮下來，垮下來，
倫敦鐵橋垮下來，
我美麗的淑女。

Build it up with iron bars.
Iron bars, iron bars.
Build it up with iron bars.
My fair lady.

用鐵條建起來，
垮下來，垮下來，
倫敦鐵橋垮下來，
我美麗的淑女。

Iron bars will bend and break.
Bend and break, bend and break.
Iron bars will bend and break.
My fair lady.

鐵條會彎壞，
垮下來，垮下來，
倫敦鐵橋垮下來，
我美麗的淑女。

Build it up with gold and silver.
Gold and silver, gold and silver.
Build it up with gold and silver.
My fair lady.

用金銀建起來，
垮下來，垮下來，
倫敦鐵橋垮下來，
我美麗的淑女。

fair [fɛr] (a.) 美麗的

bend [bɛnd] (v.) 彎曲
- *He bent the iron bar.* 他將鐵棒折彎。

漫漫東流的泰晤士河（River Thames）上最古老的倫敦橋，從西元一世紀羅馬統治時期興建完成開始，歷經多次洪水與戰禍，多次重建之後，橋的材質從木頭、石頭到花崗岩，結構也多次變更。1300年時，橋上已經開滿了 140 間商店，有些還達三層樓高。「gold and silver」就是形容橋上繁華的貿易景況。

13 世紀英王亨利三世的皇后伊蓮娜（Queen Eleanor）挪用了保養經費，成為歌詞中惡名昭彰的「My fair lady」。今日，倫敦的地標為倫敦塔橋（Tower Bridge），而非倫敦橋，但其建造的創意和壯麗，仍讓英國人引以為傲。

48 The Farmer in the Dell

The farmer in the dell.
The farmer in the dell.
Heigh-ho, the derry-o,
The farmer in the dell.

The dog takes a cat.
The dog takes a cat.
Heigh-ho, the derry-o,
The dog takes a cat.

The farmer takes a wife.
The farmer takes a wife.
Heigh-ho, the derry-o,
The farmer takes a wife.

The cat takes a rat.
The cat takes a rat.
Heigh-ho, the derry-o,
The cat takes a rat.

The wife takes a child.
The wife takes a child.
Heigh-ho, the derry-o,
The wife takes a child.

The rat takes the cheese.
The rat takes the cheese.
Heigh-ho, the derry-o,
The rat takes the cheese.

The child takes a nurse.
The child takes a nurse.
Heigh-ho, the derry-o,
The child takes a nurse.

The cheese stands alone.
The cheese stands alone.
Heigh-ho, the derry-o,
The cheese stands alone.

The nurse takes a dog.
The nurse takes a dog.
Heigh-ho, the derry-o,
The nurse takes a dog.

那農夫在小山谷，
那農夫在小山谷，
嗨喔，得力喔，
那農夫在小山谷。

那農夫帶個妻，
那農夫帶個妻，
嗨喔，得力喔，
那農夫帶個妻。

那妻子帶個子，
那妻子帶個子，
嗨喔，得力喔，
那妻子帶個子。

那孩子帶個護士，
那孩子帶個護士，
嗨喔，得力喔，
那孩子帶個護士。

那護士帶隻狗，
那護士帶隻狗，
嗨喔，得力喔，
那護士帶隻狗。

那隻狗帶隻貓，
那隻狗帶隻貓，
嗨喔，得力喔，
那隻狗帶隻貓。

那隻貓帶隻鼠，
那隻貓帶隻鼠，
嗨喔，得力喔，
那隻貓帶隻鼠。

那隻鼠帶了片起司，
那隻鼠帶了片起司，
嗨喔，得力喔，
那隻鼠帶了片起司。

那起司沒得帶，
那起司沒得帶，
嗨喔，得力喔，
那起司沒得帶。

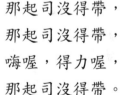

dell [dɛl] (n.) 小谷地
- *There's stream in the dell.*
  谷地有條小溪。

rat [ræt] (n.) 老鼠
- *The cat chased two rats.*
  那隻貓追著兩隻老鼠。

這首歌的歌詞描述一位山谷中的農夫，他帶著老婆、小孩、護士、狗、貓、老鼠和起司的故事。在英國，這首歌曲有些微不同，歌名為〈The Farmer's In His Den〉（那農夫在他的破房間）；Heigh-ho、the derry-o 在倫敦為「Ee-i, tiddly-I」，在英國北部為「Ee-i, the addio」，在西部鄉下為「Ee-i, ee-I」；最後一輪中，rat 被 dog 取代。大家可以輕拍狗或者狗骨頭，當作結尾。

137

49 A Sailor Went to Sea

A sailor went to sea, sea, sea,
To see what he could see, see, see.
But all that he could see, see, see,
Was the bottom of the deep blue sea, sea, sea.

一個水手出海去，去，去，
看看他所能看，看，看。
但所有他能看，看，看，
還是深藍海底的海，海，海。

bottom ['bɑtəm] (n.) 底部
• *Can a submarine go to the bottom of the sea?* 潛水艇能深入海底嗎？

deep [dip] (a.) 深的
• *Is the sea deep and wide?* 海洋是深而廣闊的嗎？

♥ the sea!

140

中世紀時，水手是最艱困的一項工作，他們一出海就是一年半載。在大海上，水手們與大海搏鬥，在船上擔任各自的工作，例如，監看員就得從日出到日落、日落到日出地觀看船的方位和前進方向，水手們在海上得忍受一成不變的單調工作與生活。

在海軍艦隊成形之前，水手大多在君主或貴族的船上工作，他們的薪資因職務等級而各有不同。十字軍戰爭過後，水手工作的重要性增加了，他們得穿越敵方的水域，擺渡到安全的碼頭停靠，補充物資和食物。

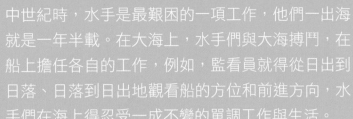

這是一首拍手歌，進行方式如下：

💙 一起拍自己的雙手
💙 同時拍夥伴的雙手
💙 一起拍自己的雙手
💙 用右手拍夥伴的右手
💙 一起拍自己的雙手
💙 用左手拍夥伴的左手

看看誰的反應速度最快，大人們也可以加上拍大腿或身體其他部位的動作。see 跟 sea 組成了這首饒口令，在唱誦時，可以將 see 和 sea，替換成其他發音相似的字，然後加以練習，也可以逐漸加快速度，來訓練孩子們的聽力和語感。例如：

💙 chop-chop-chop
💙 knee-knee-knee
💙 China-China-China

50 German Cradle Song

Lul-la-lul-la-by,
Hush, my baby, and do not cry.
In your cradle now you rock.
Until you sleep,
I'll softly sing
A gentle lullaby.

搖籃曲……
噓，我的寶貝，不要哭，
在你的搖籃裡，搖啊搖。
等到你睡著前，
我都會輕聲唱，
輕柔的搖籃曲。

搖籃和熟睡的嬰兒臉龐，觸動著人心底最柔軟的感動。那麼搖籃的起源是什麼呢？搖籃出現得很早，古羅馬的記載就提過，安撫嬰兒的三個方法：哺育、搖動和唱搖籃曲。為什麼嬰兒可以在搖籃中獲得安全感呢？胎兒在母親體內時就能感受到母親的呼吸、心跳和移動，而嬰兒出生一年後，內耳前庭的平衡感才建立完成，所以嬰兒喜歡搖動的床。這首歌謠中的 lullaby 是「搖籃曲」的意思，出現於十九世紀，意指哄睡嬰兒的歌曲。搖籃曲的旋律要類似輕輕搖動嬰兒的節奏，曲調溫和迴旋，讓嬰兒輕輕搖晃，進入夢鄉。

hush [hʌʃ] (int.) 噓
- *Hush, be quiet.* 噓，安靜。

cradle [`kredḷ] (n.) 搖籃
- *My baby sleeps in a cradle.* 我的寶貝在搖籃中睡著了。

rock [rɑk] (v.) 搖擺
- *I sing and rock my baby's cradle.* 我邊唱邊搖晃寶寶的搖籃。

lullaby [`lʌlə‚baɪ] (n.) 搖籃曲
- *I will sing a lullaby for my sweet baby.* 我要唱首搖籃曲給我的寶寶聽。

51 Hickory, Dickory, Dock

Hickory, dickory, dock.　　　　唏瀝，滴瀝，噹！
The mouse ran up the clock.　　老鼠跑上時鐘。
The clock struck one,　　　　　時鐘敲了一下，
And down he ran.　　　　　　　老鼠跑了下來。
Hickory, dickory, dock.　　　　唏瀝，滴瀝，噹！

Hickory, dickory, dock.　　　　唏瀝，滴瀝，噹！
The mouse ran up the clock.　　老鼠跑上時鐘。
The clock struck two,　　　　　時鐘敲了兩下，
And down he ran.　　　　　　　老鼠跑了下來。
Hickory, dickory, dock.　　　　唏瀝，滴瀝，噹！

Hickory, dickory, dock.　　　　唏瀝，滴瀝，噹！
The mouse ran up the clock.　　老鼠跑上時鐘。
The clock struck three,　　　　時鐘敲了三下，
And down he ran.　　　　　　　老鼠跑了下來。
Hickory, dickory, dock.　　　　唏瀝，滴瀝，噹！

Hickory, dickory, dock.　　　　唏瀝，滴瀝，噹！
The mouse ran up the clock.　　老鼠跑上時鐘。
The clock struck four,　　　　　時鐘敲了四下，
And down he ran.　　　　　　　老鼠跑了下來。
Hickory, dickory, dock.　　　　唏瀝，滴瀝，噹！

這是一首教導孩子們看時鐘和練習加減法的韻文，1744 年，於美國初次出版。第四句的「And down he ran」，也可唱成「The mouse ran down」或「down the mouse ran」。想像一下，老鼠跑到時鐘裡面，拉住了運行中的時鐘鏈條，時鐘發出了聲音，老鼠嚇得往下逃跑。在老祖父昏黃的客廳裡，滴滴答答的鐘聲，配上押韻的歌謠，增添了童趣。

5,000 到 6,000 年前，中東和北非的古文明就開始製造時鐘。蘇美人最早發明計時工具，但是埃及人才開始正式劃分時間，類似現在的小時。蘇美人的方尖塔建於西元前 3,500 年，尖塔陰影的移動類似日晷，將一天的時間劃分為早上和下午。一年之中，中午的陰影最長和最短的那一天，也是一年之中最長和最短的日子。

埃及人的日晷在西元前 1500 年出現，這可能是最早的可攜式計時器。這個設備將陽光照射的時間分為十等分，加上二等分的薄暮和黎明。夜晚時，埃及人用一種名為 Merkhet 的天文儀器計時。他們在柱子上架上一塊平板，放成南北向，從板縫得知某星辰過子午線的時刻，又從星辰與平板間所形成的角度，得知地平高度。

接著，古埃及人、希臘人和羅馬人發明了日晷、水鐘等早期的計時工具，西方人延伸這些技術，進而發明更精確、更實用的現代計時工具。

52 Baa, Baa, Black Sheep

Baa, baa, black sheep,
Have you any wool?
Yes, sir. Yes, sir.
Three bags full:
One for my master,
One for my dame,
And one for the little boy
Who lives down the lane.

咩，咩，黑羊兒，
羊毛你可有？
有，有，先生有，
滿滿有三袋。
一袋給主人，
一袋給夫人，
一袋給巷底小男生。

sheep [ʃip] (n.) 綿羊
- *The sheep is black.* 這是隻黑色綿羊。

wool [wʊl] (n.) 羊毛
- *This farmer shaves the wool from the sheep.* 這個農夫在剪羊毛。

bag [bæg] (n.) 袋子
- *The farmer gets three bags full.* 農夫剪了三袋滿滿的羊毛。

從中世紀到十九世紀，羊毛產業一向是歐洲國家的重要產業。1275 年，英國金雀花王朝的國王愛德華一世（Edward I）加重羊毛出品稅捐，這首歌謠即是諷刺當時的苛捐繁稅。

三分之一的稅歸地主所有（以歌謠中的 master 為象徵），三分之一的稅捐獻給教堂（以歌謠中的 dame 為象徵），剩下的三分之一才屬於農民（以歌謠中的 the little boy 為象徵）所有。

因為政治諷刺意味濃厚,這首童謠常常成為政治角力的幌子。2000 年,英國伯明罕市議會想禁播這首歌謠,理由是有種族歧視之嫌。後來,許多黑人父母挺身而出,指出這個理由荒唐可笑,市議會於是撤回禁令。

從這首歌謠中,孩子們可以學到許多關於羊的知識,譬如羊咩咩的叫聲(baa),還有羊毛的來源。透過模仿動物的叫聲,讓孩子們去認識動物,並徜徉在學習的樂趣中。

1744 年,這首童謠的初版〈Have you any wool?〉,美式英語應該是「Do you have any wool?」,英語在不同地域的變化,也反應在這首歌裡面。

53 One, Two, Buckle My Shoe

One, two, buckle my shoe.
Three, four, shut the door.
Five, six, pick up sticks.
Seven, eight, lay them straight.
Eight, seven, six, five, four, three, two, one.
All done!

一，二，綁緊鞋。
三，四，關上門。
五，六，撿樹枝。
七，八，排整齊。
八，七，六，五，四，三，二，一。
好了！

buckle [`bʌkl̩] (v.) 扣住
- *She buckled herself into her seat.* 她繫上位子的安全帶。

shut [ʃʌt] (v.) 關上
- *Would you please shut the door?* 可以麻煩你把門關上嗎？

stick [stɪk] (n.) 樹枝

這是一首教導孩子們數數兒的歌謠，以實用又有趣的方式，讓孩子們在日常生活中，藉由穿鞋的連續動作，記憶並活用數字。古代歐洲人穿木底的鞋，通常稱為木屐（clogs），木屐的上面釘了一層皮革，以利於長時間穿著，這些簡便的手工製鞋後來進口到美國。木屐可以當作主要的鞋子穿，裡面可以穿長襪，也可以不穿。有時候也會套在其他鞋子的外面，讓泥土不易沾附到內層的鞋子。

clogs

開拓新大陸的殖民者很快就發現，印第安人鍾愛的鹿皮軟鞋（moccasin）容易製造又耐用，於是也開始穿起鹿皮軟鞋。1790 年，鞋帶問世，到了 1800 年代，廣為流行。美國開拓先驅者穿鞋子時，需要綁緊鞋帶固定住，既然要綁鞋帶，必然有帶釦。帶釦有條狀的、分岔狀的，容易損壞，常常一雙鞋子得配上三副帶釦。考古學者在歐洲和美國的繪畫中，發現了各式各樣鞋子的裝飾品，例如用珠寶裝飾的帶釦，而這通常是上流社會身分地位的象徵。

moccasins

在早期，鞋子常常需要修理，一方面是因為一般人擁有的鞋子數量不多，另一方面是鞋子本身也很容易損壞。鞋子是鞋匠製作的，並沒有尺寸或左右腳之分。直到 1800 年代中期，鞋子才開始分左右腳，並大量製造。有些人會在鞋子裡穿上長襪，長襪通常由羊毛（富人用絲）編織而成，但長襪需要用吊襪帶支撐。

54 A Tisket, a Tasket

A tisket, a tasket,　　　　　　　提斯克，塔斯克，
A green and yellow basket.　　　一個綠又黃的籃子。
I wrote a letter to my love,　　　我寫了封信給情人，
And on the way I dropped it.　　在路上卻掉了。
I dropped it,　　　　　　　　　掉了，
I dropped it,　　　　　　　　　掉了，
And on the way I dropped it.　　我半路上弄掉了。
A little boy picked it up　　　　小男孩撿到了，
And put it in his pocket.　　　　放進他的口袋。

A tisket, a tasket,　　　　　　　提斯克，塔斯克，
A green and yellow basket.　　　一個綠又黃的籃子。
I wrote a letter to my love,　　　我寫了封信給情人，
And on the way I dropped it.　　在路上卻掉了。
I dropped it,　　　　　　　　　掉了，
I dropped it,　　　　　　　　　掉了，
And on the way I dropped it.　　我半路上弄掉了。
A little girl picked it up　　　　小女孩撿到了，
And put it in her pocket.　　　　放進她的口袋。

basket [ˋbæskɪt] (n.) 籃子
- *I always put the letters in the basket.*
  我一向把信件放在籃子裡。

pocket [ˋpɑkɪt] (n.) 口袋
- *I put them in my pocket before I go to the post office.*
  去郵局之前，我會把信放在口袋裡。

籃子在歷史上扮演了重要的角色。在聖經裡記載著，摩西（Moses）的母親為了逃避法老王的追殺，將摩西放進柳條編織的籃子裡，藏在尼羅河畔的蘆葦叢中。

傳道先驅者保羅（Paul）重返大馬士革宣揚神蹟及教義時，遇到憤怒的猶太人追殺，趁著半夜，信徒們讓保羅坐在籃子裡，用繩索從城牆上的窗口，將他吊到城牆外的地面上，讓他得以順利逃往耶路撒冷。

古埃及人的墓葬，用泥磚做牆壁、用木柱做屋頂，並使用草蓆、柳條籃子保護屍體，偶而也有簡單的木棺、陶棺。西元前 30 年，渥大維佔領了亞歷山大後，埃及豔后的情人安東尼逃到一個狹長的半島上拔劍自刎。在古埃及的壁畫中，可以看到悲傷的克婁巴特拉和籃子中的眼鏡蛇握手。

在古代社會，籃子是攜帶食物和日常必需品的重要工具。現在，籃子的另一個重要角色是禮物籃，在紀念日或特別的日子裡，在籃子裡置入精心準備的食物或禮物，覆上五彩玻璃紙，加以蝴蝶結點綴，送給他人，窩心又體面。

這是一首十九世紀的英國童謠，歌中的 tisket 和 tasket 是為了和 basket 押韻腳而拼出來音，本身沒有特別意義。Van Alexander 和爵士天后艾拉・費茲傑羅（Ella Fitzgerald）以這首童謠稍加增添歌詞，譜寫成著名的同名爵士歌曲，隨即成為膾炙人口的成名曲。

55 Rain, Rain, Go Away

(55)

Rain, rain, go away.
Come again another day.
Little Johnny wants to play.
Rain, rain, go away.

Rain, rain, go to Spain.
Never show your face again.
Little Johnny wants to play.
Rain, rain, go away.

Rain, rain, on the green grass,
And rain on the tree.
Rain on the housetop,
But not on me!

雨啊，雨啊，快走開，
改天再來吧，
小強尼想要玩。
雨啊，雨啊，快走開。

雨啊，雨啊，去西班牙，
別再露臉吧，
小強尼想要玩。
雨啊，雨啊，快走開。

雨啊，雨啊，下到綠草上，
下到樹上去，
下到屋頂上，
可別下在我身上。

housetop [ˋhaʊsˌtɑp] (n.) 屋頂
● *From my treehouse, I can look down on the housetop.*
從我的樹屋看去，我可以看到屋頂。

都鐸王朝最後一位君主伊莉莎白女王一世統治時期（1533–1603），西班牙與英國的海上對抗非常激烈。1588 年，西班牙組成的無敵艦隊（Spanish Armada）下水，競爭達到白熱化。西班牙無敵艦隊挾著許多大型帆船，由 Medina Sedonia 公爵領軍，企圖侵略英國。浩浩蕩蕩的西班牙艦隊超過 130 艘船，由總司令 Lord Howard 領導的英國艦隊只有寥寥 34 艘小海軍艦艇和 163 艘武裝的商船。

激戰後，西班牙無敵艦隊落敗，殘敗的 65 艘帆船和一萬名士兵倉皇撤軍。西班牙此次的敗北，除了英國的小艦艇反應敏捷，艦隊遭遇到暴風雨，險惡天候打亂了艦隊的布局，也是主因。當綿綿細雨為心情蒙上陰影時，不妨陪著孩子哼唱這首歌謠，遙想十六世紀烽火連天的時代。

56 Twelve Months

by Dennis Le Boeuf

January, January, it gets cold.

February, February, the cold gets old.

March, March, the snow is going.

April, April, flowers are growing.

May, May, birds sing and fly for miles.

June, June, summer days bring smiles.

July, July, it is time for a swim.

August, August, it is hot for Kim.

September, September, school starts for Paul.

October, October, the leaves fall.

November, November, it makes us cold.

December, December, old Santa is bold.

一月，一月，漸漸冷。

二月，二月，別再冷了。

三月，三月，雪溶化。

四月，四月，花盛開。

五月，五月，鳥啼唱，飛遠去。

六月，六月，夏天到，人歡笑。

七月，七月，游泳去。

八月，八月，金好熱。

九月，九月，保羅上學天。

十月，十月，落葉飄。

十一月，十一月，讓人冷。

十二月，十二月，聖誕老人很勇敢。

January

一月（January）

名稱源自 Janus，他是古羅馬神話中一位具有兩張臉、掌管天堂宮殿的門神，代表最初與最終。

February

二月（February）

名稱源自古義大利神 Februusc 或 februa，是一位掌管淨化和貞潔的神，意謂著羅馬在當月潔淨的慶祝活動。

March

三月（March）

名稱源自 Mars，他是羅馬神話中掌管征戰、農業的戰神。這是古羅馬曆法中的第一個月。

April

四月（April）

名稱源自拉丁語 aperire（打開）。意指這是一個樹木抽芽、花蕊綻放的仲春之月。

May

五月（May）

名稱源自 Maiesta，羅馬神話中象徵榮耀與尊嚴的女神。這是古羅馬曆法中的第三個月。

June

六月（June）

名稱源自 Juno，她是古羅馬神話中一位守護婚姻及女性的女神。這是古羅馬曆法中的第四個月。

July

七月（July）

這是羅馬共和國凱撒大帝（Julius Caesar）出生的月分，他被暗殺後，人們為了紀念他，便以凱撒的名字命名此月分。

August

八月（August）

為紀念羅馬大帝奧古斯都（Augustus），而以他的名字命名。在奧古斯都皇帝任內，八月分是幸運的月分，遇事總能逢凶化吉。

September

九月（September）

名稱源自 septem，拉丁文「七」的意思，古羅馬一年只有十個月。

October

十月（October）

名稱源自 octo，拉丁文「八」的意思。

November

十一月（November）

名稱源自 novem，拉丁文「九」的意思。

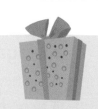

December

十二月（December）

名稱源自 decem，拉丁文「十」的意思。

57 To Market, to Market

To market, to market, to buy a fat pig;
Home again, home again, jiggety jig.
To market, to market, to buy a fat hog;
Home again, home again, jiggety jog.

To market, to market, to buy a white cake;
Home again, home again, it was never baked.
To market, to market, to buy a plum bun;
Home again, home again, market is done.

去市場，去市場，買隻肥豬；
回了家，回了家，跳吉格舞。
去市場，去市場，買隻肥豬；
回了家，回了家，輕快跳舞。

去市場，去市場，買白蛋糕；
回了家，回了家，還未烤過。
去市場，去市場，買梅子麵包；
回了家，回了家，市場打烊。

jig [dʒɪg] (n.) 吉格舞
jog [dʒɑg] (n.) 輕搖
plum [plʌm] (n.) 梅子
● *Plums are now in season.*
梅子正盛產。

中世紀時，大部分的人都是務農的，村落和城鎮一星期舉行市集一次。到了 1300 年，船隻從義大利西北部的熱那亞（Genoa）和義大利東北部的威尼斯（Venice），載運地中海沿岸珍貴的金屬、絲等奢侈品，到英國和比利時的東法蘭德省與西法蘭德省，交換羊毛、煤和木材。德國和荷蘭的船隻，則載運了鐵和銅製品到地中海區域，交換酒、油和鹽。

在市場裡，人們可以買到蔬菜、活牲口、壺、鍋、工具等各種用品。農夫們帶著自製產品去市場販賣，當然，在這裡賣東西需要繳交租費給攤位店主。通常一年會有一到兩次大型博覽會，這種大型博覽會是國際性的市集，常常持續數個星期，吸引了歐洲各地王公貴族的使者和商人前來買賣物品。

當時，不論貧富，這個市集是一個有趣的好玩地方，這裡可以看到各種戲法，像是吞火吞劍、雜技、踩高蹺、滑稽劇，也欣賞到各種音樂，還可以看到人們爭相鬥雞下注，為摔角選手加油歡呼，觀看狗逗弄熊的節目，好不熱鬧。

這種市集的買賣形式成為後來商店的前身。十字軍東征時期，促進了絲、香料、繡帷和糖等貨品的貿易，隨著物品種類的增加，人們精益求精，產品工藝和品質隨之提升。

58 Miss Mary Mack

Miss Mary Mack, Mack, Mack,
All dressed in black, black, black,
With silver buttons, buttons, buttons,
All down her back, back, back.

She asked her mother, mother, mother,
For fifteen cents, cents, cents,
To see the elephants, elephants, elephants,
Jump over the fence, fence, fence.

They jumped so high, high, high,
They reached the sky, sky, sky,
And they never came back, back, back,
Till the fourth of July-ly-ly.

瑪莉‧麥克小姐，麥克，麥克，
全身穿著黑色，黑色，黑色。
有著銀色鈕扣，鈕扣，鈕扣。
全在她的背後，背後，背後。

她跟媽媽，媽媽，媽媽，
要十五分錢，錢，錢，
想看大象，大象，大象，
跳圍籬，圍籬，圍籬。

大象跳好高，好高，好高，
碰到天空，天空，天空，
回不來，回不來，回不來，
等到七月四日才回來。

button ['bʌtṇ] (n.) 鈕釦
- *Is it a pretty silver button?* 是一顆漂亮的銀鈕扣嗎？

fence [fɛns] (n.) 圍籬
- *Daddy built a fence around the fence.* 爸爸在園中造了圍籬。

reach [ritʃ] (v.) 碰到
- *I can reach the button on the back of my dress.*
  我摸得到我洋裝背後的那顆鈕釦。

這是一首英語系國家孩子們玩的拍手歌，孩子們兩兩對站或對坐，依著節奏拍手的押韻歌，也可以用在跳繩活動上。

Mary Mack 起源於 Merrimack 這個字，Merrimack 是早期的黑色裝甲艦，鉚釘是銀色的。這首歌謠在美國內戰時期迅速流傳，黑奴的小朋友們時常一邊工作、一邊唱拍手歌，可以說是美國黑人的民族音樂。在非洲，這首歌的根源是西非的迦納，音樂經過代代相傳，混合了歐洲風格，唱出奴隸心聲和農村生活寫照。

大部分的黑人遊戲都是起源於歐洲，但加入了非洲濃重的口音傳統和歌謠創作的特色，這首歌謠結合西班牙孩子們的拍手遊戲和黑人小孩押韻的節奏感。孩子們也可以圍成一圈，讓中間的小朋友跳舞或表演，呈現出非洲舞蹈的傳統。

59 One Elephant Went Out to Play

One elephant went out to play,
Out on a spider's web one day.
He had such enormous fun.
He called another elephant to come.

Two elephants went out to play,
Out on a spider's web one day.
They had such enormous fun,
They called another elephant to come.

Three elephants went out to play,
Out on a spider's web one day.
They had such enormous fun,
They called another elephant to come.

一隻大象出去玩，
踩到蜘蛛網上去，
開開心心多快活，
呼朋引伴一起玩。

兩隻大象出去玩，
踩到蜘蛛網上去，
開開心心多快活，
呼朋引伴一起玩。

三隻大象出去玩，
踩到蜘蛛網上去，
開開心心多快活，
呼朋引伴一起玩。

web [wɛb] (n.) 蜘蛛網
- *Is it a magic web?* 這是個神奇的蜘蛛網嗎？

fun [fʌn] (n.) 樂趣
- *Is the elephant having lots of fun?* 大象玩得開心嗎？

enormous [əˋnɔrməs] (a.) 巨大的
- *Their bedroom is enormous.* 他們的臥房超大。

大象是陸地上最大型的動物，在英文中，大象的象徵意義包括「大」、「遲鈍」、「大而無當」等，例如：

You can't paint an elephant.	→	你沒有藝術天賦。
white elephant gift	→	指貴而不實的禮物
see the elephant	→	見過世面；大開眼界
There's an elephant in the room.	→	指粗獷的身軀擁有細緻的情感，但被忽略了；或指眾人皆知，卻沒人敢討論的話題。

這首是培養孩子數數兒、身體律動和培養友誼的團體活動歌。進行方式是讓所有小朋友圍成圓圈坐下，其中一位小朋友站起來，一手懸盪著假裝是象鼻，另一手放在後面假裝是象尾巴。全體小朋友一起歌唱，大象小朋友則繞著圓圈跳躍。

當唱到「He called another elephant to come.」時，大象小朋友要選另一位小朋友加入大象的行列，扮演第二隻大象。繼續遊戲，直到所有小朋友都變成大象為止，可以在結尾加上「But the web it broke and they all fell down.」，所有小朋友假裝跌到地上，當作滑稽的結局。

60 Skidamarink

Skidamarink a-dink-a-dink,
Skidamarink a-doo,
I love you. (I love you.)
Skidamarink, a-dink-a-dink,
Skidamarink a-doo,
I love you. (I love you.)
I love you in the morning and in the afternoon;
I love you in the evening and underneath the moon.
Oh, skidamarink, a-dink-a-dink,
Skidamarink a-doo,
I love you. (I love you.)

Skidamarink a-dink-a-dink，
Skidamarink a-doo，
我愛你，（我愛你。）
Skidamarink a-dink-a-dink，
Skidamarink a-doo，
我愛你。（我愛你。）
我早晨下午都愛你，
我晚上月光下也愛你。

喔，Skidamarink a-dink-a-dink，
Skidamarink a-doo，
我愛你。（我愛你。）

underneath [ˈʌndɚˌniθ]
(prep.) 在……之下
* *The baby likes to sit underneath the table.* 寶寶喜歡坐在桌子底下。

love 這個字最早出自古希臘劇作家阿里斯多芬尼斯（Aristophanes）：
在一次宴會中，眾人輪番演講致詞，宣誓效忠愛神（Eros），內容說
到人類本來是由兩個人背對背結合而成，有兩個臉和八個手腳。兩面
都是男性的人，來自於太陽；兩面都是女性的人，來自於地球；一面
男性、一面女性的人，來自於月亮。諸神妒忌人類的完美，宙斯於是
決定把人一分為二，從此人類便開始了尋找自己的「另一半」的歷程。

「Skidamarink a-doo」沒有特別意義，是練習舌頭靈活的繞口令。這
是一首情人節的歌曲，可製作情人節卡片來增加學習趣味。也可以加
強早上、下午和傍晚的時段說法，設計成遊戲，用圖片來表示關聯性。
活潑溫馨的旋律，適當運用肢體語言，可以增加團體的向心力。

61 If You're Happy and You Know It

If you're happy and you know it,
   clap your hands. (clap, clap)
If you're happy and you know it,
   clap your hands. (clap, clap)
If you're happy and you know it,
   then your face will surely show it.
If you're happy and you know it,
   clap your hands. (clap, clap)

If you're happy and you know it,
   tap your toes. (tap, tap)
If you're happy and you know it,
   tap your toes. (tap, tap)
If you're happy and you know it,
   then your face will surely show it.
If you're happy and you know it,
   tap your toes. (tap, tap)

clap [klæp] (v.) 拍手
- *Clap your hands when you are happy.*
   高興時，你就拍拍手。

If you're happy and you know it,
nod your head. (nod, nod)
If you're happy and you know it,
nod your head. (nod, nod)
If you're happy and you know it,
then your face will surely show it.
If you're happy and you know it,
nod your head. (nod, nod)

如果你很快樂就拍拍手，（拍拍）
如果你很快樂就拍拍手，（拍拍）
如果你很快樂臉兒就會笑，
如果你很快樂就拍拍手。（拍拍）

如果你很快樂就踏踏腳，（踏踏）
如果你很快樂就踏踏腳，（踏踏）
如果你很快樂臉兒就會笑，
如果你很快樂就踏踏腳。（踏踏）

如果你很快樂就點點頭，（點點）
如果你很快樂就點點頭，（點點）
如果你很快樂臉兒就會笑，
如果你很快樂就點點頭。（點點）

tap [tæp] (v.) 踏腳
• *Tap your toes when you smile.* 笑的時候踏踏你的腳。
nod [nɑd] (v.) 點頭
• *Nod your head if you agree with me.*
如果你同意我，就點點你的頭。

作曲家 Alfred B. Smith 創作了這首童謠，經過時代的更迭，內容和用途出現了各種版本，其節奏鮮明、琅琅上口，經常運用在政治活動場合中。最早的版本是由美國開始的，歌詞如下：

If you're happy and you know it,
*　　clap your hands.*
If you're happy and you know it,
*　　clap your hands.*
If you're happy and you know it,
And you really want to show it,
If you're happy and you know it,
*　　clap your hands.*

「clap your hands」可以改為「stomp your feet」。進行這首歌謠時，鼓勵孩子們用面部表情來表達喜怒哀樂，並加上手腳動作，來加強情緒的表達。有的版本中，適時加入「Hurray」、「Amen」等聲音，增添樂趣。在這首歌謠中，孩子可以學到如何透過面部表情和身體語言，來表達自己的情緒。

十九世紀時，在女性的英文名字中出現了 Happy 這個名字，意思是「興高采烈的、輕鬆愉快的」，美國第 41 屆副總統洛克斐勒（Nelson Rockefeller）的妻子，她的名字就叫 Happy。Happy 較常用於暱稱，較少用於名字或姓氏。

62 Looby Loo

Here we go Looby Loo,
Here we go Looby Light,
Here we go Looby Loo,
All on a Saturday night.
You put your right hand in,
You put your right hand out,
You give your right hand a shake,
   shake, shake,
And you turn yourself about. Oh!

我們來玩嚕比嚕，
我們來玩嚕比賴，
我們來玩嚕比嚕，
在星期六的晚上。
把你的右手放進去，
把你的右手拿出來，
右手兒，搖一搖，
全身轉一圈。喔！

Here we go Looby Loo,
Here we go Looby Light,
Here we go Looby Loo,
All on a Saturday night.
You put your left hand in,
You put your left hand out,
You give your left hand a shake,
   shake, shake,
And you turn yourself about. Oh!

我們來玩嚕比嚕，
我們來玩嚕比賴，
我們來玩嚕比嚕，
在星期六的晚上。
把你的左手放進去，
把你的左手拿出來，
左手兒，搖一搖，
全身轉一圈。喔！

Here we go Looby Loo,
Here we go Looby Light,
Here we go Looby Loo,
All on a Saturday night.
You put your right foot in,
You put your right foot out,
You give your right foot a shake,
   shake, shake,
And you turn yourself about. Oh!

我們來玩嚕比嚕，
我們來玩嚕比賴，
我們來玩嚕比嚕，
在星期六的晚上。
把你的右腳放進去，
把你的右腳拿出來，
右腳兒，搖一搖，
全身轉一圈。喔！

Here we go Looby Loo,
Here we go Looby Light,
Here we go Looby Loo,
All on a Saturday night.
You put your left foot in,
You put your left foot out,
You give your left foot a shake, shake,
   shake,
And you turn yourself about. Oh!

我們來玩嚕比嚕，
我們來玩嚕比賴，
我們來玩嚕比嚕，
在星期六的晚上。
把你的左腳放進去，
把你的左腳拿出來，
左腳兒，搖一搖，
全身轉一圈。喔！

Here we go Looby Loo,
Here we go Looby Light,
Here we go Looby Loo,
All on a Saturday night.
You put your head in,
You put your head out,
You give your head a shake, shake, shake,
And you turn yourself about. Oh!

我們來玩嚕比嚕，
我們來玩嚕比賴，
我們來玩嚕比嚕，
在星期六的晚上。
把你的頭放進去，
把你的頭拿出來，
頭兒，搖一搖，
全身轉一圈。喔！

Here we go Looby Loo,
Here we go Looby Light,
Here we go Looby Loo,
All on a Saturday night.
You put your whole self in,
You put your whole self out,
You give your whole self a shake,
    shake, shake,
And you turn yourself about. Oh!

我們來玩嚕比嚕，
我們來玩嚕比賴，
我們來玩嚕比嚕，
在星期六的晚上。
把你的全身放進去，
把你的全身拿出來，
全身，搖一搖，
全身轉一圈。喔！

這是一首美國的遊戲歌（play party），充滿動感和歡樂，描述在星期六夜晚，家庭成員提水桶洗澡的情景。大家輪流放入手腳試水溫（put your hand in），接著又因被燙傷而紛紛抽回手腳（put your hand out）。

從這首歌謠中，可以學習到手腳等身體部位和左右邊的英文說法，也可以練習身體的反應速度。

在 looby loo 的引申用法中，通常當作動詞，表示「謹慎小心地做事，而且從他人那兒，獲得好處」。

shake [ʃek] (v.) 搖擺
• *Now, shake your head.* 現在，搖搖你的頭。
whole self 全身
• *And turn your whole self around.* 然後整個人轉一圈。

63 Old MacDonald Had a Farm

63

Old MacDonald had a farm, E-I-E-I-O.
And on his farm he had some cows, E-I-E-I-O.
With a "moo-moo" here and a "moo-moo" there,
Here a "moo," there a "moo,"
Everywhere a "moo-moo."
Old MacDonald had a farm, E-I-E-I-O.

Old MacDonald had a farm, E-I-E-I-O.
And on his farm he had some pigs, E-I-E-I-O.
With a "oink-oink" here and a "oink-oink" there,
Here a "oink," there a "oink,"
Everywhere a "oink-oink."
Old MacDonald had a farm, E-I-E-I-O.

Old MacDonald had a farm, E-I-E-I-O.
And on his farm he had some quack, E-I-E-I-O.
With a "quack-quack" here and a "quack-quack" there,
Here a "quack," there a "quack,"
Everywhere a "quack-quack."
Old MacDonald had a farm, E-I-E-I-O.

Old MacDonald had a farm, E-I-E-I-O.
And on his farm he had some chicks, E-I-E-I-O.
With a "chick-chick" here and a "chick-chick" there,
Here a "chick," there a "chick,"
Everywhere a "chick-chick."
Old MacDonald had a farm, E-I-E-I-O.

老麥先生有農場，伊呀伊呀喔。
農場裡頭有母牛，伊呀伊呀喔。
這兒哞哞，那兒哞哞，
這兒哞哞，那兒哞哞，
到處哞哞哞。
老麥先生有農場，伊呀伊呀喔。

老麥先生有農場，伊呀伊呀喔。
農場裡頭有鴨子，伊呀伊呀喔。
這兒呱呱，那兒呱呱，
這兒呱呱，那兒呱呱，
到處呱呱呱。
老麥先生有農場，伊呀伊呀喔。

老麥先生有農場，伊呀伊呀喔。
農場裡頭有豬兒，伊呀伊呀喔。
這兒齁齁，那兒齁齁，
這兒齁齁，那兒齁齁，
到處齁齁齁。
老麥先生有農場，伊呀伊呀喔。

老麥先生有農場，伊呀伊呀喔。
農場裡頭有小雞，伊呀伊呀喔。
這兒咕咕，那兒咕咕，
這兒咕咕，那兒咕咕，
到處咕咕咕。
老麥先生有農場，伊呀伊呀喔。

farm [fɑrm] (n.) 農場
everywhere [ˈɛvrɪˌhwɛr] (adv.) 到處
chick [tʃɪk] (n.) 小雞

這首歌在中文裡，就是大家耳熟能詳的〈王老先生有塊田〉。老麥當勞應該是全世界最著名的農夫了，這首繽紛熱鬧的農莊歌謠，隨著時代與地域的轉換，出現了許多版本，歌詞中描述的農莊動物越來越多，叫聲越來越嘈雜，也出版為不同的韻文、歌曲和書籍。在 1952 出版的《Frank C. Brown Collection of North Carolina Folklore》一書中，有一首歌叫作〈McDonald's Farm〉，歌詞內容如下：

Old McDonald had a farm, E-i-ei o,
And on that farm he had some chicks, E-i ei o,
With a chick chick here and a chick chick there,
And a here chick, there chick, everywhere chick chick.
Old McDonald had a farm, E-i-ei o.

在 1917 年的《Tommy's Tunes》中，收集了第一次世界大戰時的歌曲，其中的 Ohio 歌詞如下，與本歌略有不同：

Old Macdougal had a farm in Ohio-i-o,
And on that farm he had some dogs in Ohio-i-o,
With a bow-wow here, and a bow-wow there,
Here a bow, there a wow, everywhere a bow-wow.

這首歌的歌詞、曲調有許多語言的改編版本，用來教導孩子們認識各種農莊的動物和動物的叫聲，讓孩子們可以沉浸在模仿動物叫聲的歡樂中。

64 The Wheels on the Bus

(64)

The wheels on the bus go round and round,
Round and round,
Round and round.
The wheels on the bus go round and round,
All through the town!

The people on the bus go up and down,
Up and down,
Up and down.
The people on the bus go up and down,
All through the town!

The horn on the bus goes beep, beep, beep.
Beep, beep, beep,
Beep, beep, beep.
The horn on the bus goes beep, beep, beep,
All through the town!

wheel [hwil] (n.) 輪胎
* *The wheels on the bus are very big.*
  公車的輪胎很大。

公車的輪子轉啊轉，
轉啊轉，
轉啊轉。
公車的輪子轉啊轉，
繞了整個鎮！

公車的人們上又下，
上又下，
上又下。
公車的人們上又下，
繞了整個鎮！

公車的喇叭嗶嗶叫，
嗶嗶叫，
嗶嗶叫。
公車的喇叭嗶嗶叫，
繞了整個鎮！

這首歌曲頻繁使用狀聲詞，活靈活現地刻畫公車和乘客的舉止和情景。大人們可以設計情境學習活動，介紹描述位置的介系詞，例如 in、out、under，用來增加孩子的字彙量、聽力和語感。其中「All through the town」也可以唱成「All day long」。

西元前 3500 到 3000 年間，美索不達米亞平原最早出現了輪子。早期的手推車或運貨車是以人或牲畜拖曳的，時至今日，還是有許多地方保持了以牲畜拖曳的習慣。手推車或運貨車本來是用來托運貨物的，後來才演變為載運人。四輪馬車比運貨車快多了，在戰場上戰車。四輪戰車最早出現於西元前 2000 年的美索不達米亞平原，後來迅速流傳至埃及、波斯、希臘、羅馬和其他古文明地區。

雖然輪子的發明對歐洲和亞洲的交通發展非常重要，但在北美洲和南美洲的古文明卻不見蹤影。人們在北美洲和南美洲通常用簡單的雪橇運送動物或貨品，直到十六世紀，歐洲人才將輪子帶到新大陸。美國舊時的驛馬車和篷車，在拓展西部土地的歷史上，扮演了重要的角色，托運的重量可達七噸。

1928 年五月，英國孔雀斯特鎮（Colchester）淘汰了使用 24 年的有軌電車（tram）系統，購買四輛 20 個座位的丹尼斯（Dennis）單層公車取而代之，是英國公車出現之始。

65 Old Brass Wagon

Circle to the left, the old brass wagon.
Circle to the left, the old brass wagon.
Circle to the left, the old brass wagon.
You're the one, my darling.

Circle to the right, the old brass wagon.
Circle to the right, the old brass wagon.
Circle to the right, the old brass wagon.
You're the one, my darling.

Everybody in, the old brass wagon.
Everybody in, the old brass wagon.
Everybody in, the old brass wagon.
You're the one, my darling.

Everybody out, the old brass wagon.
Everybody out, the old brass wagon.
Everybody out, the old brass wagon.
You're the one, my darling.

向左繞，老黃車。
向左繞，老黃車。
向左繞，老黃車。
就是你，我親愛的。

向右繞，老黃車。
向右繞，老黃車。
向右繞，老黃車。
就是你，我親愛的。

大家進來，老黃車。
大家進來，老黃車。
大家進來，老黃車。
就是你，我親愛的。

大家出去，老黃車。
大家出去，老黃車。
大家出去，老黃車。
就是你，我親愛的。

brass [bræs] (a.) 黃銅的
- *Claire loves that old brass wagon over there.*
  克蕾兒很愛那邊那台舊黃銅馬車喔！

wagon [ˈwægən] (n.) 運貨馬車
- *Whose cool brass wagon is in front of our school?*
  那台在學校前面的酷黃銅車是誰的啊？

搭貨車便車，到現在還很常見。這是一首美國的民族音樂，適合大家圍成圓圈跳舞時唱和。民族音樂在歌唱中傳述著歷史，在歌手賴白里（Lead-belly）和伍迪（Woody Guthrie）的歌曲中，會口述傳說中的故事。民族音樂源自於民間，具地域性，總因廣泛人們的加入而顯得更加豐富，常見的題材包括戰爭、工作、美國內戰、公民權利、經濟的困頓、諷刺作品和愛情等。

在美國，田裡工作的黑奴們會唱黑人的聖歌，例如〈Down by the Riverside〉、〈We Shall Over-come〉等，這些歌曲具體抒發了生活中艱苦的掙扎，但也充滿了希望。在聆聽這些歌曲之際，我們除了看到黑奴現實中的困厄之外，也可以感受到他們對人生所抱有的深切期許和憧憬。

66 Apples, Peaches

Apples, peaches, pears and plums,
Tell me when your birthday comes.
February–F-e-b-r-u-a-r-y.

Apples, peaches, pears and plums,
Tell me when your birthday comes.
June–J-u-n-e .

Apples, peaches, pears and plums,
Tell me when your birthday comes.
August –A-u-g-u-s-t.

Apples, peaches, pears and plums,
Tell me when your birthday comes.
November–N-o-v-e-m-b-e-r.

January, February, March, April, May,
June, July, August, September, October,
November, December.

蘋果，桃子，梨子，梅子，
你的生日是何時？
二月（F-e-b-r-u-a-r-y）

蘋果，桃子，梨子，梅子，
你的生日是何時？
六月（J-u-n-e）

蘋果，桃子，梨子，梅子，
你的生日是何時？
八月（A-u-g-u-s-t）

蘋果，桃子，梨子，梅子，
你的生日是何時？
十一月（N-o-v-e-m-b-e-r）

一月、二月、三月、四月、五月、
六月、七月、八月、九月、十月、
十一月、十二月。

peach(es) [pitʃ] (n.) 桃子
* *Eat a ripe peach, and you'll feel sweet.* 吃顆熟桃，很甜喔。

pear [pɛr] (n.) 梨子
* *Please share this pear with Claire.* 請和克蕾兒分享這顆梨子吧。

plum [plʌm] (n.) 梅子
* *I like plums, and so does my brother Mike.*
  我很愛吃梅子，我弟弟麥克也是。

最早的生日蛋糕可以溯源至古希臘，人們製作圓形或月亮形狀的蜂蜜蛋糕或麵包，供奉月亮女神 Artemis。有學者認為，生日蛋糕源自中世紀的德國，人們將香甜的生麵糰做成耶穌在襁褓中的模樣，用來慶祝耶穌的生日。這種特殊的生日蛋糕後來在孩童的嘉年華會或生日中出現，用來慶生。

德國人也烘培另一種叫做 Geburtstagorten 的蛋糕，這是分層烘烤的，當時大部分的蛋糕都很粗糙、狀似麵包，而這種蛋糕除了外型不同外，也比較甜。

蛋糕綴上水果、乾果、蜂蜜和核果的歷史，可以追溯到遠古時代，食品歷史學家認為，水果蛋糕起源於中世紀。十三世紀時，乾果才由葡萄牙和東地中海區域傳入英國。十八世紀之後，水果蛋糕就用在婚禮等慶典活動上，由水果麵包演變而來。

蛋糕上插蠟燭的傳統，要溯至古希臘。古希臘人將燃亮的蠟燭插在蛋糕上，看來絢爛得更像月亮。以插上蠟燭的蛋糕來祭祀月神，將人們的祈願傳達到神界。有些人認為，德國傳統習俗會在蛋糕中心插上一根大蠟燭，象徵「生命之光」。

中世紀慶祝生日的原因，是為了感謝守護天使或神祇。聖壇上用花或花圈來裝飾，獻祭給節慶之神。朋友們會帶著禮物和祝福前來，國王的生日會舉辦遊行、盛宴、馬戲團表演和狩獵，這種慶祝方式尤其盛行於早期的基督教社會。

67 He's Got the Whole World

He's got the whole world in His hands.
He's got the whole world in His hands.
He's got the whole world in His hands.
He's got the whole world in His hands.

He's got the little, bitty baby in His hands.
He's got the little, bitty baby in His hands.
He's got the little, bitty baby in His hands.
He's got the whole world in His hands.

He's got everybody here in His hands.
He's got everybody here in His hands.
He's got everybody here in His hands.
He's got the whole world in His hands.

He's got the wind and rain in His hands.
He's got the wind and rain in His hands.
He's got the wind and rain in His hands.
He's got the whole world in His hands.

204

He's got the sun and the moon in His hands.
He's got the sun and the moon in His hands.
He's got the sun and the moon in His hands.
He's got the whole world in His hands.

He's got the whole world in His hands.
He's got the whole world in His hands.
He's got the whole world in His hands.
He's got the whole world in His hands.

祂手上握有全世界；　　　　祂手上握有呼風又喚雨；
祂手上握有全世界；　　　　祂手上握有呼風又喚雨；
祂手上握有全世界；　　　　祂手上握有呼風又喚雨；
祂手上握有全世界。　　　　祂手上握有全世界。

祂手上握有小寶寶；　　　　祂手上握有主宰日和月；
祂手上握有小寶寶；　　　　祂手上握有主宰日和月；
祂手上握有小寶寶；　　　　祂手上握有主宰日和月；
祂手上握有全世界。　　　　祂手上握有全世界。

祂手上握有所有人；　　　　祂手上握有全世界；
祂手上握有所有人；　　　　祂手上握有全世界；
祂手上握有所有人；　　　　祂手上握有全世界；
祂手上握有全世界。　　　　祂手上握有全世界。

bitty [ˋbɪtɪ] (a.) 微小的
- *She fills her bag with tulips and little bitty things like paper clips.*
  她在包包中塞了鬱金香，還有一些小東西，像是迴紋針。

這是一首黑人聖歌，1958 年，美國 Laurie London 演唱之後，這首歌開始大受歡迎，而 Laurie London 錄製這首歌時，年紀只有 13 歲。之後，陸續有 Marian Anderson、Odetta、Perry Como 和 Nina Simone 等人的演唱版本問世。

聖歌的起源可以追溯到十七世紀中葉，那時候教育不普及，許多參與禮拜的教徒並不識字。於是領唱者便一次一句地帶唱聖歌，搭配世俗熟悉的旋律來吟唱。黑人聖歌擷取了白人讚美詩的傳統，但在音質、聲音效果、節拍和伴奏上，有很大出入。黑人聖歌不僅在教堂做禮拜時可以聽到，在工作時也常傳唱，而歌曲的內容也會反映現實生活狀態。

黑奴來自非洲西岸，在新開墾地或城鎮中工作。在一些文獻中，忠實記錄了黑奴們代代口耳相傳的詩歌，他們的生活狀況也歷歷在目。雖然身為奴隸，他們仍會進入教堂從事宗教活動。農村的奴隸習慣於例行的禮拜活動後，在教堂內或農園的讚美之家（praise houses）繼續唱歌跳舞。但是奴隸主人並不允許他們像在非洲一樣打鼓跳舞。他們需要分享彼此的快樂、痛苦和希望，所以會在祕密的地方集會，譬如紮營集會（camp meetings）或灌木叢集會（bush meetings）。

在農村的集會中，許多的奴隸聚集在一起，聆聽巡迴傳教士的福音，一起唱聖歌。1700 年代後期，他們唱的玉米小調（corn ditties）成為現代黑人靈歌的前身。

68 Eight Fat Sausages

Eight fat sausages sizzling in a pan.
Eight fat sausages sizzling in a pan.
One went pop,
And the other went bang!
There were six fat sausages sizzling in a pan.

Six fat sausages sizzling in a pan.
Six fat sausages sizzling in a pan.
One went pop,
And the other went bang!
There were four fat sausages sizzling in a pan.

Four fat sausages sizzling in a pan.
Four fat sausages sizzling in a pan.
One went pop,
And the other went bang!
There were two fat sausages sizzling in a pan.

Two fat sausages sizzling in a pan.
Two fat sausages sizzling in a pan.
One went pop,
And the other went bang!
There were no fat sausages sizzling in a pan.

八條肥香腸，正在鍋裡煎，　　　四條肥香腸，正在鍋裡煎，
八條肥香腸，正在鍋裡煎，　　　四條肥香腸，正在鍋裡煎，
一條啪一聲，　　　　　　　　　一條啪一聲，
一條碰一聲。　　　　　　　　　一條碰一聲。
六條肥香腸，正在鍋裡煎。　　　兩條肥香腸，正在鍋裡煎。

六條肥香腸，正在鍋裡煎，　　　兩條肥香腸，正在鍋裡煎，
六條肥香腸，正在鍋裡煎，　　　兩條肥香腸，正在鍋裡煎，
一條啪一聲，　　　　　　　　　一條啪一聲，
一條碰一聲。　　　　　　　　　一條碰一聲。
四條肥香腸，正在鍋裡煎。　　　沒有肥香腸，正在鍋裡煎。

sizzle [ˋsɪzl̩] (v.) 滋滋響

pan [pæn] (n.) 鍋子

- *The monkey Dan asks, "How many sausages are in the pan?"*
  猴子丹問：「鍋子裡有多少香腸啊？」

sausage [ˋsɔsɪdʒ] (n.) 臘腸

- *Dan begs, "May I please have all these sausages and peas?"*
  丹懇求道：「我可以把這些香腸和豆子都吃掉嗎？」

209

這首韻文透過琅琅上口的韻文，來增進孩子們的算數和讀寫能力。香腸（sausage）這個字來自拉丁文 salsicia，指「鹽味的」（salted）或「保存的」。在沒有冰箱的時代，香腸是保存肉類的主要方式，可說是文明世界最早的便利食品之一。

香腸源自西元前三千年的蘇美人。巴比倫人記載了國王尼布甲尼撒（Nebuchadnezzar）偏好的香腸種類，類似今日義大利的蒜味香腸薩拉米（salami）。古希臘詩人荷馬（Homer）在《奧德賽》（Odyssey）中，也提到血香腸（blood sausage）。

salami

西元前 589 年，中國史籍中出現了以羊肉做成的香腸。西西里島詩人埃庇卡摩斯（Epicharmus）在喜劇作品中，有一部就是以「香腸」為題。在古希臘和古羅馬時期，香腸已經是很普遍的食品了。

blood sausage

在古羅馬皇帝尼祿（Nero）統治時期，香腸用來慶祝牧神節（Lupercalia）。後來，天主教廷宣布牧神節非法，而且吃香腸是一種罪惡。於是，羅馬皇帝康斯坦汀（Constantine）順水推舟禁止食用香腸。

因應不同的氣候和原料，人們製造出不同的香腸，有新鮮的，也有乾燥的，有軟的，也有硬的。例如，含牛、豬肉的燻製粗香腸（bologna）和義大利蒜味香腸（salami）是硬的，早餐香腸則是軟的。波隆納香腸來自義大利北部，而里昂香腸來自法國，至於柏林人，理所當然就是德國風味的香腸囉！

bologna

69 Georgie Porgie

Georgie Porgie, pudding and pie,
Kissed the girls and made them cry.
When the boys came out to play,
Georgie Porgie ran away.

喬治·波治，布丁和派，
偷親女孩，弄哭使壞；
當男孩們出來玩耍，
喬治·波治跑掉了。

這首歌謠起源於英國，可以說是早期描述性騷擾的作品。Georgie Porgie 指第一世白金漢公爵喬治·維爾斯（George Villiers, 1592–1628），他長相俊美，是國王詹姆士一世的寵臣，但是他道德操守不佳。他最惡名昭彰的事件，是和法王路易士十三世的妻子私通，這件事對男女雙方的名譽傷害都很大，後來被十九世紀的法國作家大仲馬（Alexander Dumas）寫進《三劍客》（*The Three Musketeers*）。他靠著英王的寵愛，獲得不少特權。英國國會最後失去耐性，出面制止英王對他的縱容。這首歌詞中，便諷刺了白金漢公爵的妄為行徑。

70 Skip to My Lou

Lou, Lou, skip to my Lou.
Lou, Lou, skip to my Lou.
Lou, Lou, skip to my Lou.
Skip to my Lou, my darling
Lost my partner, what'll I do?
Lost my partner, what'll I do?
Lost my partner, what'll I do?
Skip to my Lou, my darling!

Lou, Lou, skip to my Lou.
Lou, Lou, skip to my Lou.
Lou, Lou, skip to my Lou.
Skip to my Lou, my darling
I'll find another one, and prettier, too.
I'll find another one, and prettier, too.
I'll find another one, and prettier, too.
Skip to my Lou, my darling!

Lou, Lou, skip to my Lou.
Lou, Lou, skip to my Lou.
Lou, Lou, skip to my Lou.
Skip to my Lou, my darling!
Can't get a red bird, a blue bird will do.
Can't get a red bird, a blue bird will do.
Can't get a red bird, a blue bird will do.
Skip to my Lou, my darling!

Lou, Lou, skip to my Lou.
Lou, Lou, skip to my Lou.
Lou, Lou, skip to my Lou.
Skip to my Lou, my darling!
Flies in the sugar bowl, shoo, shoo, shoo.
Flies in the sugar bowl, shoo, shoo, shoo.
Flies in the sugar bowl, shoo, shoo, shoo.
Skip to my Lou, my darling!

Lou, Lou, skip to my Lou.
Lou, Lou, skip to my Lou.
Lou, Lou, skip to my Lou.
Skip to my Lou, my darling!

skip [skɪp] (v.) 跳躍
sugar bowl (n.) 糖罐

露，露，跳向我的露。
露，露，跳向我的露。
露，露，跳向我的露。
跳向我的露，我親愛的。
失去夥伴，怎麼辦？
失去夥伴，怎麼辦？
失去夥伴，怎麼辦？
跳向我的露，我親愛的。

露，露，跳向我的露。
露，露，跳向我的露。
露，露，跳向我的露。
跳向我的露，我親愛的。
找到另一個，更漂亮的。
找到另一個，更漂亮的。
找到另一個，更漂亮的。
跳向我的露，我親愛的。

露，露，跳向我的露。
露，露，跳向我的露。
露，露，跳向我的露。
跳向我的露，我親愛的。
捉不到紅鳥，藍鳥也行。
捉不到紅鳥，藍鳥也行。
捉不到紅鳥，藍鳥也行。
跳向我的露，我親愛的。

露，露，跳向我的露。
露，露，跳向我的露。
露，露，跳向我的露。
跳向我的露，我親愛的。
糖罐裡的蒼蠅，咻，咻，咻。
糖罐裡的蒼蠅，咻，咻，咻。
糖罐裡的蒼蠅，咻，咻，咻。
跳向我的露，我親愛的。

這首歌可以說是美國最著名的舞會歌曲（play-party），是即席演出的典型。loo 源自於蘇格蘭語，意指 love。據信是美國西南部北歐裔英語系美國人的祖先，將 loo 的拼法改成現在的 lou。lou 後來引申為甜心（sweetheart），所以 skip to my lou 的意思，就是興高采烈地蹦跳著奔向心上人。

在美國早期的新教徒社區土風舞會中，樂器和舞蹈被認為是惡魔欺詐的騙局。由於這種社交上的宗教偏見，新潮的年輕人發展出一種表演舞會（play-party）。在表演舞會中，所有方塊舞（square dance）中可能引起反感的動作，都被取消或戴面具進行，從而得到保守的長輩首肯。

舞會中沒有樂器，舞者拍手唱自己的音樂，形成特有的方式，也是十幾歲的青少年和新婚夫妻理想的娛樂方式。獵熊的獵人、印第安戰士、貨船上幹粗活的工人、鄙野的牛仔，都可以和自己的女伴跳舞，就像學校週日野餐的孩子一樣。play-party 的舞者要繞圈，並交換舞伴，這種舞蹈不分男女老幼，人人能跳的，所以在美國的土風舞界佔有不墜的地位。

〈Skip to My Lou〉是一種偷舞伴的簡單遊戲。一開始中間站著一位落單的男孩，其餘的人和自己的舞伴雙雙對對地手牽手，繞著圓圈跳舞。當女孩們繞過落單的男孩時，落單的男孩就要考慮要不要偷這個女孩。如果不要，就唱道：「I'll get another one prettier than you.」當他找到中意的對象時，就可以將鍾意的女孩拉走，留下那女孩落單的男伴。新的落單男孩要站到圓圈中間，繼續遊戲。這是很好的團康遊戲，在搖擺的舞蹈中，可以迅速拉近彼此的距離。

71 The More We Get Together

The more we get together, together, together;
The more we get together, the happier we'll be.
Cause your friends are my friends
And my friends are your friends.
The more we get together, the happier we'll be!

我們愈常在一起，在一起，在一起；
我們愈常在一起，就愈快樂。
因你朋友就是我朋友，
而我朋友也是你朋友。
我們愈常在一起，就愈快樂。

中世紀的歐洲人，如何和朋友共享美好時光呢？在忙碌的日常工作之餘有許多休閒活動，西洋棋（chess）是很普遍的遊戲，遊戲的方式有傳統規則的，也有用骰子進行的。此外還有保齡球、抓俘虜遊戲（prisoner's base）、瞎盲者的騙局（blind man's bluff, hoodman's blind）和簡單的惡作劇（horseplay），至今仍興盛不衰。西洋跳棋也是很受歡迎，當時稱為西洋雙陸棋戲（backgammon）。

chess

backgammon

孩子們會玩摔角、游泳、釣魚，和一種介於網球和手球之間的遊戲。中世紀的騎士，寓訓練於娛樂、體操和跑步活動中。中世紀最吸引觀眾的，不外乎鬥雞和嗾犬逗牛（bullbaiting）的遊戲。大部分人在收成季節時，會去小酒館喝兩杯。村民們玩咬住擺動中的蘋果來當遊戲。如果地主允許，還可以在附近的森林狩獵。中世紀的城堡有養獵鷹的人，人們會配合這種休閒活動而飼養幼鳥。當時的聖誕節遊戲還包括了「國王的豆子」，誰吃到了藏在烘培麵包或蛋糕中的豆子，誰就是慶典中的國王哦！

72 Twelve Green Bottles

Twelve green bottles hanging on the wall.
Twelve green bottles hanging on the wall.
If three green bottles should accidentally fall,
There'd be nine green bottles hanging on the wall.

Nine green bottles hanging on the wall.
Nine green bottles hanging on the wall.
If three green bottles should accidentally fall,
There'd be six green bottles hanging on the wall.

Six green bottles hanging on the wall.
Six green bottles hanging on the wall.
If three green bottles should accidentally fall,
There'd be three green bottles hanging on the wall.

Three green bottles hanging on the wall.
Three green bottles hanging on the wall.
If three green bottles should accidentally fall,
There'd be twelve green bottles lying on the floor.

十二個綠瓶子掛在牆上。
十二個綠瓶子掛在牆上。
若有三個意外掉下來，
還有九個掛在牆上。

九個綠瓶子掛在牆上。
九個綠瓶子掛在牆上。
若有三個意外掉下來，
還有六個掛在牆上。

六個綠瓶子掛在牆上。
六個綠瓶子掛在牆上。
若有三個意外掉下來，
還有三個掛在牆上。

三個綠瓶子掛在牆上。
三個綠瓶子掛在牆上。
若有三個意外掉下來，
有十二個綠瓶子躺在地上。

bottle [ˋbɑtl̩] (n.) 瓶子
- *Can tall Claire get her bottle down from the wall?*
  高高的克蕾兒有辦法把她牆上的瓶子拿下來嗎？

hang [hæŋ] (v.) 吊著
- *Why is Claire's small bottle hanging on the wall?*
  為何克蕾兒的小瓶子會掛在牆上呢？

fall [fɔl] (v.) 掉落
- *Will Claire fall off the chair?* 克蕾兒會從椅子上摔下來嗎？

這是一首起源於英國的歌謠，主要是教導孩子們練習減法。透過反覆的旋律和遞減數量的歌詞，牆上瓶子一一減少，讓孩子們熟練減法和訓練反應。

這首歌在不同的地區有不同的版本，例如，在美國是〈99 個啤酒瓶〉（99 Bottles of Beer）。針對不同的年齡孩子，可以替換不同的歌詞，例如將 twelve 換成 ten，或是將「green bottles」換成「Teddy bears」。

基本上是一次減少一定數量的東西，在內容上可以自由做變化，因時、因地制宜，發展各種面貌和想像。

73 The Animals Went In Two by Two

The animals went in two by two.
Hurrah! Hurrah!
The animals went in two by two.
Hurrah! Hurrah!
The animals went in two by two.
The elephant and the kangaroo,
And they all went into the ark,
    just to get out of the rain.

The animals went in three by three.
Hurrah! Hurrah!
The animals went in three by three.
Hurrah! Hurrah!
The animals went in three by three.
The wasp, the ant, and the bumblebee,
And they all went into the ark,
    just to get out of the rain.

The animals went in four by four.
Hurrah! Hurrah!
The animals went in four by four.
Hurrah! Hurrah!
The animals went in four by four.
The huge hippopotamus stuck in the door,
And they all went into the ark,
    just to get out of the rain.

動物兩兩走進去。
好哇！好哇！
動物兩兩走進去。
好哇！好哇！
動物兩兩走進去。
大象和袋鼠，
為了避雨，一起走進那方舟。

動物四隻、四隻走進去。
好哇！好哇！
動物四隻、四隻走進去。
好哇！好哇！
動物四隻、四隻走進去。
巨大的河馬塞住了門，
為了避雨，一起走進那方舟。

動物三隻、三隻走進去。
好哇！好哇！
動物三隻、三隻走進去。
好哇！好哇！
動物三隻、三隻走進去。
黃蜂、螞蟻和蜜蜂，
為了避雨，一起走進那方舟。

ark [ɑrk] (n.) 木舟

huge [hjudʒ] (a.) 巨大的
- *Mark said, "I want to go into that huge ark."*
  馬克說：「我想進去那艘方舟。」

hippopotamus [ˌhɪpəˈpɑtəməs] (n.) 河馬
- *Clark and Mark followed a hippopotamus onto the ark.*
  克拉克和馬克跟著河馬上走進方舟了。

這首歌謠的內容是描述聖經中諾亞方舟的故事，藉由歌詞中「two by two」、「three by three」、「four by four」的遞增數字，訓練孩子們的數學加法能力。

上帝創造人類，但是人類世代繁衍之後，德行越來越敗壞，痛心的神於是決定用洪水淹沒地面上的人類和飛禽走獸。但神垂憐諾亞，因為諾亞是篤信神的義人。神囑咐諾亞，建造一艘三層高的方舟，長 135 公尺、寬 22.5 公尺、高 13.5 公尺。諾亞花了一百二十年，建造了避難的方舟，在諾亞六百歲那一年，按照神的指示，諾亞一家八口，和每種各一公一母的動物，進入了方舟，並帶上足夠的食物。二月十七日時，大雨連降了四十晝夜，除了諾亞方舟上的倖存者之外，所有生物都被毀滅了。

大雨過後，方舟停留在今天土耳其境內的亞拉臘山（Mount Ararat）。諾亞和方舟內的生物都出來了，諾亞於是築壇獻祭。耶和華聞到馨香後很歡喜，不再詛咒世間生物，並且以彩虹當作誓約的象徵，讓各種生物從此繁衍不絕，生生不息。

74 She'll Be Coming Around the Mountain

74

She'll be coming round the mountain when she comes.
She'll be coming round the mountain when she comes.
She'll be coming round the mountain,
She'll be coming round the mountain,
She'll be coming round the mountain when she comes.

She'll be driving six white horses when she comes.
She'll be driving six white horses when she comes.
She'll be driving six white horses,
She'll be driving six white horses,
She'll be driving six white horses when she comes.

Oh, we'll all go out to meet her when she comes.
Oh, we'll all go out to meet her when she comes.
Oh, we'll all go out to meet her,
Oh, we'll all go out to meet her,
Oh, we'll all go out to meet her when she comes.

She'll be wearing red pajamas when she comes.
She'll be wearing red pajamas when she comes.
She'll be wearing red pajamas,
She'll be wearing red pajamas,
She'll be wearing red pajamas when she comes.

She will have to sleep with Grandma when she comes.
She will have to sleep with Grandma when she comes.
She will have to sleep with Grandma,
She will have to sleep with Grandma,
She will have to sleep with Grandma when she comes.

她來時，將繞山而來。   她來時，穿著紅色睡衣來。
她來時，將繞山而來。   她來時，穿著紅色睡衣來。
她將繞山而來，   她穿著紅色睡衣來，
她將繞山而來，   她穿著紅色睡衣來，
她來時，將繞山而來。   她來時，穿著紅色睡衣來。

她來時，駕著六匹白馬來。   她來時，要和祖母睡一起。
她來時，駕著六匹白馬來。   她來時，要和祖母睡一起。
她駕著六匹白馬來，   她要和祖母睡一起，
她駕著六匹白馬來，   她要和祖母睡一起，
她來時，駕著六匹白馬來。   她來時，要和祖母睡一起。

她來時，我們出去迎接她。
她來時，我們出去迎接她。
我們出去迎接她，
我們出去迎接她，
她來時，我們出去迎接她。

pajamas [pəˋdʒæməs]
(n.) 睡衣 (= pj's)

這是一首美國的傳統民俗音樂，寫於 1850–1900 年間，改編自古老的黑人靈歌〈When the Chariot Comes〉。1900 年之後，在美國西部的阿帕拉契山區衍生為現今的版本。歌詞中的 she，有兩種可能的意義：

1 指即將蜿蜒在鐵道上的新完工火車。

2 指美國勞工運動中的女先驅瑪麗·哈里絲·瓊斯（Mary Harris Jones, 1837–1930），描繪她前往阿帕拉契山區煤礦營區的情景。

瓊斯女士駕馭的六匹白馬，這是虛構的神化境界，歌詞的其他部分還描述了她到訪後隨之而來的慶祝活動。

美國西部早期交通不便，鎮上遇有火車或馬車到訪，總是令人歡欣鼓舞的事，因為這代表著可以見到親戚朋友，或接到遠方來的信件。

1890 年，這首歌在中西部鐵路工人間流傳開來，運用懷舊的「對唱」（call and response）方式，對唱指是兩個人採取談話問答式的演唱形式。「呼喚」的唱法用於「She'll be driving six white horses」，「回應」的唱法用於「When she comes」。「call and response」的唱法，是接連交互地歌唱不同的旋律，增添樂曲的張力，營造出多人合唱的效果。

75 Little Tommy Tucker

75

Little Tommy Tucker	小湯米・塔克,
Sings for his supper.	唱歌為了晚飯。
What shall we give him?	我們該給什麼？
White bread and butter.	奶油白麵包。
How will he cut it	他要怎麼切割,
Without a knife?	沒有半支刀子？
How will he marry	他要怎麼結婚,
Without a wife?	沒有半個妻子？

這首歌謠最早出版於 1829 年，「Little Tommy Tucker」在口語上是指孤兒，他們淪落街頭，乞討維生，或靠歌唱賣藝，只為填飽肚子，連娶妻生子都是一種奢望。而孤兒在古代社會中的境遇如何呢？羅馬人顯然不庇護孤兒和寡婦，希臘人則很早就有照顧孤兒的共識了，他們認為這是愛國行為。古希臘哲學家柏拉圖認為，孤兒應該由公眾監護，監護者應該愛護那些不幸的孤兒。在現在，世界上各地都有孤苦無依的孤兒，「Little Tommy Tucker」的悲歌仍在四處傳唱著。

supper [ˋsʌpɚ] (n.) 晚餐
- *He wants to have his supper.* 他想吃晚餐了。

butter [ˋbʌtɚ] (n.) 奶油
- *He eats his bread and butter and then goes to bed.*
  他吃完奶油麵包就上床睡覺了。

knife [naɪf] (n.) 刀子
- *He picks up the knife and cuts a piece of bread.*
  他拿起刀子，切了一片麵包。

76 Humpty Dumpty

Humpty Dumpty sat on a wall.
Humpty Dumpty had a great fall.
All the King's horses and all the King's men
Couldn't put Humpty together again.

蛋頭人坐牆上，
蛋頭人摔下來；
國王馬兒和侍衛，
全都無法修復他。

西元 1642–1652 年間，英國議會黨與保皇黨發動內戰，
烽火四起。1648 年，議會黨員為了抵禦保皇黨的圍城
之困，在聖瑪麗教堂（St. Mary's at the Wall Church）
上架設了 Humpty Dumpty 砲台，但教堂高塔還是被敵
軍摧毀，Humpty Dumpty 也滾落地面。匆忙趕來的英
國國王步兵團和騎兵部隊，努力想要修復 Humpty
Dumpty，但已回天乏術。這首歌謠隱喻高位者終將跌
落而支離破碎。到了 18 世紀，此韻文演變為謎語，謎
底就是「蛋」。Humpty Dumpty 長得就像蛋頭人，在
英語俚語中，也成為了「又矮又胖的人」的寫照。

put together 組合

- *Glen put the pieces together.* 葛倫把碎片組合起來。

77 Little Cat, Little Cat

(77)

Little cat, little cat,
Where have you been?
I've been to London to visit the queen.
Little cat, little cat,
What did you do there?
I frightened a little mouse under her chair.

小貓兒，小貓兒，
你去哪兒？
我去倫敦看皇后。
小貓兒，小貓兒，
你在那裡做了什麼？
嚇壞她椅下的小老鼠。

故事發生在十六世紀英國的都鐸王朝。女王伊利莎白一世
（Queen Elizabeth I）的女侍養了一隻老貓，牠總是在溫莎
堡（Windsor Castle）閒晃。有一天，女王坐在寶座上問政
時，老貓鑽進寶座底下嬉戲，牠的尾巴冷不防地掠過女王的
腳，女王被嚇了一跳。伊利莎白一世在眾臣面前失態，但是
她機智又富幽默感，除了替自己找台階下，也展現她宅心仁
厚的王者之風。於是女王下令，那隻貓可以在御座下漫步，
以免老鼠來訪。這段小小的插曲，和著歌謠，流傳不墜。

78

Little Miss Muffet

Little Miss Muffet sat on a tuffet,
Eating her curds and whey.
Along came a spider who sat down beside her,
And frightened Miss Muffet away.

瑪菲小小姐坐凳上，
吃著凝乳和乳漿。
一隻蜘蛛坐身旁，
嚇走瑪菲小小姐。

tuffet [ˋtʌfɪt] (n.) 矮凳
* *Is that cute Claire sitting on the tuffet over there?*
  坐在那邊小凳上的是可愛的克蕾兒嗎？

curd [kɝd] (n.) 凝乳（牛奶變酸後形成的厚厚一層物質）

whey [hwe] (n.) 乳漿（牛奶變酸後移去固體後留下的液體）

beside [bɪˋsaɪd] (prep.) 旁邊
* *Look, there is a spider beside Claire!* 看，克蕾兒身旁有一隻蜘蛛！

frighten [ˋfraɪtn̩] (v.) 驚嚇
* *Yes, I guess the spider may frighten her away.*
  對呀，我在想這隻蜘蛛搞不好會嚇走她。

Little
Miss Muffet..

•••• sat on a tuffet
reading a picture book
there came a spider-
and sat down beside her
and said, "May I have a look"?

這首歌謠的起緣有二說：一說是十六世紀時，蘇格蘭的皇后瑪莉（Mary I of Scotland, 1542–1587）和宗教改革家約翰‧諾克斯（John Knox, 1505–1572）因宗教理念不合，所以諾克斯想藉蜘蛛之力，將瑪莉皇后從寶座上嚇跑。

另一說是，這是英國第一部科學目錄的作者湯瑪仕‧瑪菲特博士（Dr. Thomas Muffet, 1553–1604），為繼女 Patience Muffet 所寫的歌謠。瑪菲特博士也是一位昆蟲學家，他在實驗室中養了許多昆蟲，有一天，Patience Muffet 坐在矮凳子上吃凝乳和乳漿早餐時，被突如其來的蜘蛛嚇到，便哭哭啼啼地逃跑了。

在通俗文化和民間傳說中，蜘蛛有不同的象徵意義。蜘蛛結網捕食，象徵耐心與毅力；牠致命的劇毒和緩慢致死的特性，代表敵意與怨恨；牠用網捕食到獵物後，會將獵物以網包裹住，帶到洞穴享用，則象徵占有欲。

這首歌謠可說是最早描寫恐蜘蛛者（arachnophobia）的作品了，最早的版本出現於 1805 年，收錄於《Songs for the Nursery》。

79 Twinkle, Twinkle, Little Star

Twinkle, twinkle, little star,
How I wonder what you are!
Up above the world so high,
Like a diamond in the sky.
Twinkle, twinkle, little star,
How I wonder what you are!

一閃，一閃，小星星。
我多麼想知道你是誰！
高高掛在那天空，
就像天空一顆顆鑽石。
一閃，一閃，小星星。
我多麼想知道你是誰！

twinkle [ˋtwɪŋkḷ] (v.) 閃耀
- *Did Ed see anything twinkling under his bed?*
  愛德有沒有在他的床底下看到什麼閃閃發亮的東西？

wonder [ˋwʌndɚ] (v.) 猜想
- *Ed wonders how a big diamond got under his bed.*
  愛德在想這顆大鑽石怎麼會跑到他床底下。

diamond [ˋdaɪəmənd] (n.) 鑽石
- *Look, Ed has the huge big diamond on his head!*
  看，愛德的頭上有一顆大鑽石。

這首歌謠是很受歡迎的英語童謠，曲調起源於 1761 年的法國旋律〈Ah! vous dirai-je, Maman〉（Ah! Will I tell you, Mother）。作詞者是珍·泰勒（Jane Taylor, 1783–1824），原詩名為〈The Star〉。1806 年，珍和姊妹安（Ann）出版了《童謠韻文》（Rhymes for the Nursery）一書，收錄了這首童謠。

這首童謠以雙韻方式寫成，世界各地有各種語言的版本，優美的文字和曲調，歷久不衰。歌詞使用 like a diamond in the sky 的明喻法，將天空中的星星比喻為閃亮的鑽石，開啟了孩童們的想像空間。本書收錄的這一段，是我們最常聽到，也是最容易唱的版本。以下是原詩的完整版本：

Twinkle, twinkle, little star,
How I wonder what you are!
Up above the world so high,
Like a diamond in the sky!

When the blazing sun is gone,
When he nothing shines upon,
Then you show your little light,
Twinkle, twinkle, all the night.

Then the traveler in the dark,
Thanks you for your tiny spark,
He could not see which way to go,
If you did not twinkle so.

In the dark blue sky you keep,
And often through my curtains peep,
For you never shut your eye,
Till the sun is in the sky.

As your bright and tiny spark,
Lights the traveler in the dark,
Though I know not what you are,
Twinkle, twinkle, little star.

80 To Babyland

How many miles to Babyland,
Anyone can tell?
Up one flight,
To the right,
Then please ring the bell.

What do they do in Babyland?
Dream and wake and play.
Laugh and crow,
Fonder grow,
Jolly times have they.

What do they say in Babyland?
Why, the oddest things.
Might as well,
Try to tell,
What a birdie sings.

Who is the queen in Babyland?
Mother, kind and sweet.
And her love,
Born above,
Guards the baby's sleep.

嬰兒之鄉幾哩遠，有誰會知道？
騰空飛行，往右去，
請你按按鈴。

他們在嬰兒之鄉做什麼？
做夢、清醒和玩耍。
歡笑和歡叫，熱愛成長，
他們多快活。

他們在嬰兒之鄉說什麼？
哎呀，什麼奇事都可說。
不妨也可以，
聽聽小鳥兒唱什麼。

誰是嬰兒之鄉的皇后？
是仁慈又溫柔的媽媽。
她的愛產生於上天，
保衛嬰兒入夢鄉。

crow [kro] (v.) 歡呼

guard [gɑrd] (v.) 保衛

Mom's smile will guard us today while we play.
今天媽媽的笑容會在我們玩樂時護衛著我們。

Babyland 這個「嬰兒之鄉」，是嬰兒還未出生前的居住地，各個民族對此有許多神秘的信仰和傳說。美國阿拉斯加的印第安部落因加利克人（Ingalik）認為，有一個地方充滿了小孩的靈魂，這些小孩按捺不住興奮的心情，等待被唱名出生。西北部的印第安人傳說有一處 babyland，還未出生到的小孩們都住在這裡。

北美印第安的契努克人（Chinook）認為，小孩們出生前的居住地是在白晝的太陽裡。東蕭尼族印第安人（Eastern Shawnee）流傳著，未出生的嬰孩住在銀河的星星裡，也有人認為孩子們和造物者在一起。

加拿大溫哥華島北部和英屬哥倫比亞沿岸的瓜基烏圖人（Kwakiutl）相信，在森林的深處有一間神秘的房子，這裡舉行著出生的儀式，所有人類、動物和植物都由這裡誕生。越南山區的原住民族 Montagnais，他們認為孩子們來自雲端。

81 Little Boy Blue

Little Boy Blue, come blow your horn.
The sheep's in the meadow, and the cow's
   in the corn.
Where is the boy that looks after the sheep?
He's under the haystack,
fast asleep.

小男孩布魯，快快吹號角。
羊兒在草原上，牛兒在穀堆中。
牧羊的小男孩呢？
他在乾草堆下，
沈睡著了。

blow [blo] (v.) 吹鳴
- *If you blow your horn loudly, your sheep can't sleep.*
  如果你的號角吹得太響，你的羊兒會睡不著。

meadow [ˈmɛdo] (n.) 草原
- *It's fun to go to play in a meadow.*
  在草原上玩好有趣。

haystack [ˈheˌstæk] 乾草堆
- *Slide down the haystack, and then you can hide.* 從乾草堆上滑下來，然後躲起來。

Thomas Wolsey (1475–1530)

這首童謠起源自中世紀英國的都鐸王朝，Little Boy Blue 指天主教樞機主教沃爾西（Thomas Wolsey, 1475–1530），當時在位者為亨利七世（King Henry VII, 1485–1509）。沃爾西很富有，但是為人高傲，人緣不佳，樹敵甚多。他十五歲時，拿到牛津大學學位，便有了「小學士」（Boy Bachelor）的暱稱。

「Blowing one's own horn」描述沃爾西的自吹自擂的行徑。1514–1525 年，他將莊園宅第改建成漢普敦皇宮（Hampton Court Palace），鋪張地炫耀財富與權勢。，是出現了用來諷刺他的順口溜：

Come ye to court? Which Court?
The King's Court or Hampton Court?

要去皇宮？誰的皇宮？
國王的皇宮，還是漢普敦皇宮？

這樣口耳相傳的譏諷，讓亨利七世的面子也掛不住。1529 年，亨利七世宣布沒收沃爾西的財產。當時，英國主要的貿易輸出產品為羊毛，貿易與稅收充實了國庫，也進了沃爾西的口袋，「Where is the boy who looks after the sheep?」就是指沃爾西富可敵國。天主教的主教長袍為鮮紅色的，但沃爾西的長袍表面有四隻藍色美洲豹，所以被稱為 Little Boy Blue。中世紀的英國，公開批評貪官的異議人士會遭到監禁、沒收財產，甚至處死，所以人們就用這首童謠來暗諷。

Hampton Court Palace

82 Here Is the Beehive

Here is the beehive. Where are the bees?
Hidden away where nobody sees.
Watch and you'll see them come out of the hive.
One, two, three, four, five.
Bzzzzzzzz . . . all fly away!

蜂窩在這裡，蜜蜂在哪裡？
藏在沒人看到的地方。
看，你會看到他們飛出蜂窩。
一，二，三，四，五。
嗡嗡嗡……全飛走了！

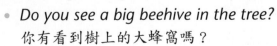

beehive [ˋbihaɪv] (n.) 蜂窩
- *Do you see a big beehive in the tree?*
  你有看到樹上的大蜂窩嗎？

蜜蜂是少數從新石器時代延續至今的生物。
西元 7000 年前的遠古時代，人們即採集並
食用野外的蜂蜜和蜂巢，這是當時唯一的
甜食。青銅器時代的社會，人們慶祝勝利
時會飲用蜂蜜酒（從蜂蜜發酵而來）。事
實上，在許多語言中，mead（蜂蜜酒）和
mellifera 這兩個字經常交替使用，字根均意
指蜜蜂、酒精飲料和有療效的飲料等。

mead

蜜蠟（beeswax）在古代的民間傳說和神話中
占有重要的地位。在基督教以前的時代，蜜
蠟用來獻祭給神祇、慶祝分娩、割禮、婚禮、
淨身和用於葬禮。另外，也用於塗屍防腐、
封棺和木乃伊化。蜜蠟的使用到基督教時代
仍沿用，牧師和僧侶也經常自己養蜂，以確保
製作宗教用的蠟蜜原料不虞匱乏。

beeswax

在過去，人們經常使用蜜蠟作為交易媒介和課稅，蜜蠟在書
寫、繪圖、雕刻、保護藝術作品和照明上，有不可磨滅的功
勞。自西元前 2700 年之後，蜂蜜、蜜蠟和蜂蠟（樹脂和蜜
蜂用來築巢的蜜蠟的混合物），廣泛出現於各種藥典裡。
1530 年，蜂蜜正式被引進南美洲，1638 年，荷蘭拓殖者將
之引進北美洲，蜂蜜更加普及至全世界。

83 Rock a Bye, Baby

Rock a bye baby, on the tree top.
When the wind blows, the cradle will rock.
When the bough breaks, the cradle will fall,
And down will come the baby, cradle and all.

搖啊搖，寶貝，在樹頂上。
輕風吹拂，搖晃搖籃。
樹枝斷了，搖籃摔落，
寶貝、搖籃全都掉落。

這首又名 Hush-a-Bye Baby，起源有兩種說法：

〔英國版〕一場政治風暴前的寧靜後，詹姆斯二世（James II）的兒子安然地睡在搖籃裡，對將至的風雨渾然未覺。當王朝衰落，各殖民地紛紛起義獨立，人們透過童謠來暗諷顢頇的朝政。

〔美國版〕1620 年，英國清教徒搭乘五月花號前往新大陸，看到印第安人用搖籃板將嬰兒背在背後，天氣好時，就將搖籃懸掛在樹枝上，然後去忙農事，任由微風輕拂搖籃和嬰兒，安撫嬰兒入睡。

bough [bau] (n.) 大樹枝

- *When the wind blows and sings, the bough swings.*
  當風咆哮時，樹枝會晃動。

84

Little Bo-Peep

Little Bo-Peep has lost her sheep,
And doesn't know where to find them.
Leave them alone, and they'll come home
Wagging their tails behind them.

小波比丟了羊兒，
不知道該往哪找。
不管他們，
他們就會搖著尾巴回家。

Martello Tower

這首歌謠字面上的意思，是描述一位走失羊的牧羊女，接受建議，靜待羊群歸來。這首歌的內容可以追溯至英國維多利亞時代的英格蘭東南的居民，他們當時哈斯丁斯城市的貿易是走私，所以蓋了座圓形石堡（Martello Tower），當作海關人員的住處，後來也用來拘禁走私者。這座圓形石堡被暱稱為 Bo Peep，Little Bo Peep 指「海關人員」，the sheep 指「走私者」，the tails 指「違禁品」，走私者碰到海關臨檢，往往會丟下違禁品逃跑。

lose [luz] (v.) 遺失

- *I lost my favorite doll somewhere in the sky.*
  我在天上的某個地方遺失了我心愛的洋娃娃。

leave [liv] (v.) 遺留

- *Did I leave it on the moon with Eve?*
  我是不是把它留在月亮上面的伊芙那邊了？

wag [wæg] (v.) 搖擺

- *Eve's small dog likes to wag its tail and lick my doll.*
  伊芙的小狗喜歡搖搖尾巴，舔我的娃娃。

85 Who Stole the Cookies From the Cookie Jar?

Group Who stole the cookies from the cookie jar?
Sue stole the cookies from the cookie jar.

Sue Who? me?
Group Yes, you!
Sue Not me!
Group Then Who?

Tome Tippi stole the cookies from the cookie jar.
Tippi Who? me?
Group Yes, you!
Tippi Not me!
Group Then Who?

Sue Tom stole the cookies from the cookie jar.
Tom Who? me?
Group Yes, you!
Tome Not me!
Group Then Who?

Tippi Jacky stole the cookies from the cookie jar.
Jacky Who? me?
Group Yes, you!
Jacky OK, me!
Group Jacky stole the cookies from the cookie jar.
He is not going to get the chocolate bar.

Group 誰偷走了罐子裡的餅乾？

　　　　蘇偷走了罐子裡的餅乾！

Sue 我嗎？

Group 對，是你。

Sue 不是我。

Group 那是誰？

Sue 湯姆偷走了罐子裡的餅乾！

Tom 我嗎？

Group 對，是你。

Tom 不是我。

Group 那是誰？

Tom 緹比偷走了罐子裡的餅乾！

Tippi 我嗎？

Group 對，是你。

Tippi 不是我。

Group 那是誰？

Tippi 傑奇偷走了罐子裡的餅乾！

Jacky 我嗎？

Group 對，是你。

Jacky 好吧，是我。

Group 傑奇偷走了罐子裡的餅乾！

　　　　他別想得到巧克力棒。

cookie [ˋkʊkɪ] (n.) 餅乾
- *Mom baked a lot of cookies.* 媽媽幫烤了許多餅乾。

jar [dʒɑr] (n.) 罐子

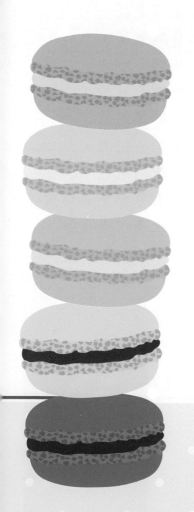

這首童謠適合認識新朋友時進行。大家一同唱歌遊戲之際，歌詞中被點名的新朋友要及時反應，並說出下一位偷餅乾的嫌疑犯。藉由歌曲的循環唱誦，歌詞不斷地變換成每一位小朋友的名字，加深同儕間的熟稔度和情感。

餅乾罐起源於英國，原本稱為 biscuit jars，十八世紀末期開始被使用。早期的餅乾罐通常用玻璃製成，蓋子是金屬製的，在雜貨舖就可以買到。更早的餅乾罐是圓柱型的，上面有彩繪花點綴以綠葉。1930 年之後，陶製的餅乾罐占美國餅乾罐大宗。

第一個陶製餅乾罐，是由美國俄亥俄州的 Zanesville 城的「刷子製陶公司」（Brush Pottery Company）生產的，綠色的罐身前後皆有餅乾（Cookies）的字眼，此後，各種外觀形狀的餅乾罐，如雨後春筍般出現在市面上，在 1940–1970 年間，製罐業達到鼎盛。

從收藏家喜好的葡萄酒或可口可樂罐，到各式各樣的餅乾罐，一個大餅乾罐是家庭必備用品。從動物圖騰，像羊啊、熊啊、牛啊、雞啊、貓啊，人們可以輕而易舉地從罐海中，找到心儀的餅乾罐。現在深受歡迎的餅乾罐，常見的有維尼熊（Winnie the Pooh）和貝蒂（Betty Boop）等。創意十足的製陶業，也在實用與美感的工業設計間，不斷尋找驚艷的平衡點。

86 Three Blind Mice

Three blind mice,
Three blind mice,
See how they run!
See how they run!
They all ran after the farmer's wife,
Who cut off their tails with
   a carving knife.
Did you ever see such a thing
   in your life
As three blind mice?

三隻瞎老鼠，
三隻瞎老鼠，
看牠們怎麼跑！
看牠們怎麼跑！
牠們追著農婦跑，
她拿了一把刀，
剪了牠們尾巴。
你今生可曾見過這等事，
這般三隻瞎老鼠？

韻文中的農夫和妻子，影射英王亨利八世之女瑪麗皇后一世（Mary I），和她的西班牙夫婿腓力二世（Felipe II）。信仰天主教的瑪麗在獲得王位後，迫害新教徒，被稱為血腥瑪麗。兩百多年前，忠誠追隨新教徒的三位主教 Hugh Latimer、Nicholas Ridley 和 Thomas Cranmer，只因為誤闖捕鼠陷阱，被判造反罪，後來被矇眼處刑。

Mary I (1516–1558)

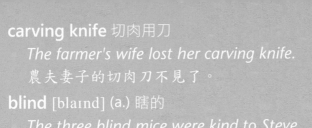

carving knife 切肉用刀
The farmer's wife lost her carving knife.
農夫妻子的切肉刀不見了。

blind [blaɪnd] (a.) 瞎的
The three blind mice were kind to Steve.
那三隻瞎老鼠對史蒂夫很好。

87 Little Jack Horner

Little Jack Horner sat in a corner
Eating a Christmas pie.
He put in his thumb and pulled out a plum
And said, "What a good boy am I!"

傑克‧霍納坐在角落，
吃著聖誕派。
拇指插進，挖出梅子，
說：「我真是個好孩子！」

歌謠中的小傑克‧霍納，傳說是英國格拉鎮
（Glastonbury）最後一位修道院長 Richard
Whiting 的管家。亨利八世即位後想解散修
道院，緊張的院長想到了一則妙計：送給國
王一份特別的聖誕禮物，一個內藏十二份莊
園租地契據的餡餅。孰料在前往倫敦的路上，
信差小傑克‧霍納敵不過貪婪人性，竟將拇
指戳進餡餅中，使勁挖出 Mells Manor 莊園
的租地契據，他的後代於是便落腳在此地。

Christmas pie

corner [ˋkɔrnɚ] (n.) 角落

● *Jack ran to the bakery at the corner.*
傑克跑到轉角處的麵包店。

88 You Are My Sunshine

You are my sunshine,
My only sunshine.
You make me happy
When skies are gray.
You'll never know, dear,
How much I love you.
Please don't take my sunshine away.

你是我的陽光，
我唯一的陽光。
你使我快樂，
當天空陰暗。
你永遠不會知道，
我是多麼愛你啊。
請你別帶走我的陽光。

The other night, dear,
As I lay sleeping,
I dreamed I held you in my arms.
When I awoke, dear,
I was mistaken,
And I hung my head and cried.

有一天晚上，親愛的，
當我躺著睡覺，
我夢見我擁你入懷。
當我醒來，親愛的，
發現我弄錯了，
我垂著頭哭泣。

sunshine [ˈsʌnˌʃaɪn] (n.) 陽光
- *I always feel fine when I'm walking in the sunshine.*
  走在陽光下，我總是覺得很好。

1940 年，這首膾炙人口的歌曲開始發片，被美國路易斯安那州選為州歌，前州長暨鄉村音樂歌手吉米．戴維斯（Jimmie Davis, 1899–2000）功不可沒。根據資料顯示，戴維斯向 Paul Rice 買下這首歌的版權，然後掛上自己的名字。這種現象在第二次世界大戰之前的音樂市場，並不罕見。

這首歌更早的版本掛名 Rice Brothers，還有資料顯示，單簧管手 Pud Brown 也參與這首歌的早期編曲階段。戴維斯熱愛這首歌曲，他在 1987 年的自傳中提到，州長任內的每次大集會，他都騎著他名叫陽光（Sunshine）的馬，高歌著這首歌，真是浪漫熱情的路易斯安那州陽光呀。

89 John Jacob Jingleheimer Schmidt

(89)

John Jacob Jingleheimer Schmidt,
That is my name too.
Whenever I go out,
The people always shout,
John Jacob Jingleheimer Schmidt!
Da, da, da, da, da, da, da, da!

約翰雅各金哥海默史密特，
那也是我的名。
只要我一出去，
人們就會大叫，
約翰雅各金哥海默史密特，
在那裡！在那裡！在那裡！

John Jacob Jingleheimer Schmidt,
His name is my name too.
Whenever we go out,
The people always shout,
John Jacob Jingleheimer Schmidt!
Da, da, da, da, da, da, da, da!

約翰雅各金哥海默史密特，
他的名也是我的名。
只要我們一出去，
人們就會大叫，
約翰雅各金哥海默史密特，
在那裡！在那裡！在那裡！

shout [ʃaut] (v.) 大叫
- *My neighbors shout, "Hello, Dee!" whenever they see me.*
  我鄰居看到我就會叫著：「哈囉，蒂。」

歌中的「Da!」是德文，是「There!」的意思。John Jacob Jingleheimer Schmidt 是德國名字，因又長又饒舌，成為取笑、模仿的對象。在社區遠足、郊遊、短途旅遊搭乘公車時，常歡唱這首歌助興，童軍活動也經常可以聽到，這首歌還是美國賓夕法尼亞州的經典遊行歌曲。唱時可以更換歌詞中的代名詞，增添趣味。

90 Hey, Diddle, Diddle

Hey, diddle, diddle,
The cat and the fiddle.
The cow jumped over the moon,
The little dog laughed to see such sport,
And the dish ran away with the spoon.

嘿，滴朵，滴朵，
小貓和小提琴；
牛兒跳過月亮；
小狗看了笑開懷；
盤子跟著湯匙跑走了。

fiddle [ˋfɪdl̩] (n.) 小提琴
* *play the fiddle* 演奏小提琴
laugh [læf] (v.) 大笑
dish [dɪʃ] (n.) 盤
* *my favorite dish* 我喜歡吃的菜

Elizabeth I (1533–1603)

The dish ran away with the spoon.

在英國宮廷裡，人們給政治人物取詼諧的綽號是慣例。伊麗莎白一世（Elizabeth I）就常常被稱為「貓」（The Cat），因為她總是像貓玩老鼠般地玩弄朝臣於股掌之中。

這首童謠是諷刺一椿宮廷醜聞。歌謠中的牛、月亮和狗，都是這場猜字謎遊戲中的角色，貓理所當然是伊麗莎白一世，狗影射羅伯特·杜得利（Robert Dudley），他是英國列斯特郡（Leicester）的伯爵，女王有一次就稱他為她的「lap dog」，意思是「供她玩賞用的小狗」。

文中的 dish（餐盤）指伊麗莎白一世的女侍，spoon（湯匙）指皇室的嚐味者。他們兩個私奔，結果東窗事發，就被伊麗莎白一世軟禁在倫敦塔上。在一場場的遊戲中，女王永遠是贏家！

這首童謠最早出版於 1765 年，藉由現實中不可能發生的現象，像是牛飛越過月亮、小狗見了哈哈大笑、餐盤跟著湯匙跑等，這些畫面刺激孩童們天馬行空、詼諧有趣的想像。這本歌謠的原作為〈High Diddle Diddle〉，原來是口語體，後來因為時代變遷而改變了面貌，這在英國民謠中很常見。

91 Hey, Lolly, Lolly

Hey lolly lolly lolly, hey lolly lolly lo
Hey lolly lolly lolly, hey lolly lolly lo

The cat on the bridge holds a cage,
Hey lolly lolly lo.
She's talking to the birdies,
Hey lolly looly lo.

Hey lolly lolly lolly, hey lolly lolly lo
Hey lolly lolly lolly, hey lolly lolly lo

The dog with the hat looks at the cat,
Hey lolly lolly lo,
He's waiting to get the cage,
Hey lolly lolly lo.

Hey lolly lolly lolly, hey lolly lolly lo
Hey lolly lolly lolly, hey lolly lolly lo

嘿，蘿麗蘿麗蘿麗，嘿，蘿麗蘿麗羅，
嘿，蘿麗蘿麗蘿麗，嘿，蘿麗蘿麗羅。

橋上的貓拿著鳥籠，
嘿，蘿麗蘿麗羅，
她對著鳥兒說話，
嘿，蘿麗蘿麗羅。

嘿，蘿麗蘿麗蘿麗，嘿，蘿麗蘿麗羅，
嘿，蘿麗蘿麗蘿麗，嘿，蘿麗蘿麗羅。

戴帽的狗看著貓咪，
嘿，蘿麗蘿麗羅，
他正等著拿鳥籠，
嘿，蘿麗蘿麗羅。

嘿，蘿麗蘿麗蘿麗，嘿，蘿麗蘿麗羅，
嘿，蘿麗蘿麗蘿麗，嘿，蘿麗蘿麗羅。

hold [hold] (v.) 裝著
- *I can hold my little cat called Pat in my straw hat.*
  我可以用草帽裝我那隻叫做蓓特的小貓。

cage [kedʒ] (n.) 鳥籠
- *My straw hat is like a cage for little Pat.*
  我的草帽對小蓓特來說就像是一個鳥籠。

這首是很典型的「對唱」（call and response song）
的歌曲，對唱通常是由兩個人採取談話問答式的演唱，
形式活潑。由一個人自由編唱出一句韻文，其他人接
著一起唱和出「hey lolly lolly lo」，每個人輪流對
唱，看能編出多長的歌，饒富歡樂的氣息。

在英文俚語中，lolly 指「棒棒糖」或「錢」。
現在，就讓我們看看棒棒糖的起源！在美國南部
和中西部，吮吸者（sucker）也可以用來指棒棒糖
（lollipop）。在這些區域，lollipop 適用於圓盤狀的
糖果，sucker 則指球狀的糖果。棒棒糖有櫻桃、葡萄、
橘子、西瓜和青蘋果等口味。在北歐，例如德國和荷
蘭等地，甚至還有味道像複方甘草合劑口味的棒棒糖。

lollipop

1769 年，英國最早有棒棒糖的紀錄，意指棒棒糖以糖
或糖蜜為主要成分。loll 指「懸盪」（to dangle，指像
舌頭一樣的懸盪），lolly 在美國北部的方言，也是指「舌
頭」，起源可能來自舌頭舔或吸吮的聲音。第一支自
動化生產的棒棒糖產地眾說紛紜，美國威斯康辛州和
加州的舊金山都宣稱自己搶得頭彩，製作了第一支棒
棒糖。

92 Down by the Station

Down by the station early in the morning,
See the little puffer bellies all in a row.
See the engine driver pull the little throttle;
Puff, puff, toot, toot.
Off we go!

大清早，車站旁，
小火車頭排排站，
看看火車長拉拉油門，
噗，噗，嗆，嗆
出發囉！

station [`steʃən] (n.) 車站
- *in the crowded train station* 在擁擠的火車站

puffer [`pʌfɚ] (n.) 噴氣物

row [ro] (n.) 排（列）
- *wait in a row to get on the train* 排隊等著上火車

driver [`draɪvɚ] (n.) 司機

throttle [`θrɑtl̩] (n.) 油門

本歌發行於 1948 年，作曲者是 Slim Gaillard，由 Lee Ricks 填詞。一般流傳版本的第二段，和本書版本略有不同：

See the station master
Turn the little handle
Puff, puff, toot, toot
Off we go!

火車站，可以稱為 train station（英式和美式英語）、railway station、railroad station 或 rail station（英式英語）。火車停靠在火車站，便利乘客上下車或裝卸貨物。早期的火車站是客貨兼用的，但隨著貨運方式多樣化，現今歐美的貨運已逐漸集中於主要車站。

最早的鐵路車站，建築物少，設施簡陋。第一條商營鐵路是「史托頓及達靈頓鐵路」（Stockton and Darlington Railway），但並沒有正式的火車站。英國曼徹斯特的利物浦火車站，是現存最古老的火車站，建於 1830 年。時至今日，利物浦火車站已經被保留成科學博物館。

歐美國家現存的火車站大多建於十九世紀，在藝術的角度上，這些車站保留了當時的建築風格，外觀宏偉寬闊、美侖美奐。從巴洛克式、實用主義到現代主義，不一而足。

93 Five Little Monkeys

93

Five little monkeys jumped on the bed.
One fell off and bumped his head.
Mama called the Doctor and the Doctor said:
"No more monkeys jumping on the bed!"

Four little monkeys jumped on the bed.
One fell off and bumped his head.
Mama called the Doctor and the Doctor said:
"No more monkeys jumping on the bed!"

Three little monkeys jumped on the bed.
One fell off and bumped his head.
Mama called the Doctor and the Doctor said:
"No more monkeys jumping on the bed!"

Two little monkeys jumped on the bed.
One fell off and bumped his head.
Mama called the Doctor and the Doctor said:
"No more monkeys jumping on the bed!"

One little monkey jumped on the bed.
One fell off and bumped his head.
Mama called the Doctor and the Doctor said:
"Put those monkeys straight to bed!"

五隻小猴子，床上跳不停。
一隻摔下來，撞傷他的頭。
媽媽打電話給醫生，醫生告誡說：
「不要再有猴子在床上跳。」

四隻小猴子，床上跳不停。
一隻摔下來，撞傷他的頭。
媽媽打電話給醫生，醫生告誡說：
「不要再有猴子在床上跳。」

三隻小猴子，床上跳不停。
一隻摔下來，撞傷他的頭。
媽媽打電話給醫生，醫生告誡說：
「不要再有猴子在床上跳。」

二隻小猴子，床上跳不停。
一隻摔下來，撞傷他的頭。
媽媽打電話給醫生，醫生告誡說：
「不要再有猴子在床上跳。」

一隻小猴子，床上跳不停。
猴子摔下來，撞傷他的頭。
媽媽打電話給醫生，醫生告誡說：
「把所有小猴子全都送上床去。」

這是一首教導孩子們減法的歌謠。琅琅上口的曲調、通俗幽默的故事情節，描繪出一幅可愛、頑皮又逗趣的小猴子浮世繪。倦極又受傷的小猴子們，在醫生的最後通牒和母親的悉心照顧下，終於筋疲力竭地沉沉進入夢鄉。第一句流傳的版本是「Five little monkeys jumping on the bed」，本書版本改 jumping 為 jumped。Jumping 比較好唱，但不符文法，所以改成 jumped。

猴子除了是我們熟知的靈長類動物，如獼猴、狒狒、長尾猴、猿和大猩猩之外，在西方文化中，猴子也指惡作劇、調皮、淘氣的小孩或模仿者。

They made a monkey out of him.
他們愚弄他。

→ 在俚語中，指模仿並愚弄受害者。

He has a monkey on his back.
他毒癮重。

→ 當做名詞用時，可以暗指毒癮。

Stop monkeying around!
不要搞蛋！

→ 當作動詞用時，指行為淘氣、調皮像猴子一樣。

1857 年，在 C. A. Abbey 的書中首次出現「brass monkey」的字眼，用來形容嚴寒，書中説道：「It would freeze the tail off a brass monkey.」（天氣冷到可以凍僵 brass monkey 的尾巴。）

以「brass monkey」的字眼形容酷熱，則可以回溯到 1847 年，「hot enough to melt the nose off a brass monkey」（天氣熱到可以融化 brass monkey 的鼻子）。儘管起源眾説紛紜，莫衷一是，透過文學作品之脈絡，可以看到文字隨時代變化的多元性。

94 Little Cabin in the Woods

Little cabin in the woods,
Little man by the window stood.
Little rabbit hopped by,
Knocking at the door.
"Help me! Help me, sir!" he said,
"Before the farmer bops my head."
"Come on in," the little man cried,
"Warm up by the fire."

森林裡的小木屋，
窗前站著小矮人，
小小兔子跳過去，
敲啊敲啊敲敲門。
「救我！救我！」兔子說，
「就在農夫還沒打我的頭前。」
「快快進來，」那小矮人喊，
「快去火邊取取暖。」

cabin [ˋkæbɪn] (n.) 小屋
wood [wʊd] (n.) 森林
bop [bɑp] (v.) 輕輕敲打
warm up 取暖（暖身）

小木屋原本是簡單的小木房子，起源於瑞典，瑞典移民將小木屋的使用傳統，帶到美國德拉瓦灣沿岸地區。1663 年，馬里蘭州的法令規定，小木屋的興建規模為 20 平方呎，才正式將小木屋納入管理。

逐漸地，小木屋由附屬功能逐漸轉變為住屋。在維吉尼亞州 1770 年的一份文件中載明：「a log cabin twenty four feet long and twenty wide for a Court House」（小木屋的興建規模為長 24 呎、寬 20 呎）。

之後在西部開拓邊疆的拓荒運動中，小木屋的規格也受到此法令的約束。於是，小木屋成了美國拓荒者的象徵──樸素而不矯飾，平實而堅固。

這首歌謠是以手指舞蹈進行，和孩子們遊戲時，可以依據歌詞的涵義，用手指或整個身體扮演兔子、獵人與小木屋，將遊戲融入情境，增添學習樂趣。

第三句的「Little rabbit hopped by」，原流傳版本為「Little rabbit hopping by」，為符合文法改唱為 hopped。

唱歌時可配合動作律動，例如：

Little cabin in the woods,	以食指作出小木屋
Little man by the window stood.	假裝用望遠鏡眺望找人
Little rabbit hopped by,	食指和中指假裝兔子耳朵跳啊跳
Knocking at the door.	做敲敲門的動作
"Help me! Help me, sir!" he said,	張開手臂作求救狀
"Before the farmer bops my head."	作敲頭狀
"Come on in," the little man cried,	揮揮手招喚小兔子
"Warm up by the fire."	雙手交叉在胸前感覺很溫暖

95 I've Been Working on the Railroad

I've been working on the railroad
All the livelong day.
I've been working on the railroad
Just to pass the time away.

Can't you hear the whistle blowing,
Rise up so early in the morning?
Can't you hear the captain shouting,
Dinah, blow your horn?

Dinah, won't you blow,
Dinah, won't you blow,
Dinah, won't you blow your horn?
Dinah, won't you blow,
Dinah, won't you blow,
Dinah, won't you blow your horn?

Someone's in the kitchen with Dinah.
Someone's in the kitchen I know.
Someone's in the kitchen with Dinah.
Strumming on the old banjo and singing.

Fie, fi, fiddly i o,
Fie, fi, fiddly i o,
Fie, fi, fiddly i o,
Strumming on the old banjo.

banjo

我在鐵路上工作，
漫長的一整天。
我在鐵路上工作，
只為消磨時間。

你沒聽那汽笛在鳴叫？
一大清早就起床。
你沒聽到火車長在喊？
黛娜，快吹號角吧！

黛娜，妳不吹嗎？
黛娜，妳不吹嗎？
黛娜，妳不吹號角嗎？
黛娜，妳不吹嗎？
黛娜，妳不吹嗎？
黛娜，妳不吹號角嗎？

有人和黛娜在廚房。
我知道有人在廚房。
有人和黛娜在廚房。
彈奏五弦琴唱著歌。

非，非，非得力，意，喔。
非，非，非得力，意，喔。
非，非，非得力，意，喔。
正彈奏著五弦琴。

livelong [ˈlɪvˌlɔŋ] (a.) 漫長的

whistle [ˈhwɪsl̩] (n.) 汽笛

strum [strʌm] (v.) 彈奏

因為口音的更迭，這首歌謠最早的名稱為〈I've Been Working on the Levee〉，而於 1894 年首次出版的歌名為〈The Levee Song〉。歌曲的來源，有一說是出自愛爾蘭民謠，是愛爾蘭工人在西部鋪設鐵路時所唱。還有一說是來自非裔美國人，是他們在路易斯安那州築堤壩時，一邊工作，一邊吟唱的歌。不論起源為何，這首歌已是膾炙人口的美國民謠。

歌詞中 Dinah 和 Someone's in the Kitchen 這些歌詞是後來才加上去的，曲調和德克薩斯人的〈The Eyes of Texas Are Upon You〉相符。Dinah 可能是指女子的姓名或是火車頭，horn 是指用來通知午餐時間到了的號角聲。

96 The Mulberry Bush

96

Here we go round the mulberry bush,
The mulberry bush, the mulberry bush.
Here we go round the mulberry bush,
So early in the morning.

This is the way we wash our clothes,
We wash our clothes, we wash our clothes.
This is the way we wash our clothes,
So early Monday morning.

This is the way we iron our clothes,
We iron our clothes, we iron our clothes.
This is the way we iron our clothes,
So early Tuesday morning.

This is the way we wash our face,
We wash our face, we wash our face.
This is the way we wash our face,
So early Wednesday morning.

This is the way we comb our hair,
We comb our hair, we comb our hair.
This is the way we comb our hair,
So early Thursday morning.

This is the way we brush our teeth,
We brush our teeth, we brush our teeth.
This is the way we brush our teeth,
So early Friday morning.

This is the way we tie our shoes,
We tie our shoes, we tie our shoes.
This is the way we tie our shoes,
So early Saturday morning.

This is the way we walk to church,
We walk to church, we walk to church.
This is the way we walk to church,
So early Sunday morning.

我們就是這樣繞桑椹樹，
桑椹樹，桑椹樹，
我們就是這樣繞桑椹樹，
這麼一大清早。

我們就是這樣洗衣服，
洗衣服，洗衣服，
我們就是這樣洗衣服，
星期一清早。

我們就是這樣燙衣服，
燙衣服，燙衣服，
我們就是這樣燙衣服，
星期二清早。

我們就是這樣洗洗臉，
洗洗臉，洗洗臉，
我們就是這樣洗洗臉，
星期三清早。

我們就是這樣梳頭髮，
梳頭髮，梳頭髮，
我們就是這樣梳頭髮，
星期四清早。

我們就是這樣刷刷牙，
刷刷牙，刷刷牙，
我們就是這樣刷刷牙，
星期五清早。

我們就是這樣綁鞋帶，
綁鞋帶，綁鞋帶，
我們就是這樣綁鞋帶，
星期六清早。

我們就是這樣去教堂，
去教堂，去教堂，
我們就是這樣去教堂，
星期天清早。

clothes [kloz] (n.) 衣物
- *They hang the clothes out to dry under the blue sky.*
  他們在藍天下晾乾衣服。

iron [ˈaɪən] (v.) 燙衣服
- *Today I'll iron the clothes and then put them away.*
  今天我要燙衣服，然後收起來。

這首著名的童謠源自威克費爾監獄（Wakefield Prison）。獄友們在茂盛的桑樹叢中操練，竟譜出絕妙樂章，讓世世代代的兒童，傳唱不止。

威克費爾監獄座落於英國的約克郡西邊，於 1594 年興建，原為英國國會下議院，現為英國安全措施最嚴密的監獄。此建築完工於維多利亞時代，收容英國重大罪犯 600 人，英國小報暱稱這個監獄為怪獸大廈（Monster Mansion）。

歌詞中，「So early in the morning」原為「On a cold and frosty morning」。歌詞的最後一句，用星期一到星期日輪替練習，在和孩子們唱遊時，可以將孩子們星期一到星期日的各式活動，代換進歌詞中，一方面練習星期一到星期日的英文說法，另一面也可以藉此熟練日常生活作息的規律性，是教導孩子們生活規則的好教材。

97 Oats, Peas, Beans, and Barley Grow

Oats, peas, beans, and barley grow.
Oats, peas, beans, and barley grow.
Do you or I or anyone know
How oats, peas, beans, and barley grow?

First the farmer sows his seeds
And stands erect and takes his ease.
He stamps his foot and claps his hands
And turns around to view his lands.

Next the farmer hoes the weeds
And stands erect and takes his ease.
He stamps his foot and claps his hands
And turns around to view his lands.

Last the farmer harvests his crops
And stands erect and takes his ease.
He stamps his foot and claps his hands
And turns around to view his lands.

Cereals

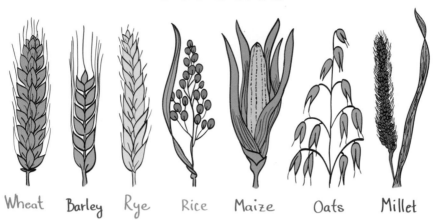

Wheat   Barley   Rye   Rice   Maize   Oats   Millet

Oats, peas, beans, and barley grow.
Oats, peas, beans, and barley grow.
Do you or I or anyone know
How oats, peas, beans, and barley grow?

燕麥、豌豆、豆子、大麥長啊長；
燕麥、豌豆、豆子、大麥長啊長，
你、我或任何人可知道
燕麥、豌豆、豆子、大麥怎麼長？

農夫先播種，
站挺喘口氣，
踏腳又拍手，
轉圈看大地。

seed [sid] (n.) 種子
weed [wid] (n.) 雜草
harvest [ˈhɑrvɪst] (v.) 收穫

接著農夫鋤鋤地，
站挺喘口氣，
踏腳又拍手，
轉圈看大地。

最後農夫來收割，
站挺喘口氣，
踏腳又拍手，
轉圈看大地。

燕麥、豌豆、豆子、大麥長啊長；
燕麥、豌豆、豆子、大麥長啊長，
你、我或任何人可知道
燕麥、豌豆、豆子、大麥怎麼長？

這是一首描述農夫播種、鋤草和收割莊稼過程的韻文。小
朋友們可以邊唱歌、邊做遊戲，遊戲方式如下：

小朋友們圍成一圈，先選一位小朋友站在圓圈中央，扮演
農夫。其餘小朋友手牽手合唱這首韻文，扮演農夫的小朋
友則根據歌詞，表演播種、站立休息、跺腳拍手等動作，
之後再輪番由各個小朋友來扮演。

這個唱遊遊戲可以讓小朋友們熟悉農作物的種類、來源和
農夫的辛勤工作，是一首寓教於樂的典型童謠。

中世紀的歐洲，隨時都籠罩在飢荒的威脅中，不論是市井小民還是貴為王公大臣的存糧，都不足以度過饑饉時代。1300 年初期，大量增加的人口，使得農作物唯在最佳狀態下收成，才能勉強維持供需平衡。換句話說，農作物的耕種與收成不允許有任何意外。然而，當時莊稼的變數有多變的天氣、濕冷的夏天和早秋的暴風雨，任何一項天災，都會使社會陷入饑饉的恐慌。

1315–1317 年，春夏季特別濕冷，大量農作物無法收成，使得整個社會都受到了影響。當時人們甚至靠吃耕牛和穀粒維生。貓狗經常失蹤，有的村落甚至流傳著人吃人的謠言。中世紀的童話故事《糖果屋歷險記》（Hansel and Gretel）和《格林童話》（Grimm's Fairy Tales）中大部分的故事，都具體而微地描繪了當時飢荒的情景。

98 All the Pretty Little Horses

Hush-a-bye, don't you cry.
Go to sleep, little baby.
When you wake up,
You shall have all the pretty little horses,
Blacks and bays,
Dapples and grays,
A coach and six little horses.
Hush-a-bye, don't you cry.
Go to sleep, little baby.

噓，乖乖別哭哭。
乖乖睡，小寶貝。
等你醒來，
就有全部漂亮小馬兒。
有黑馬和棗紅馬，
有花斑馬和灰馬，
還有大馬車和六隻小馬。
噓，乖乖別哭哭。
乖乖睡，小寶貝。

bay [be] (n.) 棗紅色小馬

- *Faye wants to raise another bay, but her dad says no.*
  菲想要養隻棗紅色小馬，但她爸爸說不行。

dapple [ˋdæpḷ] (n.) 斑紋

- *"Horses with dapples are prettier," says Faye's dad.*
  「有斑紋的馬兒比較漂亮。」菲的爸爸說。

coach [kotʃ] (n.) 馬車

- *"A bay looks lovely pulling Mom's reddish-brown coach," notes Faye.*
  「一隻棗紅色小馬拉著媽媽棕紅色的馬車，
  看起來很可愛。」菲說道。

314

這是一首哄嬰兒入睡的搖籃曲。母親藉由各色各樣的馬匹，來構築一個奇幻迷離的夢中仙境。這是一首美國傳統民謠，根據美國歷史現存最早的文件指出，這首歌謠起源自殖民時期到南北內戰期間，由 John A Scott 在 1963 年收錄於《三叉報刊》（ Trident Press ），是美國民謠研究者 Alan Lomax（1915–2002）從母親那裡學來的，母親將這首歌從北卡羅萊納州帶來了德州。這篇韻文還有其他版本，增加了以下的內容：

Way down yonder, down in the meadow,
There's a poor little lamby.
The bees and the butterflies peckin' at its eyes,
The poor little thing cried for her mammy.

歌詞中的 lamby（小羊）被蜜蜂和蝴蝶啄了眼睛，哭喊著要找媽咪的情景，穿插於這首溫馨的歌詞中，顯得突兀。事實上，這也是這首韻文的喻意所在。在南北戰爭之前，黑奴制度普遍存在於美國南方各州，黑奴一方面要是從事生產勞動的工作，另一方面也要打理白人家庭的家務。

於是，黑奴婦女被迫丟下自己的孩子，轉而去照顧白人的孩子。主人的寶寶得到完善的照顧，自己的孩子卻失去了屏蔽。這首韻文，就透露出了黑奴的這種悲哀。
當時這類暗喻的作品為數不少，囿於黑奴的政經狀況和社會地位，他們不能抒發胸臆之情，便在迂迴的樂曲中，創造出反映現實的深度作品。

99 Lavender's Blue

99

Lavender's blue, dilly dilly.
Lavender's green.
When you are King, dilly dilly,
I shall be Queen.
Who told you so, dilly dilly,
Who told you so?
It was my own heart, dilly dilly,
That told me so.

薰衣草的藍，滴嚦滴嚦，
薰衣草的綠。
若你是國王，滴嚦滴嚦，
我就是皇后。
誰告訴你的，滴嚦滴嚦？
誰告訴你的？
是我的心，滴嚦滴嚦，
這麼告訴我。

Call up your friends, dilly, dilly.
Set them to work.
Some to the plow, dilly dilly,
Some to the fork,
Some to the hay, dilly dilly,
And some to thresh the corn,
While you and I, dilly dilly,
Will keep ourselves warm.

召喚你的朋友來，滴嚦滴嚦，
安排去工作。
有些到耕地，滴嚦滴嚦，
有些去耙草，
有些去割草，滴嚦滴嚦，
有些去打穀。
而你和我，滴嚦滴嚦，
相互在取暖。

文中的 dilly，原本作 diddle，這首童謠的來源是〈Diddle Diddle〉，又稱為〈The Kind Country Lovers〉，於 1672 到 1685 年間問世。到了 1805 年，開始以簡短形式出現於童謠中。

在《Folk Songs of Old New England》一書中，作者 Eloise Linscott 認為這首歌和慶祝第十二夜（Twelfth Night，1 月 5 日晚上）有關，在慶祝活動中，有一項是選出國王和皇后。第十二夜之後是主顯節（Epiphany，聖誕節後的第 12 天，一月六日）。主顯節是為了慶祝基督的三個顯現：誕生、洗禮和第一個奇蹟。主顯節、復活節和聖誕節，為基督徒的三大主要節慶。

最受歡迎的版本由 Burl Ives 所演唱的。其中一直重複的 dilly，原指「極好的東西或傑出的人」，但在歌中沒有特殊之意，只是唱著好玩的音。

lavender [ˈlævəndɚ] (n.) 薰衣草
- *I saw the most exquisite field of lavender there.*
  我在那兒見到了最美的薰衣草園。

plow [plaʊ] (v.) 犁地
- *The farmer Joan plows all day with her strong cow.*
  農夫瓊整天都和她強壯的牛都在耕地。

fork [fɔrk] (v.) 叉起
- *Joan Lau uses her big pitchfork to fork hay to her cow.*
  瓊用她的大乾草叉，叉起乾草給她的牛吃。

thresh [θrɛʃ] (v.) 打穀
- *Joan's threshing machine will thresh a huge pile of wheat.*
  瓊的打穀機能把一大堆的小麥去穀。

古希臘人稱薰衣草為草本植物納德斯（Nardus），名稱來自於敘利亞的納達（Naarda）城市，有時也統稱為納德（Nard）。羅馬帝國時代，薰衣草的花，一磅可以賣到一百迪納里（denarii，古羅馬幣值），這個價格相當於一個農場工人的月薪，或是當地理髮師理了五十個人頭髮的報酬。羅馬人將薰衣草放到水裡沐浴，認為這樣可以消除疲勞、恢復元氣。羅馬人攻克南大不列顛（southern Britain）後，也將這種薰衣草入浴法引進英國。

在瘟疫肆虐的時代，法國格拉斯（Grasse）製作手套的工人，因為常以薰衣草油浸泡皮革，許多人因此逃過一劫，於是薰衣草又罩上能阻絕瘟疫的神秘面紗。其實，薰衣草具有驅蟲的功效，而瘟疫正是透過跳蚤傳播的，所以薰衣草防瘟疫的説法是有科學根據的唷！

LAVENDER

100 Five Little Ducks

Five little ducks went out one day,
Over the hills and far away.
Mommy duck called quack quack quack quack,
But only four little ducks came back.

Four little ducks went out one day,
Over the hills and far away.
Mommy duck called quack quack quack quack,
But only three little ducks came back.

Three little ducks went out one day,
Over the hills and far away.
Mommy duck called quack quack quack quack,
But only two little ducks came back.

Two little ducks went out one day,
Over the hills and far away.
Mommy duck called quack quack quack quack,
But only one little duck came back.

One little duck went out one day,
Over the hills and far away.
Mommy duck called quack quack quack quack,
But no little ducks came back.

Sad Mommy Duck went out one day,
Over the hills and far away.
Mommy Duck called quack quack quack quack
And five little ducks came wandering back.

五隻小鴨出門去，
爬過遠方一山又一山，
鴨子媽媽呱呱叫，
只有四隻回到家。

兩隻小鴨出門去，
爬過遠方一山又一山，
鴨子媽媽呱呱叫，
只有一隻回到家。

四隻小鴨出門去，
爬過遠方一山又一山，
鴨子媽媽呱呱叫，
只有三隻回到家。

一隻小鴨出門去，
爬過遠方一山又一山，
鴨子媽媽呱呱叫，
沒有小鴨回到家。

三隻小鴨出門去，
爬過遠方一山又一山，
鴨子媽媽呱呱叫，
只有兩隻回到家。

傷心母鴨出門去，
爬過遠方一山又一山，
鴨子媽媽呱呱叫，
五隻鴨子晃回家。

這首韻文是以鴨子為數數兒的主角。在西方社會中，鴨子象徵的意義是什麼呢？在西方文化中，鴨子常代表「弱者」，所以英文用法有：

ugly duckling	→	大器晚成的人；醜小鴨
lame duck	→	弱者；政治生命將結束的人
dead duck	→	沒有成功希望的人或物
sitting duck	→	易射擊的目標；容易被騙的人
duck soup	→	輕而易舉的事；易擊敗的對手
duck-legged	→	腿短的
break one's duck's egg	→	打破零分
be like a duck in a thunderstorm	→	垂頭喪氣；目瞪口呆

從水和鴨的關係，也衍生出許多用法。如：

be like water off a duck's back	→	沒有影響；毫無效果
take to something like a duck to water	→	如魚得水
play ducks and drakes	→	打水漂兒
play ducks and drakes with money	→	浪費、揮霍金錢
Would a duck swim?	→	這還用問嗎？
fine day for young ducks	→	雨天
in two shakes of a duck's tail	→	立即

101 Cinderella

Cinderella, dressed in yellow,
Went downstairs to kiss her fellow.
How many kisses did she get?
One, two, three . . . (Continue counting)

Cinderella, dressed in lace,
Went downstairs to powder her face.
How many pounds did it take?
One, two, three . . . (Continue counting)

Cinderella, dressed in red,
Went downstairs to bake some bread.
How many loaves did she bake?
One, two, three . . . (Continue counting)

仙度瑞拉穿黃衣，
下樓親親她朋友。
有幾個吻她得到？
一，二，三……（繼續數）

仙度瑞拉穿蕾絲，
走下樓來撲個粉。
到底用了幾磅粉？
一，二，三……（繼續數）

仙度瑞拉穿紅衣，
下樓來烤烤麵包。
她總共烤了幾條？
一，二，三……（繼續數）

downstairs [ˌdaʊnˈstɛrz] (a.) 樓下
- *Grace and Kaye are busy working downstairs.*
  葛蕾絲和凱在樓下忙著做事。

lace [les] (n.) 花邊
- *"Let's tie this lace onto the handrail to make it colorful," says Grace.*
  「把這花邊綁到手把上面，讓它看起來色彩繽紛。」葛蕾絲說。

powder [ˈpaʊdɚ] (v.) 把粉撒在……
- *"Let's put this shiny powder on the walls to make them glitter," added Kaye.*
  「我們把發光的粉撒在牆上，讓這些牆壁閃閃發光。」凱又說。

這是一首跳繩歌。孩子們喜歡在跳繩時朗誦韻文和歌謠，有些是敘述一個故事，伴隨特定的動作；有些是數數兒，愈數愈快，以此來挑戰跳繩的速度極限。這首韻文用家喻戶曉的灰姑娘故事入韻，讓孩子們在一邊跳繩之際，可以一邊練習顏色和數數兒。

《灰姑娘》（*Cinderella*）可以說是最廣為人知的童話故事，玻璃鞋、南瓜車，象徵著女孩們所夢想的幸福。女孩因為整天在廚房工作、灰燼撲面，所以被稱為灰姑娘。後母和後母兩個女兒常常欺負灰姑娘，讓她終日在廚房裡工作，任由灰燼掩蓋她的美貌和少女的綺夢。這一天，傳來了王子要舉辦舞會選妃的消息，灰姑娘在神仙教母的幫助下，終於如願以償的參加了王子的舞會。

102 The Noble Duke of York

Oh, the noble Duke of York,
He had ten thousand men.
He marched them up to the top of the hill
And marched them down again.

When you're up, you're up.
When you're down, you're down.
When you're only half way up,
You're neither up nor down.

Oh, a hunting we will go,
A-hunting we will go.
We'll catch a little fox and put him in a box,
And then we'll let him go.

喔，約克的尊爵，
他有一萬名士兵。
他領軍上山頭，
又領軍下山頭。

你們上山，就上山，
你們下山，就下山，
你們要只在半山腰，
就是不上也不下。

喔，我們打獵去，
我們打獵去。
捉隻小狐狸放進小盒子，
然後又放他走。

noble [ˋnobḷ] (a.) 高貴的
- *The noble Prince Paul has the ability to talk to animals.*
  尊貴的保羅王子擁有跟動物說話的能力。

march [mɑrtʃ] (v.) 行進
- *Paul often marches around the castle with his pet turtle.*
  保羅常帶著他的寵物烏龜繞著城堡行進。

hunting [ˋhʌntɪŋ] (n.) 打獵
- *Paul never goes hunting and killing animals.*
  保羅從不打獵、不殺害動物。

這首歌謠的起源有眾多說法，其中最常見的說法可以溯源至十五世紀英國的金雀花王朝，用來嘲弄被擊潰的約克公爵理查（Duke of York）。1455 年到 1485 年間，英國爆發玫瑰戰爭（Wars of the Roses），前後歷時三十年。玫瑰內戰是蘭開斯特家族（House of Lancaster，以紅玫瑰代表）和約克家族（House of York，以白玫瑰代表）的支持者，為了爭奪英國王位而發生的內戰。

這首歌謠的內容是指 1460 年 12 月 30 日發生在韋克菲爾德（Wakefield）附近的桑德爾城堡（Sandal Castle）之役，桑德爾城堡是建在舊諾曼第叢林上，由公爵理查所防禦的堡壘。堅實的土木工程高出了海平面十公尺，所以歌詞中寫道「He marched them up to the top of the hill.」。當時眼見蘭開斯特家族的部隊人數是理查軍隊的兩倍以上，約克情急之下，下錯了軍令，要部隊離開城堡，下山正面迎擊，此即是歌詞中的「He marched them down again.」。結果，他的軍隊在這次的戰役中潰不成軍，理查也在混戰中身亡。

歌謠的來源還另有一說，歌中的 The Noble Duke of York 指的是英國國王喬治三世的次子弗雷德里克（Frederick），他是禁衛騎兵團的統帥，個性老實和藹，但最終失敗。他娶了普魯士公主為妻，但幾年後就分居了。弗雷德里克得另覓新居，於是出現了 York House。

The Red Rose of the House of Lancaster 蘭開斯特家族紅玫瑰

The White Rose of the House of York 約克家族白玫瑰

103 Brahms' Lullaby

Lullaby and good night,
With roses bedight.
With lilies over spread is baby's wee bed.
Lay you down now and rest;
May your slumber be blessed.
Lay you down now and rest;
May your slumber be blessed.

Lullaby and good night,
Your mother's delight.
Bright angels beside my darling abide.
They will guard you at rest;
You shall wake on my breast.
They will guard you at rest;
You shall wake on my breast.

bedight [bɪˋdaɪt] (v.) 裝飾　　**wee** [wi] (a.) 極小的

spread [sprɛd] (v.) 散佈　　**slumber** [ˋslʌmbɚ] (n.) 睡眠

唱首搖籃曲道晚安，
玫瑰裝飾在旁，
百合花散滿寶貝的小床。
把你放下休息，願你好眠。
把你放下休息，願你好眠。

唱首搖籃曲道晚安，
媽媽心歡喜，
快樂天使陪伴在我寶貝旁。
他們會守護你安眠，
在我懷裡醒來。
他們會守護你安眠，
在我懷裡醒來。

「布拉姆斯的搖籃曲」是一個總稱，代表一些相同旋律和類似歌詞的搖籃曲。布拉姆斯的搖籃曲起源於德國作曲家布拉姆斯（Johannes Brahms），他一生作品甚多，包括協奏曲、奏鳴曲、交響曲、合唱作品和歌曲集。這首搖籃曲正是布拉姆斯歌曲集中的作品，原文以德文寫成，英譯如下：

Good evening, good night. With roses adorned,
With carnations covered, slip under the covers.
Early tomorrow, if God wills, you will wake once again.
Early tomorrow, if God wills, you will wake once again.
Good evening, good night. By angels watched,
Who show you in your dream the Christ-child's tree.
Sleep now peacefully and sweetly, look into dream's paradise.
Sleep now peacefully and sweetly, look into dream's paradise.

1833 年，布拉姆斯生於德國漢堡，卒於奧地利的維也納。父親 Johann Jakob Brahms 是低音提琴手，耳濡目染下，他從七歲便開始學琴，也在早年就開始作曲，但早期的作品已被他自己銷毀。布拉姆斯於二十歲時，與匈牙利小提琴家 Remenyi 合作，在德國北部第一次巡迴演出後，從此順利踏上音樂創作之路，並成為一代大師。

Johannes Brahms
(1833–1897)

335

104 Jack and Jill

Jack and Jill went up the hill
To fetch a pail of water.
Jack fell down and broke his crown,
And Jill came tumbling after.

傑克吉兒上山去，
提了一桶水。
吉兒跟著滾下來，
傑克跌倒撞到頭。

Up Jack got and home he ran
As fast as he could caper.
There his mother bound his head,
With vinegar and brown paper.

站起身，跑回家，
傑克飛快跑啊跳。
用那醋和牛皮紙，
媽媽幫他包紮頭。

Jill came in and she did grin
To see his paper plaster.
Mother was vexed and would scold
   her next
For causing Jack's disaster.

吉兒進來哈哈笑，
看見傑克的藥膏。
媽媽生氣責怪她，
害得傑克出災難。

Louis XVI (1754–1793)

這首歌謠起源於法國，和法國的歷史環環相扣。歌中的 Jack，指法王路易十六（King Louis XVI），Jill 則指法國的最後一位皇后瑪麗（Queen Marie Antoinette）。1774 年五月，路易十六登上法國的王座，但此時帝國已經債台高築，光是每年要償還的利息，就超過國庫收入的一半。路易十六不是治國的明君，但他具有精湛的製鎖技術，鎮日沉迷鑽研其中。

1789 年 7 月 14 日，暴發了法國革大命，路易十六逃亡未遂，被押在巴黎的杜伊勒裡宮。他在牆板裡面藏了一個保險箱，裝上了複雜無比的鎖，裡面正藏有企圖勾結國內外復辟勢力、阻止法國大革命的密函。但鎖還是被開啟了，路易十六也被送上了斷頭台。諷刺的是，斷頭台的設計路易十六也曾參與，為了讓斷頭台更有效率，他還命人把鍘刀改成三角形，沒想到居然自食惡果。這首童謠最早出版於 1795 年，歌詞中的「lost his crown」，正是指路易十六被斬首，「came tumbling after」指皇后隨後也被處決。

fetch [fɛtʃ] (v.) 取
- *Watch Aunt Adel fetch pails of water from the well.*
  看亞黛阿姨從井裡取了好多桶水。

tumble [ˈtʌmbl̩] (v.) 跌倒
- *Uh-oh, she tumbles over her puppy Rover.*
  喔喔，她被她的小狗狗羅弗絆倒了。

caper [ˈkepɚ] (v.) 蹦跳
- *Rover capers away, and Aunt Adel picks herself up with a laugh.*
  羅弗跳開，亞黛阿姨笑笑地爬起身來。

vexed [vɛkst] 生氣的
- *You did make me vexed yesterday.* 你昨天真的惹惱我了。

scold [skold] 責罵
- *Our teacher is always scolding us.* 老師老是責備我們。

105 Little Bunny Foo-Foo

Little bunny Foo-Foo
Came hopping through the forest,
Scooping up the field mice,
And bopping them on the head.

Then down came the Good Fairy, and she said,
"Little Bunny Foo-Foo,
I don't want to see you
Scooping up the field mice
And bopping them on the head."

"I'll give you three chances,
And if you don't behave,
I'll turn you into a goon!"
And the next day . . .

Little bunny Foo-Foo
Came hopping through the forest,
Scooping up the field mice,
And bopping them on the head.

Then down came the Good Fairy, and she said,
"Little Bunny Foo-Foo,
I don't want to see you
Scooping up the field mice
And bopping them on the head."

"I'll give you two more chances,
And if you don't behave,
I'll turn you into a goon!"
And the next day . . .

 Little bunny Foo-Foo
Came hopping through the forest,
Scooping up the field mice,
And bopping them on the head.

Then down came the Good Fairy, and she said,
"Little Bunny Foo-Foo,
I don't want to see you
Scooping up the field mice
And bopping them on the head."

"I'll give you one more chance,
And if you don't behave,
I'll turn you into a goon!"
And the next day . . .

Little bunny Foo-Foo
Came hopping through the forest,
Scooping up the field mice,
And bopping them on the head.

Then down came the Good Fairy, and she said,
"Little Bunny Foo-Foo,
I don't want to see you
Scooping up the field mice
And bopping them on the head."

"I've given you three chances,
    and you didn't behave.
So now I'll turn you into a goon!
POOF! You're a goon!"

And the moral of the story is
"Hare today, goon tomorrow!"

scoop [skup] (v.) 舀出；挖出

goon [gun] (n.)〔英〕笨蛋

小兔子富富，森林裡蹦跳，
挖出那田鼠，拍他們的頭。

善良仙女來了，說：
「小兔子富富，
我不想看你
挖出田鼠，
拍他們頭。」

「我給你三次機會，
你要是不乖乖，
我就把你變呆呆。」
到了第二天……

 小兔子富富，森林裡蹦跳，
挖出那田鼠，拍他們的頭。

善良仙女來了，說：
「小兔子富富，
我不想看你
挖出田鼠，
拍他們頭。」

「我給你再一次機會，
你要是不乖乖，
我就把你變呆呆。」
到了第二天……

 小兔子富富，森林裡蹦跳，
挖出那田鼠，拍他們的頭。

善良仙女來了，說：
「小兔子富富，
我不想看你
挖出田鼠，
拍他們頭。」

「我給你再兩次機會，
你要是不乖乖，
我就把你變呆呆。」
到了第二天……

 小兔子富富，森林裡蹦跳，
挖出那田鼠，拍他們的頭。

善良仙女來了，說：
「小兔子富富，
我不想看你
挖出田鼠，
拍他們頭。」

「我給了你三次機會，
你卻不乖乖，
所以我現在要把你變呆呆。
碰！你變呆呆了！」

這個故事的寓意是：
今天兔子，明天變呆。

這首童謠描述一隻欺負田鼠的兔子,最終遭到報應的故事。藉由輕快的音調,教導孩子們要愛護小動物。兔子(Easter Bunny)和彩蛋,是復活節最可愛的象徵。復活節期間,孩子們期待這個毛茸茸的動物,能帶來彩蛋和裝滿巧克力的禮物籃。兔子因為多產,代表著豐饒和迅速重生,成為了春分時節的吉祥物。

復活節兔子的傳說不可勝數,有些傳說說明了復活節(Easter)這個名稱的由來,來自古代歐洲專掌生育和春天的女神 Eostre,她和她的寵物兔子長伴左右。後來這隻兔子產下了第一顆彩蛋,復活節孩子們獵彩蛋的傳統遊戲也由此而來。

另一個說法來自德國,傳說復活節兔子(Easter Hare)會下蛋給孩子們尋找,他們也烘培兔子形狀的蛋糕、巧克力兔子和巧克力蛋。

106 Down by the Bay

Down by the bay
The watermelons grow.
Back to my home,
I dare not go,
For if I do,
My mother will say,
"Did you ever see a bear combing his hair?"
Down by the bay . . .

Down by the bay
The watermelons grow.
Back to my home,
I dare not go,
For if I do,
My mother will say,
"Did you ever see a bee with a sunburned knee?"
Down by the bay . . .

Down by the bay
The watermelons grow.
Back to my home,
I dare not go,
For if I do,
My mother will say,
"Did you ever see a moose kissing a goose?"
Down by the bay . . .

Down by the bay
The watermelons grow.
Back to my home,
I dare not go,
For if I do,
My mother will say,
"Did you ever see a whale with a polka dot tail?"
Down by the bay . . .

watermelon [ˈwɑtəˌmɛlən] (n.) 西瓜
- *"Knock! Knock!" The weasel knocks on the watermelon in a regular rhythm.*「叩！叩！」鼬鼠用著規律的節奏敲著西瓜。

sunburn [ˈsʌnˌbɝn] (v.) 曬傷
- *He is exposed to the sun too long and gets sunburned ears.* 他在太陽底下曬太久，結果曬傷了耳朵。

polka dot [ˈpolkə dɑt] (n.) 圓點
- *He wraps two cool wet polka dot handkerchiefs around his ears.* 他用兩張涼爽濕濕的圓點手帕包裹他的耳朵。

到那海灣邊，
西瓜生長處。
我回到了家，
卻不敢進去。
我若是進去，
媽媽準會問：
「你有沒有看到一隻梳
著頭髮的熊？」
在海灣邊。

到那海灣邊，
西瓜生長處。
我回到了家，
卻不敢進去。
我若是進去，
媽媽準會問：
「你有沒有看到一隻麋鹿
親吻鵝媽媽？」
在海灣邊。

到那海灣邊，
西瓜生長處。
我回到了家，
卻不敢進去。
我若是進去，
媽媽準會問：
「你有沒有看到一隻
膝蓋曬傷的蜜蜂？」
在海灣邊。

到那海灣邊，
西瓜生長處。
我回到了家，
卻不敢進去。
我若是進去，
媽媽準會問：
「你有沒有看到一隻有著
點點尾巴的鯨魚？」
在海灣邊。

這首歌是一首傳統歌謠，其中最後第二句「Did you ever
see a ____, ____ing a ____」，可以填入押韻的字，創造樂
趣，也考驗文字的功力。這首童謠最著名的版本由拉菲
（Raffi Cavoukian）所演唱，他於 1948 年出生在埃及的開
羅，後來隨家人移民加拿大。他投入童歌領域，如今已是世
界級的吟遊詩人、音樂製作人、作者和企業家。他被讚譽為
「英語世界最受歡迎的兒童歌手」、「加拿大永遠的兒童冠
軍」，他還曾擔任聯合國的國際環保親善大使。

107

Sing a Song of Six Pence

Sing a song of six pence,
A pocket full of rye.
Four and twenty blackbirds,
Baked in a pie.
When the pie was opened,
The birds began to sing.
Wasn't that a dainty dish to set before the king?

The king was in his counting house,
Counting out his money.
The queen was in the parlor,
Eating bread and honey.
The maid was in the garden,
Hanging out the clothes.
Down flew a blackbird and pecked off her nose.

唱首六便士的歌，
口袋滿滿是麥子。
二十四隻燕八哥
烤進一塊派。
當派被切開，鳥兒齊啼唱。
那不成了可口佳餚，可獻給國王？

國王在他帳房，
數著他的錢幣。
皇后在起居室，
吃麵包和蜂蜜。
女僕在花園裡，
把衣服晾起來，
一隻燕八哥低飛，啄了她的鼻子。

Rye

rye [raɪ] (n.) 黑麥
- *Granny bakes plenty of pastries made of rye.*
  外婆烤了許多黑麥做的酥皮點心。

dainty [ˋdentɪ] (a.) 美味的
- *All those dainty desserts look so sweet that they arouse everyone's appetite.*
  這些美味點心看起來都好甜啊，讓每個人胃口大開。

parlor [ˋpɑrlɚ] (n.) 起居室
- *Grandma Ginger decides to hold a tea party in the parlor.* 金潔外婆決定在起居室裡舉辦一個茶會。

這首著名的英國童謠，起源眾説紛紜。根據牛津字典的童謠記載，一本 1549 年出版的義大利食譜（1598 年始有英譯本）記載著，將活鳥藏進派裡面，當派被切開時，鳥會飛出來。字典中舉證，1723 年，一位廚師描述這道菜的目的：製造驚喜氣氛，娛樂賓客。1600 年，法國國王亨利四世（Henry IV）的婚禮中，當貴賓入座，打開餐巾，鳴禽接二連三飛出。

歌詞中，「a pocket full of rye」指餵食鳥兒們的黑麥。「The king was in his counting house, counting out his money. The queen was in the parlor, eating bread and honey.」指國王和王后的奢華生活，而辛勤的女僕則在戶外晾衣服。奢靡生活下的犧牲品 blackbird，於是以啄鼻來報復了。

108 Pretty Little Dutch Girl

I am a pretty little Dutch girl,	我是漂亮的荷蘭小姑娘，
As pretty as I can be.	漂亮得不得了。
And all the boys in the neighborhood	附近的男孩，
Are crazy over me.	都為我瘋狂。
My boyfriend's name is Mellow.	我男友叫梅羅，
He comes from the land of Jello.	來自果凍田園，
With pickles for his toes and a cherry for his nose,	用酸黃瓜做他的腳趾，用櫻桃做他鼻子，
And that's the way my story goes.	那就是我的故事。

neighborhood [ˈnebɚˌhud] (n.) 鄰近地區
- *The rooster Woody is holding a picnic in his neighborhood.*
  公雞伍迪正在附近舉辦野餐。

crazy [ˈkrezɪ] (a.) 瘋狂
- *All the animals on the farm are crazy about his cherry pies.*
  所有農場動物都超愛他的櫻桃派。

cherry [ˈtʃɛrɪ] (n.) 櫻桃
- *Fresh cherries are the secret to his famous cherry pies.*
  他櫻桃派有名的秘訣就是櫻桃要新鮮。

這是一首詼諧有趣的童謠。窈窕淑女，君子好逑，可是這個美麗德國女孩的男朋友居然是果凍人，腳趾是醃黃瓜，鼻子用櫻桃製成，果凍的魅力真是無法擋！類似的歌詞還有：

I am a pretty little Dutch girl,

As pretty as pretty can be,

And every boy in my hometown

Goes crazy over me!

I have a boyfriend Fatty,

He came from Cincinnati

With 48 toes and pickle on his nose,

And this is how my story goes.

One day while I was walking

I saw my boyfriend talking

To a pretty little girl with strawberry curls

And this is what he said to her:

I L-O-V-E, love you,

I K-I-S-S, kiss you.

I K-I-S-S, kiss you

On the F-A-C-E, face, face, face.

老少咸宜的果凍，是怎麼來的呢？1845 年，企業家、發明家兼慈善家彼得·庫柏（Peter Cooper）得到第一個凝膠點心（gelatin dessert）的專利。他以發明了「湯姆的拇指」（Tom Thumb）蒸汽引擎，讓火車克服了強風的陡坡地形而聞名。得到專利後，庫柏極力推廣這種凝膠點心。

1895 年，紐約「Le Roy」咳嗽糖漿製造商 Pearl B. Wait 向庫柏購買專利，將凝膠點心包裝上市，他的妻子 May David Wait 將這種凝膠點心命名為「Jell-O」。然而，產品仍然乏人問津。

法蘭克·伍華德（Frank Woodward）是一位自己創業的二十歲中輟生，他以美金 450 元購買 Jell-O 的權利，但銷售狀況還是不盡理想。伍華德打算以美金 35 元的價格將 Jell-O 賣給工廠負責人，然而就在成交前，強力的廣告促銷奏效了！

1906 年，Jell-O 的銷售量達到一百萬美金。Wood-ward Genesee Pure Food 公司在 1923 年更名為 Jell-O。如今，Jell-O 點心已經普及世界各個角落。

109 I Had a Little Nut Tree

(109)

I had a little nut tree.
Nothing would it bear,
But silver nutmegs
And golden pears.
The King of Spain's daughter
Came to visit me,
All for the sake
Of my little nut tree.

Her dress was made of crimson.
Jet black was her hair.
She asked me for my nut tree
And my golden pear.
I said, "So fair a princess never did I see.
I'll give you all the fruit
From my little nut tree."

我有棵小堅果樹，
什麼都不長。
只長銀肉荳蔻，
和金梨子。
西班牙公主，
前來拜訪我，
就為了我這棵小堅果樹。

她身穿深紅洋裝，
一頭烏溜溜黑髮。
她跟我要小堅果樹，
還有我的金梨子。
我說：「我從未見過
這麼美麗的公主。
小堅果樹上的果實
全都送給你。」

nut [nʌt] (n.) 堅果
- *Justin grows a magical and colorful nut tree in his backyard.*
  傑斯丁在他的後院種了一棵神奇的彩色堅果樹。

silver [ˈsɪlvɚ] (a.) 銀色的
- *This magic tree grows gold and silver nuts.*
  這棵神奇的樹長出金色和銀色的堅果。

princess [ˈprɪsɪs] (n.) 公主
- *"I don't see any brown nuts in the tree " says the princess.*
  「我沒有看到樹上有任何棕色的果實。」公主說。

這首歌謠是十六世紀歐洲歷史的諷刺作品，以 1506 年西班牙王室拜訪英國國王亨利七世（Henry VII）一事為背景。歌詞中的代表如下：

Nothing would it bear ➔ 指亞瑟有畸形的生殖器，無法生子。

silver nutmegs ➔ 指英國與東方的香料貿易事業。

golden pears ➔ 指英國與西方的貿易事業。

The King of Spain's daughter ➔ 指西班牙費迪南德二世國王（Ferdinand II of Aragon）和皇后伊莎貝拉（Isabella of Castile）最小的女兒亞拉岡的凱瑟琳（Katherine of Aragon）。

凱瑟琳的婚姻，促成 Aragon 和 Castile 兩個王國合併為西班牙。哥倫布發現新大陸後，一時之間，西班牙成為海上霸權。英國國王亨利七世覬覦西班牙的權勢，極力促成與西班牙的聯姻，以強大的海上貿易實力來對抗法國。於是，Aragon 的凱瑟琳與英格蘭國王亨利七世的長子訂婚，也就是王位的繼承人亞瑟王子（Prince Arthur）。

未料亞瑟王子後來驟逝，年輕的凱瑟琳便守了活寡。亨利七世怎肯讓煮熟的鴨子飛了，於是將凱瑟琳許配給次子，成為亨利八世的元配。兩個人接連生下六個孩子，其中五個不是流產，就是夭折，最後只剩下瑪莉公主（Princess Mary）長大成人。

後來亨利八世愛上女侍安妮·布林（Anne Boleyn），他為了再娶，不惜和羅馬教皇對抗，並宣布英國教會脫離羅馬教廷，由英國教會掌管英國的信仰，以達到再娶的目的。凱瑟琳深受英國人民的愛戴，韻文中也表現了對她的稱揚。反之，人們並不喜歡安妮·布妮。凱瑟琳雖然婚姻逢變，但她化成歌謠，永存不朽。

110 Rise and Shine

Rise and shine and give God the glory, glory.
Rise and shine and give God the glory, glory.
Rise and shine and give God the glory, glory.
Children of the Lord.

God said to Noah, "There's gonna be a flood, flood."
God said to Noah, "There's gonna be a flood, flood."
Get those children out of the mud, mud.
Children of the Lord.

God told Noah to build an ark, ark.
God told Noah to build an ark, ark.
Build it out of gopher bark, bark.
Children of the Lord.

God called for the animals. They came in two by two.
God called for the animals. They came in two by two.
Elephants and kangaroos.
Children of the Lord.

Rise and shine and give God the glory, glory.
Rise and shine and give God the glory, glory.
Rise and shine and give God the glory, glory.
Children of the Lord.

起床喜洋洋，獻給上帝榮耀，榮耀。
起床喜洋洋，獻給上帝榮耀，榮耀。
起床喜洋洋，獻給上帝榮耀，榮耀。
上帝的子民。

上帝告訴諾亞，將有一場洪水，洪水。
上帝告訴諾亞，將有一場洪水，洪水。
解救子民於泥濘，泥濘。
上帝的子民。

上帝告訴諾亞，要他建造方舟，方舟。
上帝告訴諾亞，要他建造方舟，方舟。
用地鼠皮革建造，皮革。
上帝的子民。

他召喚動物，牠們一對一對前來。
他召喚動物，牠們一對一對前來。
大象和袋鼠，大象和袋鼠。
上帝的子民。

起床喜洋洋，獻給上帝榮耀，榮耀。
起床喜洋洋，獻給上帝榮耀，榮耀。
起床喜洋洋，獻給上帝榮耀，榮耀。
上帝的子民。

● 一般流傳版本中二
至四段的句尾唱為
floody、arky、
barky、twosie。

rise [raɪz] (v.) 升起
- *The flag rises and flies high in the sky.* 旗子升起在高空中飄揚。

shine [ʃaɪn] (v.) 照亮
- *The sun rises and shines on Mom's face in the early hours.*
  大清早太陽升起了，照亮了媽媽的臉。

flood [flʌd] (n.) 洪水
- *The flood in that area made 10,000 people homeless.*
  該地區那場洪水，使得萬人無家可歸。

這首歌謠在描述《聖經》中諾亞方舟的故事，諾亞方舟的故事我們在前面已經介紹過，現在我們來看看諾亞方舟放出動物之後的故事吧！

話說上帝雖然吩咐諾亞要帶著所有種類的動物，每種一公、一母各一隻，以繁衍後代，但是百密一疏，諾亞還是漏掉了一些動物，例如，角獸（頭上長角的像白馬的神話動物，是純潔的化身）、斯芬克斯（sphinx，帶翼的獅身女怪，傳說常叫過路行人猜謎，猜不出的人會遭噬食）、龍（具有蛇身、蜥足、鷹爪、蛇尾、鹿角、魚鱗、口角有鬚、額下有珠的奇異動物）……等，因此牠們就絕種了。

以色列人和迦南人戰火連年的緣由，也和諾亞有關。洪水退去後，諾亞種植了一大片葡萄園，用來釀酒。有一天，酒醉的諾亞在脫掉衣服後昏睡了，他的次子含（Ham）看到了，無動於衷，其他兩個兒子雅弗（Japheth）和閃（Shem）則連忙拿衣服覆蓋父親，以防著涼。諾亞醒來後，大加稱讚雅弗和閃的孝心，並因含的不孝而詛咒其子迦南（Canaan）。根據舊約聖經，迦南人道德隳壞，又崇拜偶像，於是上帝要以色列人代替祂執行審判。時至今日，宗教的信仰力量，仍左右著國際大勢。

這是一首有時會令許多人痛苦的歌謠，為什麼呢？因為這是軍隊和營隊中常用的起床歌。在軍隊中，清晨五、六點就得起床。rise 表示起床，shine 表示軍人早上要擦亮自己的靴子。1916 年，美國海軍陸戰隊的徵兵公告上如此寫道：「He rapped at the door and in stentorian tones cried, "Rise and shine . . . Wiggle a toe."」

在營隊活動中，這首歌則是用在早餐桌上。當學員拖著闌珊的步伐走進餐廳時，指導老師或顧問就會用輕快的歌聲，輔以拍手節奏，提振學員的精神，也可以多吃幾匙燕麥粥！

111 Joy to the World

Joy to the world, the Lord is come.
Let earth receive her King.
Let every heart prepare Him room,
And heaven and nature sing,
And heaven and nature sing,
And heaven, and heaven and nature sing.

Joy to the earth, the Savior reigns.
Let men their songs employ,
While fields, floods,
Rocks, hills, and plains
Repeat the sounding joy,
Repeat the sounding joy,
Repeat, repeat the sounding joy.

He rules the world with truth and grace
And makes the nations prove
The glories of His righteousness
And wonders of His love,
And wonders of His love,
And wonders, wonders of His love.

普世歡騰，救主降臨！人間歡迎救主；
萬心為救主預備地方，宇宙萬物歌唱，
宇宙萬物歌唱，宇宙，宇宙萬物歌唱。

大地歡騰，主治萬方！萬民高聲頌揚；
田野，江河，山崗，平原，響應歌聲嘹亮，
響應歌聲嘹亮，響應，響應歌聲嘹亮。

主以真理，恩治萬方，要在萬國民中，
彰顯上主公義榮光，主愛奇妙豐盛，
主愛奇妙豐盛，主愛，主愛奇妙豐盛。

joy [dʒɔɪ] (n.) 喜樂　　　　　reign [reɪn] (v.) 統治；支配

earth [ɜθ] (n.) 土地　　　　　employ [ɪmˋplɔɪ] (v.) 使用

這是一首膾炙人口的聖誕頌歌，歌曲中以歡欣之情，傳送耶穌基督重生的喜悅。1719 年，華滋（Isaac Watts, 1674–1748）根據聖經故事填入歌詞；1841 年，梅森（Lowell Mason, 1792–1872）為這首歌譜曲，他節錄、重組韓德爾（George Frideric Handel, 1685–1759）的作品〈彌賽亞〉（Messiah），而成新曲調〈安提阿〉（Antioch），吟誦至今。

在華滋的時代，英國教會出現各種腐敗現象，講道的牧師例行公事地唸誦禱文，草草地交差了事，而信徒們不是在交頭接耳聊天，就是吃零食或打瞌睡。在華滋十八歲時，他有一次參加教會禮拜，看不過去這種墮落的景象，便向身為會堂執事的父親抱怨詩篇太沉悶，無法感動人心。父親對他說：「你要是不喜歡這些音樂，就寫一些好的音樂來聽聽啊！」

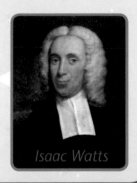

1692 年，華滋開始寫了他的第一首讚美詩，沒想到大受歡迎，一連在教會唱了 220 個禮拜天。華滋一生的作品高達八百多首，由於他的聖詩發揮了振奮人心、團結教會力量的作用，後世尊稱他為「英國聖詩之父」，可見影響之深遠。

Isaac Watts

112 Edelweiss

(112)

Edelweiss, edelweiss,
Every morning you greet me.
Small and white,
Clean and bright,
You look happy to meet me.
Blossoms of snow may you
    bloom and grow,
Bloom and grow forever.
Edelweiss, edelweiss,
Bless my homeland forever.

小白花，小白花，
每日早晨你問候我，
嬌小又潔白，
潔淨又明亮，
你見我多麼愉快。
願你在白雪中盛開成長，
永遠地開花成長。
小白花，小白花，
願你永保我家園安康。

edelweiss [ˈedḷˌvaɪs] (n.) 小白花

greet [grit] (v.) 問候

bloom [blum] (v.) 開花

- *When the edelweiss bloom,
  Ida smiles.* 只要小白花開花了，
  艾妲就笑開懷。

《小白花》這首著名歌曲，出自美國音樂劇和電影《真善美》
（The Sound of Music），Edelweiss 是高山火絨草，又名雪
絨花，生長於白雪嚴寒之地。《真善美》劇中，有兩層隱喻：
首先，當鰥夫重新發現美妙的音樂和對孩子們的愛時，他敞
開胸懷高歌，象徵他的人生就像小白花一樣，嚴雪褪盡後重
生。再者，崔普家人在面對加入第三帝國德國的壓力時，也
唱這首歌，代表奧地利愛國主義者的心聲。由於這首歌曲如
此普及，許多人誤還以為是奧地利的民歌或是官方的國歌。

113 Fiddle-de-dee

Fiddle-de-dee, fiddle-de-dee,
The Fly has married the Bumblebee.
Says the Fly, says he,
"Will you marry me and live with me,
   sweet Bumblebee?"
Fiddle-de-dee, fiddle-de-dee,
The Fly has married the Bumblebee!

Fiddle-de-dee, fiddle-de-dee,
The Fly has married the Bumblebee.
Says the Bee, says she,
"I'll live under your wing.
   You'll never know I carry a stinger."
Fiddle-de-dee, fiddle-de-dee,
The Fly has married the Bumblebee!

Fiddle-de-dee, fiddle-de-dee,
The Fly has married the Bumblebee.
And the bees did buzz,
And the blue bells did ring.
You've never heard of such a merry thing!

Fiddle-de-dee, fiddle-de-dee,
The Fly has married the Bumblebee!

Fiddle-de-dee, fiddle-de-dee,
The Fly has married the Bumblebee.
And then to think that of all of the bees,
The Bumblebee should get the prize!
Fiddle-de-dee, fiddle-de-dee,
Oh, I love you and you love me!

無聊話，無聊話，
蒼蠅娶了大黃蜂。
蒼蠅說，他說：
「你願意嫁給我，和我住在一起
嗎，甜蜜的大黃蜂？」
無聊話，無聊話，
蒼蠅娶了大黃蜂！

無聊話，無聊話，
蒼蠅娶了大黃蜂。
大黃蜂說，她說：
「我會活在你的羽翼之下，你將
永遠不會發現我帶著刺。」
無聊話，無聊話，
蒼蠅娶了大黃蜂！

無聊話，無聊話，
蒼蠅娶了大黃蜂。
蜜蜂群嗡嗡叫，藍鐘響叮噹，
你從未聽過如此樂事。
無聊話，無聊話，
蒼蠅娶了大黃蜂！

無聊話，無聊話，
蒼蠅娶了大黃蜂。
接著想到了所有的蜜蜂，
偏偏那隻大黃蜂應得獎。
無聊話，無聊話，
喔，我愛你，你也愛我。

「Fiddle-de-dee」指小提琴弦發出的聲音，引申為不具任何意義的聲響，在口語中，「Fiddle-de-dee」表示「胡說」或「無稽之談」。

至於為何會以 Fiddle 代表小提琴的聲音呢？這要溯源至小提琴的發展與語源了。西元十世紀，小提琴（violin）在歐洲首度出現，最早的用途是教會禮拜所用，在拉丁文中稱為 vitula 或 vidula。後來，小提琴越來越普及，也流行於世俗音樂。

各個不同的語言，衍生了各種名稱。在西元 1200 年，古英語中稱小提琴為 fithele；到了 1398 年的中古英語，又稱之為 fidele；演化至古高地德語，稱之為 fidula；在古北歐語，則稱之為 fithla；在義大利文中，又變成了 viola；法文叫作 vielle，之後又變成 viole。

1579 年，小提琴傳入英語世界，以當時義大利名 violino 稱之，外型是縮小版的中提琴（viola）。現在英語稱精緻的小提琴為 violin，而土氣的小提琴為 fiddle，但其實是描述同一種樂器。

🍃 小提琴的動詞 fiddle，並不是指小提琴手演奏的動作，而是古北歐語的 fitla，意思是「用手指碰觸」。

🍃 甚具貶意的 fiddle-faddle 一詞，和 fiddling 無直接聯繫，倒是與 faddle 有關，faddle 是「to trifle with」（開玩笑、戲弄）的意思。

🍃 fiddle-sticks（胡說、討厭）和 fiddle-de-dee（無聊語）的 faddle，同樣來自 fiddle-faddle（無聊事、無聊話）。

這首韻文以 Fiddle-de-dee 為名，內容是描述蒼蠅迎娶大黃蜂的故事，趣味性遠遠大於實質性，這不是剛好和「瞎扯」的主題不謀而合嗎？

fiddle-de-dee [ˈfɪdl̩ˌdidi] (n.) 無聊話；瞎說

bumblebee [ˈbʌmbl̩ˌbi] (n.) 大黃蜂

wing [wɪŋ] (n.) 翅膀

stinger [ˈstɪŋɚ] (n.) 刺

ring [rɪŋ] (v.) 響鈴

114

Six Little Ducks

Six little ducks I once knew,
Fat ones, skinny ones, and fair ones, too.
But the one little duck with the feather on his back,
He led the others with a quack, quack, quack.
Quack, quack, quack,
Quack, quack, quack,
He led the others with a quack, quack, quack.

Down to the river, they would go,
Wiggle, wobble, waddle, giggle, to and fro.
But the one little duck with the feather on his back,
He led the others with a quack, quack, quack.
Quack, quack, quack,
Quack, quack, quack,
He led the others with a quack, quack, quack.

Back from the river, they would come,
Wiggle, wobble, waddle, giggle, ho, hum, hum.
But the one little duck with the feather on his back,

He led the others with a quack, quack, quack.
Quack, quack, quack,
Quack, quack, quack,
He led the others with a quack, quack, quack.

Into the water, they would dive,
Each over and under the other five.
But the one little duck with the feather on his back,
He led the others with a quack, quack, quack.
Quack, quack, quack,
Quack, quack, quack,
He led the others with a quack, quack, quack.

Home from the river, they would go,
Wiggle, wobble, waddle, giggle, ho, hum hum.
But the one little duck with the feather on his back,
He led the others with a quack, quack, quack.
Quack, quack, quack,
Quack, quack, quack,
He led the others with a quack, quack, quack.

skinny [`skɪnɪ] (a.) 極瘦的    wobble [`wɑbl̩] (v.) 搖晃

feather [`fɛðɚ] (n.) 羽毛    waddle [`wɑdl̩] (v.) 搖擺地走

wiggle [`wɪgl̩] (n.) 扭動    giggle [`gɪgl̩] (n.) 咯咯地笑

我曾認識六隻小鴨，
胖的，瘦的，不胖不瘦的。
不過那隻背上有羽毛的小鴨，
他呱呱呱帶領著大家。
呱呱呱，呱呱呱，
他呱呱呱帶領著大家。

走下河邊去，大夥一起去。
搖搖晃晃，搖搖晃晃，去又回。
不過那隻背上有羽毛的小鴨，
他呱呱呱帶領著大家。
呱呱呱，呱呱呱，
他呱呱呱帶領著大家。

從河邊回來，大夥一起來。
搖搖晃晃，搖搖晃晃，哼哼歌。
不過那隻背上有羽毛的小鴨，
他呱呱呱帶領著大家。

呱呱呱，呱呱呱，
他呱呱呱帶領著大家。

跳入水中，一起潛下水，
大夥上下浮浮又潛潛。
不過那隻背上有羽毛的小鴨，
他呱呱呱帶領著大家。
呱呱呱，呱呱呱，
他呱呱呱帶領著大家。

從河邊回家，大夥一起回。
搖搖晃晃，搖搖晃晃，哼哼歌。
不過那隻背上有羽毛的小鴨，
他呱呱呱帶領著大家。
呱呱呱，呱呱呱，
他呱呱呱帶領著大家。

提到鴨子，最著名的非《醜小鴨》莫屬了，故事中醜小鴨變成天鵝的心路歷程，正是作者安徒生自己的寫照。安徒生（Hans Christian Andersen, 1805–1875）出生於丹麥，自幼家中貧困，年少時便輟學工作。

安徒生早期的童話多充滿炫麗的幻想和樂觀的精神，後來寫實主義的彩色逐漸濃厚。他一生共寫了 168 篇童話故事，流傳於世界各個角落。1954 年，國際兒童讀書聯盟第三次大會上設立國際安徒生獎，至今仍是兒童文學界最高榮譽，安徒生不愧為童話之王。

115 Eeny, Meeny, Miny, Mo

(115)

Eeny, Meeny, Miny, Mo,
Catch a tiger by the toe.
If it hollers, make it pay,
Fifty dollars every day.
My mother told me
    to choose the very best one.

Eeny, Meeny, Miny, Mo,
Catch a bear by the toe.
If it hollers, make it pay,
Fifty dollars every day.
My mother told me
    to choose the very best one.

Eeny, Meeny, Miny, Mo,
Catch a deer by the toe.
If it snorts, make it pay,
Fifty dollars every day.
My mother told me
    to choose the very best one.

伊尼、蜜尼、麥尼、莫，
捉住老虎腳趾頭，
他若吼叫，要他付錢，
每天要付五十元。
媽媽要我
　挑選最好的一個。

伊尼、蜜尼、麥尼、莫，
捉住熊腳趾頭，
他若吼叫，要他付錢，
每天要付五十元。
媽媽要我
　挑選最好的一個。

伊尼、蜜尼、麥尼、莫，
捉住鹿腳趾頭，
他若噴鼻息，要他付錢，
每天要付五十元。
媽媽要我
　挑選最好的一個。

這是一首教導孩童數數兒的韻文。歌詞中的 it 可以用在不同的遊戲中，挑出當「鬼」的人。遊戲方式如下：一位孩子起首唱歌，一邊唱、一邊照著歌詞將一個個字對應並指向其餘夥伴，最後一個被指到的小朋友，就要出來當「鬼」。

「Eeny, Meeny, Miny, Mo」有很多不同拼法，其意義眾說紛紜，現在只是無意義的組合音節。《The Hiram Key》一書中指出，這句話在英國前凱爾特語裡，是計數系統最早的數字。另有一說是英國督伊德教僧侶（Druid）用來決定誰是下一個獻祭給神的人的詩歌。這首歌謠最早出版的英語版本可以追溯到 1855 年，第一句話是「eeny, meeny, moany, mite」，另有版本是「hana, mana, mona, mike」。英美歐各國版本也陸續問世。

holler [ˈhɑlɚ] (v.) 吼叫
snort [ˈsnɔrt] (v.) 噴鼻息

116 Three Little Kittens

Three little kittens, they lost their mittens.
So they began to cry,
"Oh, Mother dear, come here, come here,
For we have lost our mittens."
"Lost your mittens, you naughty kittens,
Then you shall have no pie."
"Meow, meow, we shall have no pie."

Three little kittens, they found their mittens.
So they began to cry,
"Oh, Mother dear, see here, see here,
For we have found our mittens."
"Found your mittens, you darling kittens,
Now you shall have some pie."
"Meow, meow, we shall have some pie."

三隻小貓，弄丟手套，哭哭又啼啼：
「喔，親愛的媽媽，過來，過來，
我們弄丟了手套。」
「弄丟手套，調皮小貓，沒有派可吃。」
「喵，喵，沒有派可吃。」

三隻小貓，找到手套，喵喵又叫叫：
「喔，親愛的媽媽，看這邊，看這邊，
我們找到了手套。」
「找到手套，親愛小貓，來吃些派吧。」
「喵，喵，有些派可吃。」

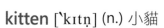

kitten [ˋkɪtn̩] (n.) 小貓
- *Why are those kittens wandering around the garbage can?*
  為什麼那些小貓徘徊在垃圾桶旁邊？

lose [luz] (v.) 遺失
- *Did they lose something?*
  牠們丟掉了什麼嗎？

mitten [ˋmɪtn̩] (n.) 手套
- *Look, they have some old mittens in their mouths.* 看，牠們嘴裡刁著舊手套。

這是一首趣味橫生的貓媽媽與小貓們互動的描寫，但在故事的背後又有警惕意味，就像平易近人的生活劇，1843 年見於《Only True Mother Goose Melodies》選集中。

故事描述三隻小貓弄丟了牠們的連指手套，「Meow, meow, meow」哭喊著告訴媽媽。媽媽為了懲戒牠們，不給牠們派吃。當手套失而復得後，三隻小貓得到了獎賞——派。

在另一種版本中，還有後續的發展。三隻小貓見獎懲分明，於是故意弄髒手套，以獲得更多獎勵的機會。顯然地，媽媽又動怒了，三隻小貓於是把手套洗乾淨並晾起來，媽媽這次除了稱讚牠們之外，也「smell a rat」開始提防著小貓們的詭計了。這也是英語「smell a rat」用法的起源。

「smell a rat」的字面意義是「聞到了老鼠味」，老鼠在人們的印象中是鬼鬼祟祟的動物。聞到了老鼠味，就是說第六感覺得不安全或起疑心，但一時之間又說不出來哪裡出了問題。

這首歌謠有深刻的教育意味，教導孩子們要妥善保管自己的東西，也告訴孩子們不可以用說謊的手段來達到目的，是寓教於樂的典範。

117 Sleep, Baby, Sleep

Sleep, baby, sleep!
Your father guards the sheep,
Your mother shakes the dreamland tree,
And from it fall sweet dreams for you.
Sleep, baby, sleep.

Sleep, baby, sleep!
Our cottage vale is deep.
The little lamb is on the green
With snowy fleece so soft and clean.
Sleep, baby, sleep.

睡吧，寶貝，睡吧！
你爸爸守護著羊群，
你媽媽搖晃著夢樹，
夢樹為你落下美夢。
睡吧，寶貝，睡吧！

睡吧，寶貝，睡吧！
我們屋前溪谷高深，
小小綿羊在綠茵上，
毛兒雪白柔軟潔淨，
睡吧，寶貝，睡吧！

cottage [`kɑtɪdʒ] (n.) 別墅
vale [vel] (n.) 溪谷
fleece [`flis] (n.) 羊毛

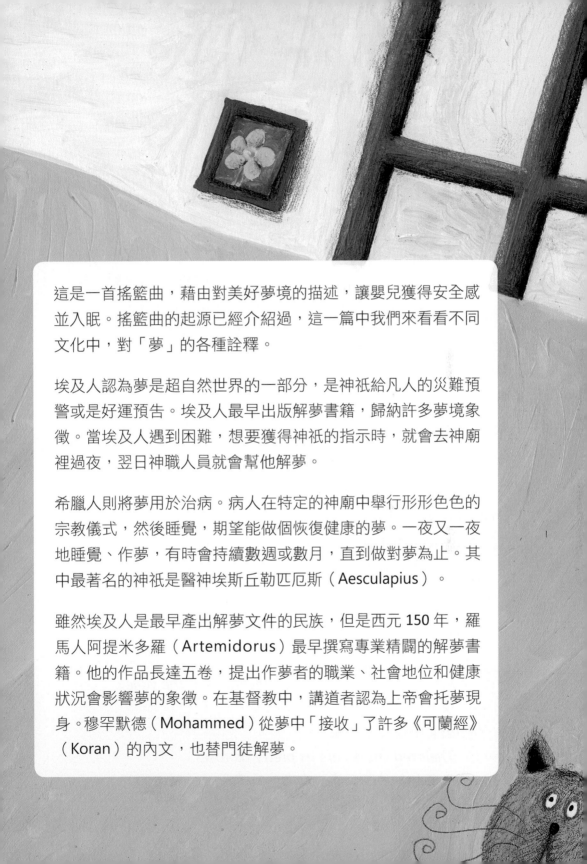

這是一首搖籃曲，藉由對美好夢境的描述，讓嬰兒獲得安全感並入眠。搖籃曲的起源已經介紹過，這一篇中我們來看看不同文化中，對「夢」的各種詮釋。

埃及人認為夢是超自然世界的一部分，是神祇給凡人的災難預警或是好運預告。埃及人最早出版解夢書籍，歸納許多夢境象徵。當埃及人遇到困難，想要獲得神祇的指示時，就會去神廟裡過夜，翌日神職人員就會幫他解夢。

希臘人則將夢用於治病。病人在特定的神廟中舉行形形色色的宗教儀式，然後睡覺，期望能做個恢復健康的夢。一夜又一夜地睡覺、作夢，有時會持續數週或數月，直到做對夢為止。其中最著名的神祇是醫神埃斯丘勒匹厄斯（Aesculapius）。

雖然埃及人是最早產出解夢文件的民族，但是西元 150 年，羅馬人阿提米多羅（Artemidorus）最早撰寫專業精闢的解夢書籍。他的作品長達五卷，提出作夢者的職業、社會地位和健康狀況會影響夢的象徵。在基督教中，講道者認為上帝會托夢現身。穆罕默德（Mohammed）從夢中「接收」了許多《可蘭經》（Koran）的內文，也替門徒解夢。

118 Down in the Valley

Down in the valley
Where the green grass grows,
There sat Susie
As pretty as a rose.
She sang, she sang,
She sang so sweet.
Along came Johnny,
And kissed her on the cheek.
How many kisses did she get?
One, two, three . . .
(Continue counting)

山谷下，
綠草生。
露西坐那兒，
像朵美玫瑰。
她歌唱，歌唱，
歌聲如此甜美。
跟著來的強尼，
親親她的臉頰。
她被親了幾下？
一，二，三……
（繼續數）

---

valley [ˈvelɪ] (n.) 山谷
- *Annie and Tracy put up a tent down in the valley.*
  安妮和崔希在山谷搭起了帳棚。

cheek [tʃik] (n.) 臉頰
- *Their red cheeks are as pretty as roses.*
  她們紅紅的臉頰就如玫瑰一般漂亮。

這是一首跳繩歌，孩童們通常邊唱歌邊跳繩，隨著跳繩的花招百出，歌詞也千變萬化。這樣的組合除了增加跳繩的樂趣外，孩童還需要手腦並用，方能勝出。這首歌曲的進行方式如下：

Down in the valley
Where the green grass grows,
There sat Susie（換成正在跳繩的人名）
As pretty as a rose.
She sang, she sang,
She sang so sweet.
Along came Johnny,（換成下一個跳繩的人名）
And kissed her on the cheek.
How many kisses did she get?
"One, two, three . . . "（數遊戲者跳繩的次數，直到腳步錯亂為止）

最早的跳繩記錄是中世紀的歐洲繪畫，可以追溯至西元 1600 年，當時的人以彈性強的竹子或藤蔓為工具跳繩。

在早期，跳繩是男性的活動，後來一度被認為是小女孩邊唱邊跳的遊戲，男孩們加入就顯得娘娘腔而有些忌諱了。

英國民間傳說，跳繩源自於猶大（Judas），他背叛了耶穌之後，上吊自殺。跳繩活動在春天流行，特別是復活節時期，在劍橋（Cambridge）和英格蘭東南的薩西克斯郡（Sussex）的幾個村落中，常常可見跳繩活動進行。事實上，在東薩西克斯郡的村落中，於復活節前的星期五耶穌受難節（Good Friday）時，還是會舉辦跳繩活動哦！

119 S-M-I-L-E

It isn't any trouble,
Just to S-M-I-L-E.
It isn't any trouble,
Just to S-M-I-L-E.
So smile when you're in trouble.
Problems vanish like a bubble,
If you'll only take the trouble just to S-M-I-L-E.

It isn't any trouble,
Just to ha-ha-ha-ha.
It isn't any trouble,
Just to ha-ha-ha-ha.
So laugh when you're in trouble.
Problems vanish like a bubble,
If you'll only take the trouble just to ha-ha-ha-ha.

It isn't any trouble,
Just to G-R-I-N.
It isn't any trouble,
Just to G-R-I-N.
So grin when you're in trouble.
Problems vanish like a bubble,
If you'll only take the trouble just to G-R-I-N.

這一點都不麻煩，
只微微笑一笑，
這一點都不麻煩，
只微微笑一笑，
所以碰到困難記得笑
困難像氣泡消失無蹤，
只要你願意努力笑笑。

這一點都不麻煩，
只要嘻嘻笑，
這一點都不麻煩，
只要嘻嘻笑，
所以碰到困難記得嘻嘻笑
困難像氣泡消失無蹤，
只要你願意努力嘻嘻笑。

這一點都不麻煩，
只哈哈笑一笑，
這一點都不麻煩，
只哈哈笑一笑，
所以碰到困難記得哈哈笑，
困難像氣泡消失無蹤，
只要你願意努力哈哈笑。

vanish [ˈvænɪʃ] (v.) 消失

bubble [ˈbʌbl̩] (n.) 氣泡

grin [grɪn] (n.) 露齒而笑

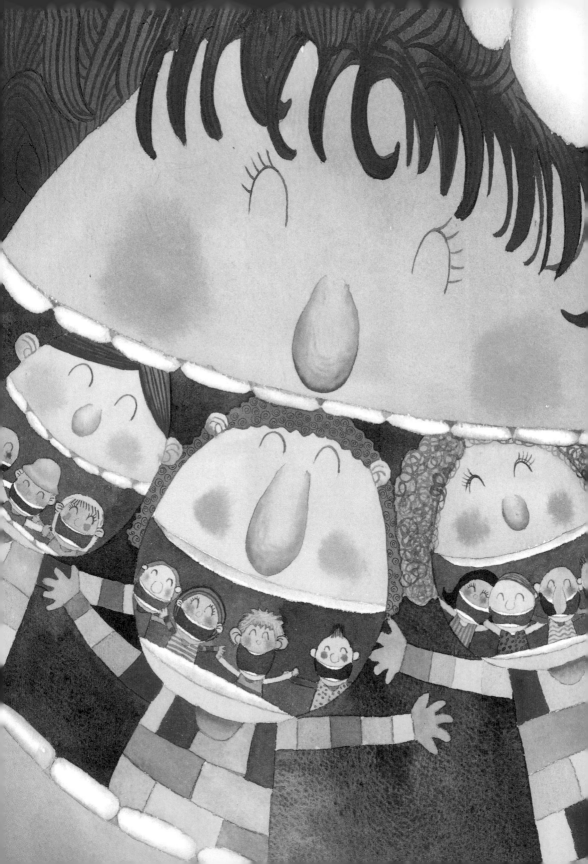

微笑，是世界共通的語言，能化解語言的藩籬。史上最著名的微笑，就屬蒙娜麗莎的微笑了。〈蒙娜麗莎的微笑〉是文藝復興時代的畫家達文西於 1503 年所繪，畫中的人物可能是佛羅倫斯一位富商的妻子麗莎（Lisa Gherardini）。據說達文西作畫時，為了化解緊張情緒、舒緩畫中人心情，還請樂師在旁奏樂呢！

現代科學家利用特殊的紅外線 3D 掃描技術，對畫作上的顏料透視掃描後，意外發現蒙娜麗莎的衣服外層，還披有一層透明的薄紗。這種穿著是 16 世紀的義大利孕婦或剛生產完的婦女的典型裝扮。此外，蒙娜麗莎的頭髮不是自然披散，而是戴著無邊軟帽。在文藝復興時期，只有年輕女孩或品行不好的婦女才會披散頭髮。

畫完成後，達文西並未將油畫交給畫中人，反而自己收藏。這幅畫在達文西在世時並未成名，而是在他於法國過世後，由他的弟子兼繼承人薩萊（Salai）賣給法王。此畫曾經收藏於楓丹白露、凡爾賽宮、羅浮宮，而且曾在羅浮宮被盜，遭到潑酸、扔石頭，至少修復過三次。

現在，這幅畫收藏於羅浮宮。義大利政府欲向法國索回這幅國寶，卻始終無法如願。1911 年，〈蒙娜麗莎〉遭竊後，在弗羅倫斯的一間旅舍被找到，沒想到蒙娜麗莎是以這種方式回義大利的！

120 Old King Cole

Old King Cole was a merry old soul,
And a merry old soul was he.
He called for his pipe,
He called for his bowl,
And he called for his fiddlers three.
Every fiddler had a fine fiddle,
And a very fine fiddle had he.
Tweedle dee, tweedle dee,
Tweedle dee, tweedle dee,
Tweedle dee, tweedle dee,
Went the fiddlers three.
Oh, there's none so rare
As can compare
With King Cole and his fiddlers three.

老柯爾國王是個快樂老人家，
快樂老人家就是他。
他要來他的菸斗，
他要來他的碗，
還招來他的三位小提琴手。
每個提琴手都有一台好提琴，
他也有一台好提琴。
滴啦，滴，滴啦，滴，
滴啦，滴，滴啦，滴，
滴啦，滴，滴啦，滴，
小提琴手們拉起了提琴。
喔，沒有人比
柯爾國王和他的三位小提琴手更奇特了。

merry [ˋmɛrɪ] (a.) 歡樂的
- *King Cole is always in a merry mood.*
  柯爾國王總是心情快活。

soul [ˋsol] (n.) 靈魂
- *King Cole believes everyone has a pure soul.*
  柯爾國王相信每個人都有純淨的靈魂。

rare [rɛr] (a.) 稀少的
- *Is King Cole's kind heart rare among all the kings?* 柯爾國王的好心腸，跟其他的國王比起來，是不是很難得呢？

科爾王（Old King Cole）的身分是個謎團，史料記載，在凱爾特（Celtic）的歷代國王中，叫做 Coel（英語中拼做 Cole）的有兩位。一位是「科徹斯特的科爾王」（King Coel of Colchester），他是西元三世紀的英國國王，住在艾薩斯郡（Essex）的科徹斯特鎮（Colchester），建立了科徹斯特。他的女兒聖海倫娜嫁給羅馬的康斯坦提皇帝（Constantius），也就是康斯坦汀大帝（Constantine）的父親。

另一位是「北不列顛的科爾王」（King Coel of Northern Britain），也就四世紀的 Coel Hen。Coel Hen 是威爾斯語，意思是「Cole the Old」，他透過聯姻和征戰，擴充領土，統治整個北英格蘭，並綿延至南蘇格蘭。直到西元 650 年，撒克遜人（Saxons）才推翻了 Cole 王朝。

這首韻文最早出版於 1709 年，將傳說中的凱爾特科爾王的性格，描述得活靈活現。韻文中的字彙代表如下：

pipe	→	指音樂，音樂在古代英國的文化活動中占有一席之地。
his bowl	→	指用來喝水的碗，暗喻科爾王的好客。
fiddlers three	→	指科爾王擁有三位樂師。事實上這三位樂師都是豎琴師，不是小提琴手。

文字中也顯示出不列頓人（Briton）的好客，他們會以伴有音樂的盛宴款待客人！

121 There Was a Crooked Man

There was a crooked man,
And he walked a crooked mile.
He found a crooked sixpence
Upon a crooked stile.
He bought a crooked cat,
Which caught a crooked mouse.
And they all lived together
In a little crooked house.

有一個駝背傢伙，
走了一哩彎曲路，
他在彎曲踢凳上，
撿到彎曲六便士，
他買了隻駝背貓，
貓捉了隻駝背鼠，
他們一起居住在
一間扭曲怪房子。

這首童謠和英國歷史有關，可溯至斯圖亞特王室（The House of Stuart）的查爾斯一世（Charles I, 1600–1649），當時治理英格蘭、蘇格蘭和愛爾蘭。歌中的「The crooked man」指蘇格蘭將軍萊斯利伯爵（Alexander Leslie, 1582–1661），他簽署了一份蘇格蘭宗教安定與政治自主的協定，「The crooked stile」指英國與蘇格蘭之間的邊界，「They all lived together in a little crooked house」指英國與蘇格蘭最終達成共識的事實，是敵對陣營和平共處的象徵。這首韻文反映了當時英國與蘇格蘭根深柢固的仇恨。

Alexander Leslie

crooked [ˈkrʊkɪd] (a.) 彎曲的
- *He walked down the crooked path.*
  他沿著蜿蜒小路走去。

stile [staɪl] (n.) 梯凳
- *He has bent the handle of the stile into a new style.*
  他將梯凳的扶手彎成新的形狀。

122 Ring Around the Roses

Ring around the roses,
A pocket full of posies.
Ashes, ashes, we all stand still.

The King has sent his daughter
To fetch a pail of water.
Ashes, ashes, we all fall down.

The bird upon the steeple
Sits high above the people.
Ashes, ashes, we all kneel down.

The wedding bells are ringing;
The boys and girls are singing.
Ashes, ashes, we all fall down.

　　圍著玫瑰花繞圈，
　　　口袋滿滿是花束，
　　　　灰燼，灰燼，我們都站好。

　　　　國王已派公主，
　　　　去提了一桶水，
　　　　　灰燼，灰燼，我們都跌倒。

　　　　尖塔上的鳥兒，
　　　　高坐人們之上，
　　　　　灰燼，灰燼，我們都跪下。

　　　婚禮鐘聲響起，
　　　男孩女孩歌唱，
　　　　灰燼，灰燼，我們都落下。

ash [æʃ] (n.) 灰燼
steeple [ˋstɪpl̩] (n.) 尖塔
kneel [nil] (v.) 跪

這首歌謠的歌詞背景，是歐洲大陸十四世紀時流行的黑死病（Black Plague）。這首韻文約成形於 1347 年，當時，黑死病奪走了 250 萬條人命，令人聞之色變。

ring around the roses → 指黑死病初期的症狀，又圓又紅的疹子，像圈圈一樣。

a pocket full of posies → 指健康的人將花或香草等放在受感染的人身旁，以防感染的迷思，因為當時的人認為黑死病是透過臭味傳送。

ashes → 模擬黑死病患者猛烈的噴嚏音，另一說是屍體的灰燼。1666 年倫敦大火，卻因禍得福將污染水源的帶病老鼠一併燒死。

we all fall down → 描述許多人因此而一病不起。

黑死病是一種淋巴腺鼠疫（bubonic plague），透過齧齒目動物攜帶的芽孢桿菌，傳播給人類。1347 年，黑死病入侵西歐，三年後便奪走了當時歐洲三分之一的人命。然而，這首韻文最早的版本，出自 1881 年出版的《Mother Goose》，距離黑死病時代相距五百年了。在這麼長的歲月裡，要追溯韻文的起源，有其困難，於是有了另一種說法：這首韻文只是單純的孩童繞圈圈遊戲，跟黑死病的歷史事件未必有關，此說法的代表人物是民俗研究學家 Philip Hiscock。

十九世紀時，歐洲和北美洲是禁止清教徒跳舞的。年輕人於是發明了一種舞會遊戲（play-party），以圍成圓圈的方式進行，與傳統方塊舞（square dances）有別，也沒有音樂伴奏。歌詞中的「Ashes, ashes」可能源自「Husha, husha」，表示停止的意思，「falling down」則指雙手放開，大家投身圓圈中央。後來，舞會遊戲大為流行，在美國的土風舞界也占了特殊地位。

123 Animal Fair

I went to the animal fair.
The birds and the beasts were there.
The big baboon by the light of the moon
Was combing his auburn hair.
The skunk bumped the monkey
And sat on the elephant's trunk.
The elephant sneezed and fell to his knees,
And what became of the skunk, the skunk,
  the skunk?

我參加動物市集，
鳥兒動物群聚首。
大狒狒倚著月光，
梳理赤褐色毛髮。
臭鼬撞上那猴子，
坐到大象象牙上，
大象打噴嚏，彎下膝蓋，
不知臭鼬下場如何，
臭鼬，臭鼬，臭鼬？

beast [bist] (n.) 怪獸
auburn [ˋɔbɚn] (a.) 赤褐色的
skunk [skʌŋk] (n.) 臭鼬
sneeze [sniz] (v.) 打噴嚏

這首歌謠是認識動物外觀和習性的絕佳教材。師長們可以製作動物面具，請小朋友們圍成圓圈，選一位自願者擔任歌詞中的主角，站在圓圈中央，其他的人小朋友依分配的動物角色，各自戴上面具。歌曲邊進行，小朋友邊唱遊，當唱到某動物時，扮演該動物的小朋友就要站到中間表演，表演錯誤的小朋友要當下一個鬼（也就是主角）。下一輪可以交換角色，也可以替換歌詞中的動物，讓活動更多元有趣。

這首歌詞的內容，是描述逛動物集市所見情景。在西方民間傳說和通俗文化中，鳥類通常被描寫為具隱藏天賦的吉祥角色，例如芝麻街中的大鳥（Big Bird）、史努比中的糊塗塔克（Woodstock）、啄木鳥伍迪（Woody Woodpecker）、唐老鴨（Donald）和達菲鴨（Daffy Duck）等角色。

有時候，鳥使人聯想到黑暗面，例如美國作家愛倫·坡（Edgar Allan Poe, 1809–1849）的詩《魔鳥》（The Raven）、漫畫書《烏鴉》（The Crow）系列，或是電影電視劇中，出現恐怖畫面時，會以夜行鳥類貓頭鷹（owl）象徵。

鵰（eagle）是大型鷹科鳥類的泛稱，鷹（hawk）是廣義意義是鷹科，牠們是王室或國家的代表。鳳凰（Phoenix）出現於神話中，而布榖鳥自鳴鐘（cuckoo clock），是熟知的計時器。

cuckoo clock

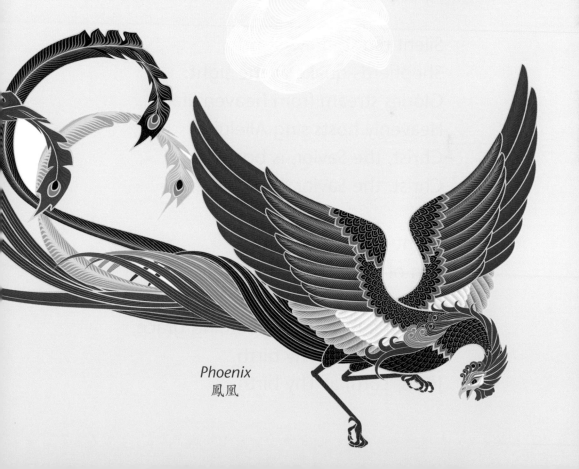

Phoenix
鳳凰

124 Silent Night

Silent night, holy night!
All is calm, and all is bright
Round yon Virgin Mother and Child.
Holy infant, so tender and mild,
Sleep in heavenly peace,
Sleep in heavenly peace.

Silent night, holy night!
Shepherds quake at the sight.
Glories stream from heaven afar.
Heavenly hosts sing Alleluia.
Christ, the Savior, is born!
Christ, the Savior, is born!

Silent night, holy night!
Son of God, love's pure light.
Radiant beams from Thy holy face
With the dawn of redeeming grace,
Jesus, Lord, at Thy birth.
Jesus, Lord, at Thy birth.

平安夜，聖善夜，
真寧靜，真光明，
光輝環照聖母聖嬰，
聖潔嬰孩純真可愛，
靜享天賜安眠，
靜享天賜安眠。

平安夜，聖善夜，
牧羊人，觸目慄，
遙遠天上榮光照下，
天軍齊唱哈利路亞，
救主已降生！
救主已降生！

平安夜，聖善夜，
神子愛，光皎潔，
這是救恩黎明光芒，
救贖恩典降臨四方，
主耶穌今降生，
主耶穌今降生。

infant [ˈɪnfənt] (n.) 嬰孩
- *Have you seen an elephant with an infant on its trunk?*
  你有看到那隻大象的鼻上有個嬰孩嗎？

shepherd [ˈʃɛpəd] (n.) 牧羊人
- *A shepherd is leading the elephant and the infant.*
  有個牧羊人帶領著那隻大象和嬰孩。

beam [bim] (n.) 光芒
- *The beams from the infant's crown light the dark night.*
  嬰孩皇冠射出的光芒照亮了夜晚。

redeem [rɪˈdim] (v.) 救贖

這首著名的聖誕歌曲，作詞者是神父莫爾（Josef Mohr, 1792–1848），作曲者是教堂風琴師格魯伯（Franz Xaver Gruber, 1787–1863）。故事發生在 1818 年，當時在奧地利薩爾斯堡（Salzburg）旁的奧本多夫（Oberndorf）小鎮高山上，有一座聖尼古拉斯（St. Nicholas）教堂。在教徒們興高采烈、準備聖誕節的慶典活動時，被視為靈魂樂器的風琴居然故障了，從外地請來的維修師，無法在聖誕節之前修復風琴，讓大家都急了。

這時候，教堂的神父莫爾拿出兩年前寫的一首詩，請教堂風琴師格魯伯譜曲。格魯伯靈光乍現，在短時間內譜成了以吉他伴奏的曲子。在聖誕夜，整個奧本多夫小鎮的居民都聚集在教堂裡，欣賞格魯伯以吉他伴奏，和神父莫爾合唱的天籟。1825 年，著名的風琴製造家 Carl Mauracher 到聖尼古拉斯教堂修繕風琴，〈Silent Night〉的手稿和散頁樂譜，才在閣樓被發現。他將〈Silent Night〉的詞曲帶走，從此開始了遠播世界的旅程。又有一說在鄉村聖堂歌詠團的抄寫本中埋沒了十多年，後來被一位喜愛音樂的人發現，就把這首聖誕歌帶到城裡的音樂會上演唱，大受歡迎，漸漸的流傳到奧地利各地，再傳到了德國。

1839 年，這首聖誕歌傳進了美國，之後經過著名歌唱家的演唱、電台的播放，這首聖誕歌曲流傳到了世界，而且各國都有翻譯的歌詞。不管是不是基督徒，這首〈平安夜〉柔美的旋律、平和的歌詞，飛揚進了每一個人的心裡。

125 Vive La Compagnie

Let every good fellow now join in the song
  "vive la compagnie!"
Success to each other, and pass it along.
Vive la compagnie!

Vive la, vive la, vive l'amour,
Vive la, vive la vive l'amour,
Vive la, vive la, vive l'amour,
Vive la compagnie!

A friend on your left and a friend on your right,
Vive la compagnie!
In love and good fellowship let us unite.
Vive la compagnie!

Vive la, vive la, vive l'amour,
Vive la, vive la vive l'amour,
Vive la, vive la, vive l'amour,
Vive la compagnie!

Now wider and wider our circle expands.
Vive la compagnie!
We sing to our comrades in far away lands
"Vive la compagnie!"

Vive la, vive la, vive l'amour,
Vive la, vive la vive l'amour,
Vive la, vive la, vive l'amour,
Vive la compagnie!

讓所有好人齊唱歌，
友情萬歲！
大家成功，傳下去吧，
友情萬歲！

愛情萬歲！
愛情萬歲！
愛情萬歲！
友情萬歲！

你左邊的朋友，你右邊的朋友，
友情萬歲！
愛和真摯友誼，我們團結一起！
友情萬歲！

愛情萬歲！
愛情萬歲！
愛情萬歲！
友情萬歲！

此刻大夥圈子越擴越大，
友情萬歲！
向遙遠國土的夥伴獻歌，
友情萬歲！

愛情萬歲！
愛情萬歲！
愛情萬歲！
友情萬歲！

fellow ['fɛlo] (n.) 人
- *Jellow is a fellow whose favorite color is yellow.*
  耶洛是個最愛黃色的人。

pass [pæs] (v.) 傳遞

unite [ju`naɪt] (v.) 聯合
- *He decides to unite all the fans of yellow to form a club.*
  他決定要結合所有黃色的愛好者組成一個俱樂部。

這是一首童軍歌曲，激勵人心的歌詞，輔以琅琅上口的曲調，讓這首歌曲更形出色。童軍歌曲眾多，在營隊行進間或營火活動時，歌曲是重要的催化劑，增強學員的向心力，並振奮精神。那麼，我們一同來看看童軍活動的起緣吧！

童子軍的創始人是英國人貝登堡（Robert Baden-Powell, 1857–1941），他是英國陸軍中將出身，後來創始了童軍運動，並擔任第一任英國童軍總會總領袖。。

Robert Baden-Powell
(1857–1941)

貝登堡從小就喜歡野外炊事、露營等大自然活動，1876 年到 1910 年之間在英國陸軍服役，曾駐防印度和非洲。他寫了許多軍事書籍，專門介紹在南非軍事生涯中的軍事偵察和偵察兵的訓練。

戰勝回國後，他發現當時英國的青少年，在國家強盛又太平無事的環境下，青少年籠罩在萎靡不振、悲觀負面的社會風氣下，這給了他想法，他希望透過野外實踐活動的舉辦，在身體、精神和智力上培訓青少年，提振青少年的精神，延續樂觀獨立、服務奉獻的美德。

1907 年，他親自率領一些青少年前往英國的桃山白浪島露營，實際運作小隊、徽章、榮譽等制度，結果令人滿意，而這次的活動也被視為是童軍運動的起源。1908 年，貝登堡集結經驗出版了《童軍警探》（Scouting for Boys），寫出他理想的教育方法。從此童子軍活動在世界各個角落生根萌芽，童子軍精神也延續不墜。

126 Oh, My Darling Clementine!

In a cavern, in a canyon, excavating for a mine,
Dwelt a miner forty niner and his daughter
    Clementine.
Light she was and like a fairy,
and her shoes were number nine.
Herring boxes, without topses,
Sandals were for Clementine.

Drove she ducklings to the water every morning
    just at nine.
She hit her foot against a splinter and fell into
    the foaming brine.
Ruby lips above the water,
Blowing bubbles, soft and fine,
But, alas, I was no swimmer,
So I lost my Clementine.

Oh, my darling, oh, my darling,
Oh, my darling Clementine!
You are lost and gone forever,
Dreadful sorry, Clementine.

洞穴中，峽谷裡，挖掘礦坑，
住著一名礦工和他的女兒克蓮婷。
她輕盈有如仙女，
腳穿九號鞋子，
鯡魚盒子，沒有蓋子，
涼鞋要送給克蓮婷。

她趕著鴨子到河邊，
每天早晨九點整，
她一腳踩到碎片，
跌入海水泡沫中。
紅唇浮上水面，
吐著泡泡，輕柔純淨，
而我哎呀不擅游泳，
故失去我克蓮婷。

喔，我親愛的，喔，我親愛的，
喔，我親愛的克蓮婷。
你已不在，永不再來，
遺憾之致，克蓮婷。

cavern [ˈkævən] (n.) 山洞

excavate [ˈɛkskəˌvet] (v.) 挖掘

forty niner 泛指在 1849 年
　　去美國淘金的人

fairy [ˈfɛrɪ] (n.) 仙女

sandal [ˈsændl̩] (n.) 拖鞋

duckling [ˈdʌklɪŋ] (n.) 小鴨

splinter [ˈsplɪntə] (n.) 碎片

brine [ˈbraɪn] (n.) 海水

這是一首美國西部民謠，據說由 Percy Montrose 作詞，曲調則是源自 1863 年 H. S. Thompson 所作的〈Down by the River Liv'd a Maiden〉，是深受歡迎的童軍及遠足活動歌曲。

這首廣受歡迎的歌謠，其實歌詞的內容是叫人心酸的，故事背景是 1849 年加州的淘金熱潮（Gold Rush）。描述在一場溺水意外中，礦工失去了所愛的女兒。那種椎心之痛，不是黃金或任何物質可以彌補的。金錢固然令人喜悅，卻買不回所愛的生命。這首歌曲後來也出現了蘇格蘭版本〈The Climbing Clementine〉，歌由開頭改成「In a crevice, high on Nevis ...」。

127 It's a Small World

It's a world of laughter and a world of tears.
It's a world of hopes and a world of fears.
There's so much that we share.
It's time we were aware
It's a small world after all.

It's a small world after all.
It's a small world after all.
It's a small world after all.
It's a small, small world.

There is just one moon and a golden sun.
And a smile means friendship to everyone.
Though the mountains are high
And the oceans are wide,
It's a small world after all.

It's a small world after all.
It's a small world after all.
It's a small world after all.
It's a small, small world.

這世界充滿笑聲，充滿淚水。
這世界充滿希望，充滿恐懼。
有多少事我們可分享，
此刻我們該意識到了，
畢竟這是個小小世界。

畢竟這是個小小世界。
畢竟這是個小小世界。
畢竟這是個小小世界。
這是個小小世界。

只有一個月亮和金陽，
微笑帶給大家友誼，
縱使山高海闊，
畢竟這是個小小世界。

畢竟這是個小小世界。
畢竟這是個小小世界。
畢竟這是個小小世界。
這是個小小世界。

fear [fɪr] (n.) 恐懼
- *Lee is fond of gathering fears.* 李著迷於收集害怕。

aware [əˋwɛr] (a.) 察覺的
- *Because they are invisible, no one is aware of them.*
  因為他們是無形的精靈，沒有人能察覺到他們。

〈小小世界〉（It's a Small World）是迪士尼樂園的主題館之一，這首歌的誕生源自主題館的設計，我們先來瞧瞧小小世界的來龍去脈吧！

〈小小世界〉源起於 1964 紐約的世界博覽會（World's Fair）。展覽結束後，這些展覽設備直接移轉給迪士尼樂園，並於 1966 年重新開幕。最初〈小小世界〉命名為「children of the world」，並以播放各個國家的國歌為號召。但是華德‧迪士尼（Walt Disney）認為，應該要有一首歌可以代表〈小小世界〉的精神。於是邀請流行歌曲作者雪曼兄弟（Sherman Brothers）獻智，為小小世界寫一首歌。

雪曼兄弟於是寫了〈It's a Small World〉這首歌，當時正在發生古巴導彈危機。〈小小世界〉這首歌問世後，立即成為演唱頻率最高、翻譯文字最多的歌曲，別具時代意義。

〈小小世界〉如此琅琅上口的祕訣，不只是因為它持續重複相同旋律，創創者羅伯特‧雪曼（Robert J. Sherman）現身說法指出，其實整首歌的架構才是關鍵所在，怎麼說呢？〈小小世界〉有韻文（verse）和合唱（chorus）部分，當兩者旋律相互對位（counterpoint）時，這首歌就會特別容易記憶，也不容易聽膩。這可以由到迪士尼樂園裡的〈小小世界〉整個行程持續十五分鐘，配樂卻百聽不厭得到驗證。

128 Down by the Old Mill Stream

(128)

Down by the old mill stream
I first met you,
With your eyes so blue,
Dressed in gingham, too.
It was there I knew
That you loved me true.
You were sixteen,
My village queen,
Down by the old mill stream.

在老磨坊的溪邊，
我初次遇見了妳，
妳的眼睛如此藍，
還身穿格紋棉布。
就在那裡我知道，
妳是真誠地愛我，
妳那時才十六歲，
是我村莊之皇后，
在老磨坊的溪邊。

這首由二十世紀初期的 Tell Taylor（1876–1937）所作，他的作品多達上百首，這首是男聲四重唱中的典型作品。1939 年，男聲合唱協會（Barbershop Harmony Society）和芝加哥 RCA Victor 唱片公司節錄國際四重奏優勝精華，這首歌即列在其中。這張專輯首度發行時，就以鋼琴與男聲四重唱版本同步發行。

這首歌曲的背景，是在俄亥俄州西北部的白蘭奇河（Blanchard River），歌詞中提及的老舊磨坊為米沙磨（Misamore）磨坊。Tell Taylor 童年時常在這裡玩耍，他將這些記憶付諸旋律，迴盪於世界各個角落。

meet [mit] (v.) 遇見
- *My mom and dad met when they were in high school.*
  我媽媽和爸爸是在他們高中時相遇的。

gingham [ˈgɪŋəm] (n.) 條紋棉布；格子棉布

true [tru] (a.) 真實的
- *It was true love, and they were meant for each other.*
  那是真愛，他們注定要成為對方的另一半。

This Old Man

This old man, he played one;
He played with a knickknack on my thumb.
With a knickknack, paddywhack,
He gave the dog a bone;
This old man came rolling home.

This old man, he played two;
He played with a knickknack on my shoe.
With a knickknack, paddywhack,
He gave the dog a bone;
This old man came rolling home.

This old man, he played three;
He played with a knickknack on my knee.
With a knickknack, paddywhack,
He gave the dog a bone;
This old man came rolling home.

This old man, he played four;
He played with a knickknack on my door.
With a knickknack, paddywhack,
He gave the dog a bone;
This old man came rolling home.

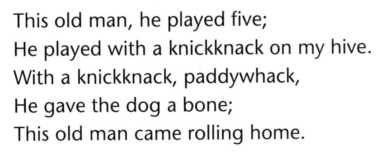

This old man, he played five;
He played with a knickknack on my hive.
With a knickknack, paddywhack,
He gave the dog a bone;
This old man came rolling home.

This old man, he played six;
He played with a knickknack on my sticks.
With a knickknack, paddywhack,
He gave the dog a bone;
This old man came rolling home.

This old man, he played seven;
He played with a knickknack on my heaven.
With a knickknack, paddywhack,
He gave the dog a bone;
This old man came rolling home.

This old man, he played eight;
He played with a knickknack on my gate.
With a knickknack, paddywhack,
He gave the dog a bone;
This old man came rolling home.

This old man, he played nine;
He played with a knickknack on my spine.
With a knickknack, paddywhack,
He gave the dog a bone;
This old man came rolling home.

This old man, he played ten;
He played with a knickknack once again.
With a knickknack, paddywhack,
He gave the dog a bone;
This old man came rolling home.

knickknack [ˋnɪkˏnæk] (n.) 小裝飾品

paddywhack [ˋpædɪˏhwæk] (n.) 打屁股 (口語)

bone [bon] (n.) 骨頭

roll [rol] (v.) 滾動

gate [get] (n.) 柵欄

這個老人，他第一次玩，
他在我拇指上玩小玩意兒，
拿著小玩意兒打屁股，
他給狗兒一根骨頭，
這個老人滾著回到家。

這個老人，他第二次玩，
他在我鞋子上玩小玩意兒，
拿著小玩意兒打屁股，
他給狗兒一根骨頭，
這個老人滾著回到家。

這個老人，他第三次玩，
他在我膝蓋上玩小玩意兒，
拿著小玩意兒打屁股，
他給狗兒一根骨頭，
這個老人滾著回到家。

這個老人，他第四次玩，
他在我門上玩小玩意兒，
拿著小玩意兒打屁股，
他給狗兒一根骨頭，
這個老人滾著回到家。

這個老人，他第五次玩，
他在我蜂窩上玩小玩意兒，
拿著小玩意兒打屁股，
他給狗兒一根骨頭，
這個老人滾著回到家。

這個老人，他第六次玩，
他在我樹枝上玩小玩意兒，
拿著小玩意兒打屁股，
他給狗兒一根骨頭，
這個老人滾著回到家。

這個老人，他第七次玩，
他在我天國上玩小玩意兒，
拿著小玩意兒打屁股，
他給狗兒一根骨頭，
這個老人滾著回到家。

這個老人，他第八次玩，
他在我大門上玩小玩意兒，
拿著小玩意兒打屁股，
他給狗兒一根骨頭，
這個老人滾著回到家。

這個老人，他第九次玩，
他在我脊椎上玩小玩意兒，
拿著小玩意兒打屁股，
他給狗兒一根骨頭，
這個老人滾著回到家。

這個老人，他第十次玩，
他再玩一次小玩意兒，
拿著小玩意兒打屁股，
他給狗兒一根骨頭，
這個老人滾著回到家。

這首歌之所以著名，是因為嚴謹的韻腳和緊密關聯的曲調。歌詞中由 1 到 10 的數字，和韻腳「on my ____」文字的替換，一方面可以讓孩子們練習 1 到 10 的數數兒，二方面又兼顧了韻腳發音的趣味性。這首歌本來在英國比較普及，1958 年後，電影《六福客棧》（*The Inn of the Sixth Happiness*）中用了這首歌，讓這首歌廣為人知。美國音樂人 Mitch Miller（1911–2010）將之出版為單曲，取名為〈孩子們的行軍樂〉（The Children's Marching Song）。

從此以後，這首歌的詞和曲都常被引用。美國電視影集《神探可倫坡》（*Columbo*），以這首歌為主旋律。兒童電視節目《邦尼與朋友》（*Barney & Friends*），主題歌採用的曲調很類似這首歌，可見其對大眾文化之影響。

130 Playmate

Oh, playmate,
Come out and play with me
And bring your dollies three.
Climb up my apple tree,
Look down at my rain barrel,
Slide down my cellar door,
And we'll be jolly friends forever more.

Oh, playmate,
Come out and play with me
And bring your dollies three.
It was a rainy day.
She couldn't come out to play.
With tearful eyes and tender sighs,
She looked terribly sad.
I could hear her say:

I'm sorry, playmate,
I cannot play with you.
My dollies have the flu,
Boo-hoo hoo hoo hoo hoo.
I can't climb on your rain barrel,
I can't slide down your cellar door,
But we'll be jolly friends forever more.

喔，玩伴，
出來陪我玩，
帶著你的三個娃娃。
爬上我的蘋果樹來，
低頭看看我的雨桶，
滑下我的地窖門去，
我們永遠是好朋友。

喔，玩伴，
出來陪我玩，
帶著你的三個娃娃。
那是一個下雨天，
她無法出來玩耍，
淚眼盈眶輕嘆息，
她看來異常哀傷，
我聽見她說：

對不起，玩伴，
我不能跟你玩。
我的娃娃感冒了，
嗚嗚嗚嗚嗚。
我無法爬上你的雨桶，
我無法溜下你的地窖門，
但我們永遠是好朋友。

playmate [ˋpleˌmet] (n.) 玩伴
- *May is my close playmate who plays with me every day.*
  梅是每天和我一起玩耍的親密玩伴。

barrel [ˋbærəl] (n.) 桶子
- *We often take our barrels to the well to fetch clean water.*
  我們時常帶著桶子去井邊取乾淨的水。

cellar [ˋsɛlɚ] (n.) 地窖
- *We also like to play hide-and-seek down in the cellar.*
  我們還愛在地窖裡面玩捉迷藏。

這是一首邀請玩伴的兒歌，轉折處是天公不作美，玩伴無法赴約。但雖然如此，友誼還是常存哦！這首歌多以拍手歌的方式進行，拍手的方式可以自己拍自己的手、雙手拍對方的手、右手拍對方右手，左手拍對方左手，或者更有創意地以手拍大腿，輔以中指與拇指彈出聲音，都是不錯的團體活動。

131 I'm a Nut

I'm an acorn, small and round,
Lying on the cold, cold ground.
Everyone walks over me.
That is why I'm cracked, you see.
I'm a nut! (click, click)
I'm a nut! (click, click)
I'm a nut! (click, click)

Called myself on the telephone,
Just to hear my golden tone.
Asked me out for a little date,
Picked me up about half past eight.
I'm a nut! (click, click)
I'm a nut! (click, click)
I'm a nut! (click, click)

Took myself to the movie show,
Stayed too late and said, "Let's go."
Took my hand and led me out,
Drove me home and gave a shout!
I'm a nut! (click, click)
I'm a nut! (click, click)
I'm a nut! (click, click)

我是一顆橡實小又圓，
躺在冰冰冷冷的地上。
每個人從我身上踏過，
所以我就這麼被踏碎。
我是個堅果！（敲，敲）
我是個堅果！（敲，敲）
我是個堅果！（敲，敲）

帶自己去看個電影，
待到很晚才說走吧，
牽我的手帶我出去，
載我回家大叫一下。
我是個堅果！（敲，敲）
我是個堅果！（敲，敲）
我是個堅果！（敲，敲）

自己打電話給自己，
只為聽我那金嗓音。
約我出去小小約會，
大概八點半來接我。
我是個堅果！（敲，敲）
我是個堅果！（敲，敲）
我是個堅果！（敲，敲）

acorn [`ekɔrn] (n.) 橡實

movie [`muvɪ] (n.) 電影

shout [ʃaut] (v.) 大叫

這是一首將核果擬人化，配合歌詞唱遊的兒歌。nut 當做名詞用時，指堅果、核果或堅果仁，是樹的種子。由於堅硬不易打開的特性，nut 又可以引申為「難事、難題、難對付的人或瘋子、傻瓜、怪人、狂熱者」等。

這首歌可搭配以下動作律動，讓小朋友圍成一圈進行：

I'm an acorn, small and round,	→ 以手掌假裝拿了一顆果實
Lying on the cold, cold ground.	→ 雙臂交叉，作發抖狀
Everyone walks over me.	→ 以雙腳用力踩地
That is why I'm cracked, you see.	→ 雙手掌貼緊從上而下作鋸齒狀移動，像破裂痕跡
I'm a nut! (click, click)	→ 以舌頭發出卡嗒聲
Called myself on the telephone,	→ 一手撥號，一手在耳旁拿話筒
Just to hear my golden tone.	→ 手摀住耳
Asked me out for a little date,	→ 手指自己
Picked me up about half past eight.	→ 聳肩作興奮狀
Took myself to the movie show,	→ 以手指舞動表示走路
Stayed too late and said, "Let's go."	→ 雙手拉住兩旁同伴的手
Took my hand and led me out,	→ 一起轉圈圈
Drove me home and gave a shout!	→ 一起跳進圈圈中央並大聲喊「吼嘿」

132 Jingle Bells

Dashing through the snow,	奔馳過雪地，
In a one horse open sleigh,	單馬無蓬橇。
Over the fields we go,	穿越那田野，
Laughing all the way.	沿路笑聲傳。
Bells on a bobtail ring,	馬兒鈴鐺響，
Making spirits bright.	心情多快活，
What fun it is to ride and sing	歡唱雪橇歌，乘坐雪橇上，
A sleighing song tonight! Oh!	今夜多快樂。喔！
Jingle bells,	叮叮噹，
Jingle bells,	叮叮噹，
Jingle all the way!	一路響叮噹！
Oh, what fun it is to ride	乘著單馬無蓬橇，
In a one horse open sleigh! Hey!	哦，有多麼快樂！
Jingle bells,	叮叮噹，
Jingle bells,	叮叮噹，
Jingle all the way!	一路響叮噹！
Oh, what fun it is to ride	乘著單馬無蓬橇，
In a one horse open sleigh!	哦，有多麼快樂！

1850 年，美國音樂人披朋（James Pierpont, 1822–1893）在波士頓附近的小鎮 Medford 上創作了這首歌，原名為〈One Horse Open Sleigh〉，目的是為了慶祝禮拜堂（Salem）大街的雪橇競賽而寫，但活動結束後這首歌就塵封了。

1857 年，披朋在教堂擔任風琴師時，計畫舉辦禮拜聯誼會，需要一首愉悅輕快的冬令歌，經過這麼多年後，這首歌的手稿被壓箱在頂樓，於是他將手稿找出來，沒想到這首歌再度大放異彩。許多人對這首歌興趣盎然，披朋於是申請版權，後來並把歌名改為〈Jingle Bells〉。兩年後，這首歌正式出版問世，成為了暢銷歌曲。披朋是美國內戰前期曇花一現的奇葩，這首歌讓他名傳千古。

dash [dæʃ] (v.) 急奔
sleigh [sle] (n.) 雪橇
bobtail [ˋbɑbˏtel] (n.) 尾巴剪短的馬

133

There was an old man named Michael Finnegan.
He had whiskers on his chinnegan.
Along came the wind and blew them in again.
Poor old Michael Finnegan.
Begin again!

There was an old man named Michael Finnegan.
He drank through all his good ginnegan,
And so he wasted all his tinnegan.
Poor old Michael Finnegan.
Begin again!

There was an old man named Michael Finnegan.
He went fishing with a pinnegan,
Caught a fish, and dropped it in again.
Poor old Michael Finnegan.
Begin again!

There was an old man named Michael Finnegan.
He grew fat and then grew thin again.
Then he died and had to begin again.
Poor old Michael Finnegan.
Begin again!

從前有個老人名叫麥可·芬尼根，
他的下巴長了小鬍鬚，
風又把鬍子吹了進去。
可憐的老麥可·芬尼根。
重頭開始！

從前有個老人名叫麥可·芬尼根，
他喝光他的全部好琴酒，
也花光了他所有的錫幣。
可憐的老麥可·芬尼根。
重頭開始！

從前有個老人名叫麥可·芬尼根，
他帶著一根針去釣魚，
捉到一隻魚又放走牠。
可憐的老麥可·芬尼根。
重頭開始！

從前有個老人名叫麥可·芬尼根，
他一下胖，一下瘦，
死掉了又重新再來。
可憐的老麥可·芬尼根。
重頭開始！

whisker [ˋhwɪskɚ] (n.) 鬍子
- *Joe looks older because of the whiskers he has grown.*
  喬因為留鬍子而看起來較老。

blow [blo] (v.) 吹
- *Joe's whiskers dance when the wind blows.*
  喬的鬍子被風吹飄動。

這首傳統童謠經常出現在營火晚會或童軍活動中。每一段末句的 begin again，可以循環歌唱，適合遊戲進行。這首歌應因時代、地域、場合的不同，版本各異，以下節選其他版本的歌詞，以窺這首歌謠的大略面貌：

There was an old man named Michael Finnegan,
Climbed a tree and barked his shin-egan,
Took off several yards of skin-egan,
Poor old Michael Finnegan, begin again.

There was an old man named Michael Finnegan.
He kicked up an awful din-egan,
Because they said he could not sing-egan,
Poor old Michael Finnegan, begin again.

There was an old man called Michael Finnegan.
Ran a race and thought he'd win again
Got so puffed that he had to go in again
Poor old Michael Finnegan, begin again.

134 The Big Rock Candy Mountains

In the Big Rock Candy Mountains,
There's a land that's fair and bright,
Where the goodies grow on the bushes
And you sleep out every night,
And where friends are all around us
And the sun shines every day.
Oh, I'm bound to go where there isn't any snow
And where the rain doesn't fall
And the wind doesn't blow.
In the Big Rock Candy Mountains.

Oh, the bees are buzzing in the peppermint trees.
Around the soda water fountains
Where the lemonade springs,
The bluebird sings.
In the Big Rock Candy Mountains.

In the Big rock Candy Mountains,
You never change your socks,
And little streams of lemonade
Come a-trickling down the rocks.

The critters there are friendly.
It's such a lovely sight.
There's a lake of stew and soda, too.
You can paddle all around them in a big canoe,
In the Big Rock Candy Mountains.

Oh, the bees are buzzing in the peppermint trees.
Around the soda water fountains
Where the lemonade springs,
The bluebird sings.
In the Big Rock Candy Mountains.

在那大冰糖山裡，
有塊美麗明亮國土。
樹叢間生長著好人，
你每晚都睡在外面。
朋友圍繞我們身邊，
每天都充滿陽光。
喔，我一定要去沒有雪，
不下雨和不起風的地方。
在那大冰糖山裡。

喔，薄荷樹裡的蜜蜂嗡嗡叫，
繞著不斷湧出檸檬水的汽水噴泉，
藍知更鳥在歌唱。
在那大冰糖山裡。

在大冰糖山裡，
你從不用換襪子。
檸檬水涓涓溪流，
沿石頭緩緩流下。
那兒的生物友善，
好一幅美好景象。
那兒還有一處燉肉和汽水湖。
你可以划著大獨木舟環遊，
在那大冰糖山裡。

喔，薄荷樹裡的蜜蜂嗡嗡叫，
繞著不斷湧出檸檬水的汽水噴泉，
藍知更鳥在歌唱。
在那大冰糖山裡。

這是首傳統民謠描述一個風和日麗、衣食無缺、友善安逸的安樂世界。由於年代久遠，原始作者已不可考，美國歌手 Harry McClintock（1882–1957）和之後的 Burl Ives（1909–1995），都整理並出版過這首歌謠。

McClintock 在 1928 年發行了的版本，還被用在 2000 年的電影《霹靂高手》（Oh Brother, Where Art Thou）中。Burl Ives 是十九世紀六〇年代的民歌演唱家和男演員，1958 年，他以《錦繡大地》（The Big Country）這部電影，榮獲奧斯卡最佳男配角獎。1949 年，他錄製了這首歌謠的唱片。而這首歌最著名的版本，要屬著名的搖滾鄉村音樂歌手 Dorsey Burnette（1932–1979）的作品了，他將這首歌謠推上了排行榜前十名。

為了配合兒童的年齡層，Harry McClintock 將部分不合宜的內容刪去，並修改了部分歌詞，例如，將原詞中的「cigarette trees」改為「peppermint trees」，「streams of alcohol」改為「streams of lemonade」，「The lake of gin」和「the lake of whiskey」也以「a lake of soda pop」替代。之後，世界上不斷有其他版本問世。這首歌所傳倡的理想大地，不就是困塞心靈的一個出口嗎？

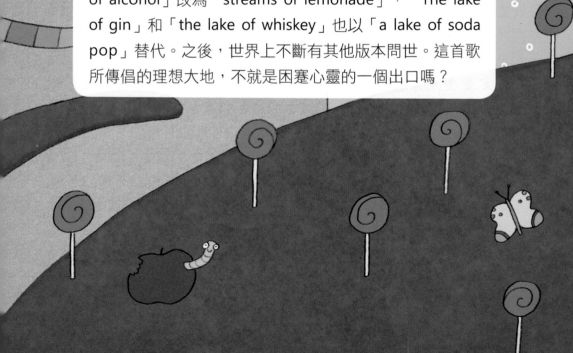

bound [baʊnd] (a.) 打算前去的
peppermint [ˈpɛpɚˌmɪnt] (n.) 薄荷
trickle [ˈtrɪkl̩] (v.) 細細地流
critter [ˈkrɪtɚ] (n.) 生物
paddle [ˈpædl̩] (v.) 用槳划

453

135 Pop Goes the Weasel

All around the cobbler's bench,
The monkey chased the weasel.
The monkey thought it was all in fun.
Pop! Goes the weasel.

A penny for a spool of thread,
A penny for a needle.
That's the way the money goes.
Pop! Goes the weasel.

A half a pound of tuppenny rice,
A half a pound of treacle.
Mix it up and make it nice.
Pop! Goes the weasel.

Up and down the London road,
In and out of the Eagle.
That's the way the money goes.
Pop! Goes the weasel.

I've no time to plead and pine.
I've no time to wheedle.
Kiss me quick, and then I'm gone.
Pop! Goes the weasel.

繞著補鞋匠的長凳，
猴子追著鼬鼠，
猴子覺得真有趣，
啪！鼬鼠跑走了。

一便士買一捲線，
一便士買一支針，
錢就是這樣花的。
啪！鼬鼠跑走了。

半磅兩便士的米，
半磅的蜜糖，
攪和一下更美味，
啪！鼬鼠跑走了。

來來去去倫敦路，
進進出出老鷹區，
錢就是這樣花的。
啪！鼬鼠跑走了。

我沒空懇求和悲哀，
我沒空說甜言蜜語，
快點親我，我要走了，
啪！鼬鼠跑走了。

bench [bɛntʃ] (n.) 長凳

weasel [ˋwizḷ] (n.) 鼬鼠

thread [θrɛd] (n.) 線

treacle [ˋθrikḷ] (n.) 蜜糖

pine [paɪn] (n.) 痛苦；悲哀

wheedle [ˋhwidḷ] (v.) 用甜言蜜語欺騙

這首歌謠起源於十七世紀英國倫敦東區的同韻俚語（Rhyming slang），以族群特有的用語，描述中下階層的生活。他們收入微薄，週末飲酒作樂，在週初就需典當借貸，如此惡性循環的生活方式，在歌詞中表露無遺。以下為幾個解讀方向：

pop	→	指 pawn，是「典當、抵押」的意思。
weasel and stoat	→	黃鼠狼和鼬鼠，指外套大衣。
pop goes the weasel	→	窮人們將自己最好的衣服拿去典當，在週末前領到工資後再贖回。
weasel	→	是紡紗工人用來丈量紗線的裝置或織布工的梭子。
popping	→	指工人們奮力工作，以 Weasel 丈量紗線或織布機梭子來回穿梭的聲音。
the Eagle	→	指 The Eagle Tavern，那是位於北倫敦哈克尼區城道（City Road）和牧羊女路（Shepherdess Walk）口的一家小酒館，後來改建成音樂廳。
the monkey	→	碼頭工人的俚語，指「喝酒」（to suck the monkey），十九世紀時也是酒館常用語。有些版本中有「to knock it off」此句，表示「一飲而盡」之意。

這首歌謠源自英格蘭，是和舞蹈搭配的歌曲，1850 年，Messrs Miller 和 Beacham of Baltimore 在美國也出版了這首歌謠。

136 Mary Had a Little Lamb

(136)

Mary had a little lamb, little lamb, little lamb,
Mary had a little lamb. Its fleece was white as snow.

And everywhere that Mary went, Mary went, Mary went,
Everywhere that Mary went, the lamb was sure to go.

It followed her to school one day, school one day, school one
    day,
It followed her to school one day, which was against the rule.

It made the children laugh and play, laugh and play, laugh
    and play,
It made the children laugh and play to see a lamb at school.

And so the teacher turned it out, turned it out, turned it out,
And so the teacher turned it out, but still it lingered near.

And it waited patiently, patiently, patiently,
And it waited patiently till Mary did appear.

"Why does the lamb love Mary so, Mary so, Mary so,
Why does the lamb love Mary so?" the eager children did cry.

"Why, Mary loves the lamb, you know, lamb you know, lamb
    you know,
Why, Mary loves the lamb, you know!" the teacher did reply.

fleece [flis] (n.) 羊毛
- *On the street, Tweety saw a lamb with zebra-like striped fleece.*
  在街上，崔弟看見一隻斑馬條紋的羊。

follow ['fɑlo] (v.) 跟隨
- *Tweety followed the lamb into the barn.* 崔弟跟隨這隻羊進入穀倉。

linger ['lɪŋgɚ] (v.) 徘徊
- *Tweety lingered in the barn to talk to the funny lamb.*
  崔弟在穀倉裡徘徊，要跟這隻有趣的羊聊天。

瑪莉有隻小綿羊，小綿羊，小綿羊，
瑪莉有隻小綿羊，牠的羊毛白如雪。

不管瑪莉去何處，去何處，去何處，
不管瑪莉去何處，小羊總要跟著走。

一天牠跟她去學校，去學校，去學校，
一天牠跟她去學校，這可違反了校規。

惹得小孩笑又玩，笑又玩，笑又玩，
惹得小孩笑又玩，看到小羊在學校。

所以老師趕走牠，趕走牠，趕走牠，
所以老師趕走牠，但牠徘徊不肯走。

牠耐著性子等，耐著性子，耐著性子，
耐著性子等下去，直到瑪莉真出現。

為何小羊愛瑪莉？愛瑪莉，愛瑪莉，
為何小羊愛瑪莉？熱切的小孩叫喊。

哦，正因瑪莉愛小羊，愛小羊，愛小羊，
哦，正因瑪莉愛小羊，老師如此回答道。

1830 年，美國女作家莎拉（Sarah Josepha Hale, 1788–1879）作了這首詩，兩年後，創立波士頓音樂學院的梅森（Lowell Mason, 1792–1872）為這首詩譜上了曲子。

這首歌謠起源於十九世紀的美國，來自一個真實故事，美國麻薩諸塞州一位叫瑪莉（Mary Sawyer）的女孩，她家中的農莊出生了兩隻雙胞胎小羊，其中一隻羸弱不堪，瑪莉便特別照顧牠，彼此形影不離。這一天在上學途中，瑪莉和哥哥發現小羊一路跟著他們，於是便帶著小羊上學，在學校引起了騷動。

137

Hush, Little Baby

Hush, little baby, don't say a word.
Papa's gonna buy you a mockingbird.

And if that mockingbird doesn't sing,
Papa's gonna buy you a diamond ring.

And if that diamond ring turns brass,
Papa's gonna buy you a looking glass.

And if that looking glass gets broke,
Papa's gonna buy you a billy goat.

And if that billy goat doesn't pull,
Papa's gonna buy you a cart and bull.

And if that cart and bull turns over,
Papa's gonna buy you a dog named Rover.

And if that dog named Rover won't bark,
Papa's gonna buy you a horse and carriage.

And if that horse and carriage falls down,
Well, you'll still be the sweetest little baby in town.

噓，小寶貝，別說話。
爸爸幫你買隻仿聲鳥。

如果那仿聲鳥不歌唱，
爸爸會幫你買只鑽戒；

如果那只鑽戒已變黃，
爸爸會幫你買面鏡子；

如果那面鏡子摔破了，
爸爸會幫你買頭公羊；

如果那頭公羊不能拉，
爸爸會幫你買台牛車；

如果那台牛車翻覆了，
爸爸幫你買隻狗叫羅福；

如果叫羅福的狗不會叫，
爸爸會幫你買一台馬車；

如果那輛馬車翻覆了，
嗯，你還是全鎮最可愛的小寶寶！

mockingbird [ˋmɑkɪŋˏbɝd] (n.) 仿聲鳥

brass [bræs] (a.) 黃銅色的

glass [glæs] (n.) 眼鏡

pull [pul] (v.) 拉

- *I pull out my big dresser drawer to get my telescope.*
  我拉出我那大衣櫃的抽屜，拿出我的單眼望遠鏡。

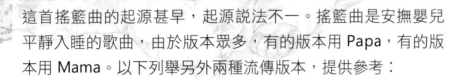

這首搖籃曲的起源甚早，起源說法不一。搖籃曲是安撫嬰兒平靜入睡的歌曲，由於版本眾多，有的版本用 Papa，有的版本用 Mama。以下列舉另外兩種流傳版本，提供參考：

Hush little baby; mama's near,
To brush your hair and calm your fears.
To kiss your cheek and hold your hand,
'Til you drift off to sleepyland.
To help you count those little white sheep,
And sing you songs 'til you're asleep.
To tell you tales of kings and queens,
Of Jack and Jill and wonderful things.
So snuggle up and hold me tight,
And dream sweet dreams all through the night.
And every night when the sun goes down,
You'll still be the sweetest little baby in town.

另一種版本較短，內容如下：

Hush little baby, don't you cry.
Within your dreams, you can touch the sky.
With you in my arms, I feel whole,
Because you are, my heart and my soul.

138 Oh, Susanna

I come from Alabama with my banjo on my knee.
I'm going to Louisiana there
My true love to see.

It rained all night, the day I left.
The weather was dry.
The sun was so hot.
I froze to death.
Susanna, don't you cry.

Oh, Susanna,
Oh, don't you cry for me,
For I come from Alabama with my banjo on my knee.

I had a dream the other night,
When everything was still.
I thought I saw Susanna dear
A-coming down the hill.
The buckwheat cake was in her mouth;
A tear was in her eyes.

Says I, I'm coming from the south.
Susanna, don't you cry.

Oh, Susanna,
Oh, don't you cry for me,
For I come from Alabama with my banjo on my knee.

Oh, Susanna,
Oh, don't you cry for me,
For I come from Alabama with my banjo on my knee.

我來自那阿拉巴馬，
膝上一把五弦琴，
我要去路易斯安那，
去見我那真愛人。

離開那晚下著雨。
天氣很乾燥，
太陽如此炎熱，
我卻冷得要死，
蘇珊娜，妳可別哭泣。

哦，蘇珊娜，
哦，請別為我哭泣。
因我來自阿拉巴馬，
膝上一把五弦琴。

有一晚我做了夢，
在萬籟俱寂之夜，
我以為見蘇珊娜，
從山丘上走下來。
嘴裡含著蕎麥餅，
眼眸還掛著淚水。
我說，我來自南方，
蘇珊娜，你別哭泣。

哦，蘇珊娜，
哦，請別為我哭泣。
因我來自阿拉巴馬，
膝上一把五弦琴。

這是首旋律輕快的美國西部歌曲，原作者是民謠歌手 Stephen Foster（1826–64），曲調可能源自蘇格蘭軍樂，適合搭配風笛演奏。歌詞內容描述離鄉背景去尋找摯愛 Susanna 的故事，後來被改編成描述淘金潮主題的歌曲〈Oh, California〉，在淘金潮時廣為傳唱，原歌詞為：

I came from Salem City
    With my washpan on my knee.
I'm going to California,
The gold dust for to see.
It rained all day the day I left,
The weather it was dry.
The sun so hot. I froze to death.
Oh, brothers, don't you cry.
Oh, California, Oh, that's the land for me!
I'm bound for San Francisco
    with my washbowl on my knee.

139 Do Your Ears Hang Low

Do your ears hang low?
Do they waggle to and fro?
Can you tie them in a knot?
Can you tie them in a bow?
Can you throw them over your shoulder
Like a Continental soldier?
Do your ears hang low?

Do your ears stick out?
Can you waggle them about?
Can you flap them up and down
   as you fly around the town?
Can you shut them up for sure
   when you hear an awful bore?
Do your ears stick out?

Do your ears stand high?
Do they reach up to the sky?
Do they hang down when they're wet?
Do they stand up when they're dry?

Can you semaphore your neighbor
With the minimum of labor?
Do your ears stand high?

你耳朵會不會垂低低？
它們會不會前後搖擺？
你可以把耳朵打個結？
你能把耳朵打蝴蝶結？
你可以把它們摔過肩？
就像美洲軍人那樣摔？
你耳朵會不會垂低低？

你耳朵會不會伸出來？
你能否前後擺動它們？
當你繞著城鎮飛行時，
你能否上下拍打它們？
當你聽到無聊的事時，
你能否完全閉起它們？
你耳朵會不會伸出來？

你的耳朵可以挺高高？
它們是否可以伸到天空？
它們濕掉時會垂下嗎？
它們乾了會挺起來嗎？
你可以輕鬆傳消息給鄰居？
你的耳朵可以挺高高？

waggle [ˋwæg!] (v.) 搖擺
knot [nɑt] (n.) 結
soldier [ˋsoldʒɚ] (n.) 軍人
semaphore [ˋsɛməfor] (v.) 發信號

這是一首琅琅上口、廣為流傳的民謠。由於民謠有地域、時間性的差異，加上口耳相傳的特色，所以版本之多不在話下。這首歌的歌詞前身為軍中歌曲，曲調方面，這首民謠可以套用〈草堆裡的火雞〉（Turkey in the Straw），或〈水手的號笛舞曲〉（Sailor's Hornpipe）等旋律。適合於夏令營的活動中帶唱，對於孩童很有吸引力。以下為結合勞作與唱遊的活動，進行方式如下：

1 在硬紙板上畫好兔子的頭和耳朵，剪下並著色。
2 耳朵部分各剪出一個適合手指進出的小洞。
3 以食指和中指插入耳朵上的小洞，邊唱歌邊讓手指隨歌詞搖擺跳動。

試試看，誰的兔子耳朵最靈活？

140 Over the River

Over the river and through the woods,
To Grandmother's house we go.
The horse knows the way to carry the sleigh
Through the white and drifted snow.
Over the river and through the woods,
Oh, how the wind does blow.
It stings the toes and bites the nose,
As over the ground we go.

Over the river and through the woods,
Trot fast my dapple gray.
Spring over the ground like a hunting hound,
For this is Thanksgiving Day.
Over the river and through the woods,
Now Grandmother's face I spy.
Hurrah for the fun, is the pudding done?
Hurrah for the pumpkin pie.

跨過河流穿過森林，
我們往祖母家走去。
馬兒熟練拉動雪橇，
穿越雪白漂流的雪。
跨過河流穿過森林，
喔風是這樣地吹著，
它刺痛腳趾凍傷鼻，
當我們穿越大地時。

跨過河流穿過森林，
我的灰斑馬兒奔馳，
像隻獵犬躍過地上，
因為今天是感恩節。
跨過河流穿過森林，
我瞧見那祖母臉龐，
打趣歡呼，布丁好了嗎？
為了南瓜派歡呼。

drifted [ˋdrɪftɪd] (a.) 漂流的
bite [baɪt] (v.) 咬
hound [haʊnd] (n.) 獵犬
pudding [ˋpʊdɪŋ] (n.) 布丁
pumpkin [ˋpʌmpkɪn] (n.) 南瓜

這首膾炙人口的歌謠由美國一位女士柴爾德（Lydia Maria Child, 1802–1880）所作，1844 年收錄於《給孩子們的花》（Flowers for Children）。歌詞描述感恩節前夕，滿心歡喜前往祖母家的兒時記憶。柴爾德是一位有名的小說家、新聞工作者，她在作品中表達了對印第安人和黑奴等弱勢團體遭遇的憐憫。她也有一些像這首歌謠的小詩作品，描寫美國新英格蘭區冬日的歡樂節慶時光。

Lydia Maria Child

141 Take Me Out to the Ball Game

Katie Casey was baseball mad,
And she had the fever and had it bad.
Just to root for the hometown crew,
Every sou Katie blew.
On a Saturday, a young beau called to see
If she'd like to go to see a show,
But Miss Kate said,
"No, I'll tell you what you can do."

"Take me out to the ball game.
 Take me out to the crowd.
 Buy me some peanuts and Cracker Jacks.
 I don't care if I never get back.
 Let me root, root, root for the home team.
 If they don't win, it's a shame,
 For it's one, two, three strikes, you're out,
 At the old ball game."

Katie Casey saw all the games,
knew the players by their first names,
And told the umpire he was wrong,
All along good and strong.
When the score was just two to two,
Katie Casey knew what to do.
Just to cheer up the boys she knew,
She made the gang sing this song.

凱蒂‧凱絲是個瘋狂棒球迷，
不但狂熱而且超級狂熱，
只為幫家鄉球隊加油，
她花光每一分錢。
星期六，一位年輕的文雅男士，
打電話來問她是否要去看一場秀，
可是凱蒂小姐說：
「不，我告訴你你能做什麼。」

「帶我去看棒球賽，
帶我至觀眾群中，
幫我買些花生和爆玉米花。
我不在乎回不回得去，
讓我為家鄉的隊伍加加油吧，
若是他們輸了會很可惜，
因為只要一好球，兩好球，
三好球，就出局，
在舊球賽中。」

凱蒂‧凱絲全部球賽都看過，
每個球員她都能直呼其名，
還告訴裁判判錯了，
說得好又強勢。
當比數來到二比二，
凱蒂‧凱絲知道她該做什麼，
只要逗她認識的男孩開心，
她請大家一起唱了這首歌。

fever [ˈfivɚ] (n.) 狂熱
sou [su] (n.)〔喻〕極少的錢
blow [blo] (v.)〔俚〕揮霍
beau [bo] (n.) 文雅的男子
Cracker Jack 爆玉米花
root [rut] (v.) 打氣；聲援
umpire [ˈʌmpaɪr] (n.) 裁判
gang [gæŋ] (n.) 一夥人

這首歌在美國可以說是人人都會唱，它和美國國歌（The Star-Spangled Banner）、生日快樂歌，並列為美國最常被唱到的三大歌曲。觀看棒球比賽時，在第七局上下攻守交換的時候，大家可以唱這首歌，順便伸伸懶腰。

這首歌的起源在 1908 年，當時歌舞劇及流行歌曲作者 Jack Norworth 在紐約搭地鐵時，瞥見一句標語：「Ballgame Today at the Polo Grounds.」（今晚在 Polo Grounds 有棒球比賽）他看了之後，靈光乍現，心中湧出歌詞，隨即拿了張便條紙抄下來，前後只花了十五分鐘。他將完成的歌詞交給作曲家 Albert Von Tilzer，兩人合力完成了這首最受歡迎的棒球歌曲。

1927 年，Jack Norworth 修改了部分歌詞，
發表了這首歌的第二個版本：

Nelly Kelly loved baseball games,
Knew the players, knew all their names,
You could see her there ev'ry day,
Shout "Hurray," When they'd play.

Her boyfriend by the name of Joe
Said, "To Coney Isle, dear, let's go,"
Then Nelly started to fret and pout,
And to him, I heard her shout.

"Take me out to the ball game,
Take me out with the crowd.
Buy me some peanuts and Cracker Jack,
I don't care if I never get back.

Let me root, root, root for the home team,
If they don't win, it's a shame.
For it's one, two, three strikes, you're out,
At the old ball game."

Nelly Kelly was sure some fan,
She would root just like any man,
Told the umpire he was wrong,
All along, good and strong.

When the score was just two to two,
Nelly Kelly knew what to do.
Just to cheer up the boys she knew,
She made the gang sing this song.

142 Polly Wolly Doodle

Oh, I'm going down south to see my Sal
And sing Polly Wolly Doodle all the day.
My Sal, she is a spunky gal.
Sing Polly Wolly Doodle all the day.

Fare thee well, fare thee well,
Fare thee well, my fairy fay,
For I'm going to Lou'siana
To see my Susyanna
And sing Polly Wolly Doodle all the day.

Oh, my Sal, she is a maiden fair,
Sing Polly Wolly Doodle all the day,
With laughing eyes and curly hair,
Sing Polly Wolly Doodle all the day.

Fare thee well, fare thee well,
Fare thee well, my fairy fay,
For I'm going to Lou'siana
To see my Susyanna
And sing Polly Wolly Doodle all the day.

Behind the barn,
Down on my knees,
Sing Polly Wolly Doodle all the day,
I thought I heard a chicken sneeze,
Sing Polly Wolly Doodle all the day.

Fare thee well, fare thee well,
Fare thee well, my fairy fay,
For I'm going to Lou'siana
To see my Susyanna
And sing Polly Wolly Doodle all the day.

這是一首南北內戰之前、1840–1850 年間的吟遊曲調。美國第一位黑人劇團的組織者艾米特（Dan Emmett, 1815–1904）在 Virginia Minstrels 劇團表演節目中，將這首歌發揚光大。這首民謠是南方黑奴經常吟詠的曲調，在《快樂的金色年代》（*These Happy Golden Years*）一書中，描寫主角興高采烈前往南方會見女友的情景。

Dan Emmett

愛米特是愛爾蘭裔的歌手兼作曲家，他最著名的作品是 1859 年寫的〈露營用大鍋〉（Dixie），南北內戰爆發後，不論南軍或北軍，都以〈Dixie〉為行軍用歌曲。後來因為艾米特支持南軍，所以 1861 年之後，〈Dixie〉成為南軍的標誌。

喔，我下南方看我的莎爾，
一整天唱著波麗烏麗杜朵。
我的莎爾她是個活力女孩。
一整天唱著波麗烏麗杜朵。

再見，再見，
再見，我美麗的精靈。
我要去路易斯安那，
去見我的蘇西安那，
一整天唱著波麗烏麗杜朵。

喔，我的莎爾是純潔少女。
一整天唱著波麗烏麗杜朵。
她有著捲捲頭髮和笑笑眼。
一整天唱著波麗烏麗杜朵。

再見，再見，
再見，我美麗的精靈。
我要去路易斯安那，
去見我的蘇西安那，
一整天唱著波麗烏麗杜朵。

在那穀倉後面，
我跪下來，
一整天唱著波麗烏麗杜朵。
我還以為我聽到雞打噴嚏，
一整天唱著波麗烏麗杜朵。

再見，再見，
再見，我美麗的精靈。
我要去路易斯安那，
去見我的蘇西安那，
一整天唱著波麗烏麗杜朵。

spunky [ˋspʌŋkɪ] (a.) 有精神的
gal [gæl] (n.)〔口〕姑娘；女孩
fare thee well 離別
fay [fe] (n.) 仙女
curly [ˋkɝlɪ] (a.) 捲的
barn [bɑrn] (n.) 穀倉

484

143 Yankee Doodle

Yankee Doodle went to town,
A-riding on a pony,
Stuck a feather in his hat,
And called it macaroni.

Yankee Doodle, keep it up,
Yankee Doodle dandy.
Mind the music and the step,
And with the girls be handy.

Father and I went down to camp,
Along with Captain Gooding.
And there we saw the men and boys,
As thick as hasty pudding.

Yankee Doodle, keep it up,
Yankee Doodle dandy.
Mind the music and the step,
And with the girls be handy.

There was Captain Washington
Upon a slapping stallion,
A-giving orders to his men.
I guess there was a million.

Yankee Doodle, keep it up,
Yankee Doodle dandy.
Mind the music and the step,
And with the girls be handy.

洋基‧杜朵進城去，
騎乘一匹小馬兒。
帽子上方插羽毛，
說那樣是時髦派。

洋基‧杜朵，不要停，
時髦的洋基‧杜朵。
留意你音樂和步伐，
輕巧地伴著女孩舞。

父親和我一起露營，
還有上尉古丁，
那兒我們看到男人和男孩，
多得像布丁一樣密集。

洋基‧杜朵，不要停，
時髦的洋基‧杜朵。
留意你音樂和步伐，
輕巧地伴著女孩舞。

上尉華盛頓在那裡，
騎在高大的雄馬上，
正向他的士兵下令，
我猜想有上百萬人。

洋基‧杜朵，不要停，
時髦的洋基‧杜朵。
留意你音樂和步伐，
輕巧地伴著女孩舞。

handy [ˈhændɪ] (a.) 靈巧的
slapping [ˈslæpɪŋ] (a.) 非常大的；非常快的
stallion [ˈstæljən] (n.) 雄馬

這首的曲調是以童謠〈Lucy Locket〉的曲子而來。在美國獨立戰爭前期，相較於英軍陣仗，美國殖民地軍隊是一群烏合之眾。這首歌據說是由一名英國的隨軍醫生 Richard Shuckburgh 所寫，用來取笑殖民地居民粗俗的衣著和舉止，貶低參加法印戰爭的新英格蘭人。不過到了美國獨立戰爭期間，美國人反而很喜歡這首歌，搖身一變成愛國歌曲，人們自豪於自己樸素的衣著和不矯揉的舉止。

Macaroni 有兩種涵意，一是指當時倫敦高級的俱樂部，意思是說 Yankee（美國人）笨到以為只要帽子別上羽毛，看起來夠炫，就可以去 Macaroni 消費。

第二種涵意是因為當時的義大利時尚代表了身分地位，因此引申為「來自上流社會、打扮時髦的人」，而美國人在帽子上別著羽毛模仿，簡直就是鄉巴佬。

doodle → 指蠢蛋。

dandy → 指時髦的男子或花花公子。

Yankee → 有二義，一是從一首關於清教徒的領袖 Oliver Cromwell 詩歌中的 Nankey 一字演變而來；二是指印第安人（另說為荷蘭人）發 English 音不準，唸成「Yengees」。到了 1700 年，就專指在美國的英國移民了。

這首歌最初是一首諷刺性的嘲笑詩文，然而現在這首慷慨激昂又幽默十足的軍樂，已經成了康乃迪克州的州歌了。

144 Miss Lucy Had a Baby

Miss Lucy had a baby.
His name was Tiny Tim.
She put him in the bathtub
To see if he could swim.

He drank up all the water,
He ate up all the soap,
He tried to eat the bathtub,
But it wouldn't go down his throat.

Miss Lucy called the doctor,
Miss Lucy called the nurse,
Miss Lucy called the lady
With the alligator purse.
"Mumps," said the doctor.
"Measles," said the nurse.
"Nothing," said the lady
With the alligator purse.

Miss Lucy punched the doctor.
Miss Lucy knocked the nurse.
Miss Lucy paid the lady
With the alligator purse.

露西小姐有個寶貝，
他名叫小提姆。
她把他放進浴缸，
看他是否會游泳。

他喝光全部的水，
他吃光整塊肥皂，
他又想吃掉浴缸，
只是他吞不下去。

露西小姐叫醫生，
露西小姐叫護士，
露西小姐叫拿鱷魚皮夾的小姐。
「腮腺炎。」醫生說。
「麻疹。」護士說。
「沒事。」拿鱷魚皮夾的小姐說。

露西小姐給了醫生一拳，
露西小姐敲了護士一記，
露西小姐付給拿鱷魚皮夾的小姐錢。

soap [sop] (n.) 肥皂
- *Today he ate a thousand bars of soap.* 今天他吃了一千塊肥皂。

throat [θrot] (n.) 喉嚨
- *He forced a pile of soap down his throat, and then he vomited up stinky bubbles.* 他硬將成堆的肥皂塞進喉嚨，然後吐出臭泡泡。

alligator [ˈæləˌgetɚ] (n.) 鱷魚
- *Ali, the monster alligator, dares to eat anything others don't and won't.* 亞力鱷魚怪獸敢吃任何人不吃、也不會吃的東西。

這是一首拍手歌和跳繩歌，特別能夠吸引學齡前幼童的注意力。當拍手歌遊戲時，可以兩兩一組，按照歌詞的節奏，相互拍擊雙手或大腿。當跳繩歌時，可以一群小朋友一起邊跳邊唱。歌詞內容乍見有些無厘頭，不過拍手歌與跳繩歌本來就著重於節奏和趣味性，至於歌詞是否合邏輯，就不重要囉。

歌詞中帶著鱷魚皮手提包的女士，指美國女權運動先驅蘇珊‧安東尼（Susan B. Anthony, 1820–1906），她於1892 到 1900 年間，任職全美婦女選舉權協會會長。蘇珊出席大大小小的演說活動、極力促成婦女選舉權時，都提著一個顯眼的鱷魚皮手提包，所以也有的版本將「Nothing, said the lady with the alligator purse.」改為「Vote! said the lady with the alligator purse.」，令人莞爾。

Susan B. Anthony

部分教育工作認為以下歌詞帶有暴力：

Miss Lucy punched the doctor.
Miss Lucy knocked the nurse.
Miss Lucy paid the lady with the alligator purse.

於是把歌詞改為以下的模樣，只是精彩程度就略顯失色了：

Out went the doctor.
Out went the nurse.
Out went the lady
With the alligator purse.

國家圖書館出版品預行編目資料

唱吧!英文歌謠：聽歌謠說故事(寂天雲隨身聽APP版) /=
Let's sing and learn English songs / Gloria Lu編著.
-- 二版. -- 臺北市：語言工場，2022.06印刷
面；　公分

ISBN 978-986-6963-82-7(20K平裝)

1.CST: 英語 2.CST: 讀本

805.18   111006640

編者 _ Gloria Lu
編輯 _ 安卡斯
製程管理 _ 洪巧玲
製作&出版 _ 語言工場出版有限公司
發行人 _ 黃朝萍
電話 _ +886-2-2365-9739
傳真 _ +886-2-2365-9835
網址 _ www.icosmos.com.tw
讀者服務 _ onlineservice@icosmos.com.tw
出版日期 _ 2022年6月 二版八刷 (寂天雲隨身聽APP版)
郵撥帳號 _ 1998620-0
　　　　　　寂天文化事業股份有限公司